THE RIVER OF ETERNITY

Book 1 of The Harem Conspiracy

BRUCE BALFOUR

Scribbling Gargoyle

Author website: https://brucebalfour.com

The characters and events portrayed in this book are fictitious. Though some characters, incidents, quotes, songs, and dialogue are based on historical record, the work as a whole is a product of the author's imagination.

ISBN 979-8-218-34658-4

Cover by Adrijus Guscia

Gargoyle logo by Eucalyp

Books by Bruce Balfour

HISTORICAL NOVELS

The River of Eternity (Book 1 of The Harem Conspiracy)

The House of Death (Book 2 of The Harem Conspiracy)

The Revenge of Sekhmet (Book 3 of The Harem Conspiracy) – upcoming

SCIENCE FICTION NOVELS

The Forge of Mars

The Digital Dead (sequel to *The Forge of Mars*)

Prometheus Road (Young Adult)

THRILLER NOVELS

Burning Season

Author's Note

I have attempted to be as accurate as possible regarding locations, historical figures, religious proceedings, judicial processes, and other minutiae of New Kingdom Egypt, and I apologize in advance for any factual errors in rendering the reality of the ancient world. Many of the characters are drawn from the oldest written record of a judicial proceeding that we have, commonly known as the Harem Conspiracy, relating to the assassination of Pharaoh Ramesses III. This story begins well before the Harem Conspiracy, and some characters are fictional, but I hope I have accurately portrayed what it was like to live during that period.

As in modern society, the ancient Egyptians didn't approve of some kinds of daily violence, while other kinds were considered appropriate and necessary. As an example, we have court proceedings, letters, and other official texts from later periods of Egyptian history that document sanctioned corporal punishments: beatings for failure to pay taxes, beatings for students who failed to study, inflicting open wounds for theft or failure to pay debts, mutilation, and execution. A criminal found to have stolen food from temple lands, tomb robbing, or having minor involvement in the Harem Conspiracy might have their nose and ears removed. A more extreme crime could lead to impalement "on the wood," as depicted in this hieroglyphic determinative (from Daniel McClellan, Brigham Young University Ancient Near Eastern Studies Program) that explains itself pretty well:

Thanks for reading.

Bruce Balfour, PhD
Phoenix, Arizona
January, 2024

Maintain your vigilance against those who should be subordinate to you,
But who turn out not to be so,
Men in whose loyalty one can place no trust;
Do not let yourself be alone with them.
Put no trust in a brother,
Acknowledge no one as a friend,
Do not raise up for yourself intimate companions,
For nothing is to be gained from them.
When you lie down at night, let your own heart be watchful over you,
For no man has any to defend him on the day of anguish.
I was generous to the pauper, I sustained the orphan,
I caused him who had nothing to become at length like a man of means.
But it was one who ate my bread who conspired against me,
One to whom I had given my support devised dread deeds thereby,
Those clad in my fine linen behaved toward me like worthless louts,
And those anointed with my myrrh made my way slippery before me.

--From *The Teaching of Pharaoh Amenemhat I for His Son Senwosret* (Hieratic copy ca. 1295-1070 BCE, New Kingdom Egypt: the original was written after the murder of Amenemhat ca. 1909 BCE when the reign of Pharaoh Senwosret I began)

PROLOGUE

1153 BCE—Royal City of Thebes, Valley of the Kings

Year 32 of His Majesty, King of Upper and Lower Egypt, the Maat of Re is Strong, Beloved of Amun, Son of Re, Ruler of Heliopolis, Pharaoh Ramesses III, Third Month of Shomu (Season of Harvest), Day 15

Even a god can die.

Far below me, in the city of the dead, my ancestors dream of eternity in their royal tombs. I wait for them here, in my chair atop the weathered orange cliffs, at the edge of the great desert, knowing that they will rise with the sunset to stand beside their chambers of eternity and look east across the Nile to the living city. Their dry voices already whisper to me on the breeze that caresses the valley—the same breeze that carries the earthy scent of fertile croplands, fried fish, and baked bread. As the slanting rays of light from Amun-Re's golden sun-boat glide across the Great Place, the glittering river turns silver, continuing its journey through rich black silt and emerald green fields beneath a crystal blue sky. On the east bank, hundreds of temple flagpoles glitter and flash where their golden tips catch the last rays of the dying day, their white pennants dancing in the wind. My sparkling city of Thebes stands proudly, the focus of a great empire rebuilt by my hand, defended by my armies from the Libu and the formidable Sea People. My great works are many, with new temples and monuments built to worship Amun-Re, Ptah, Mut, and Khonsu. I am the Living God; master of the greatest empire the world has ever known. When Anubis weighs my heart and my deeds, Osiris, the Ruler of Eternity, will welcome me as an equal, knowing that I defend Truth and hold back the chaos of Seth. As the voice of the gods in this world, I am the connection between heaven and earth, and my power is great.

But not great enough.

I am Ramesses III, Lord of the Two Lands, King of Upper and Lower Egypt, descendant of Ramesses the Great—and I am dying.

ONE

1184 BCE—Royal City of Pi-Ramesses

Year 4 of His Majesty, King of Upper and Lower Egypt, Chosen by Re, Beloved of Amun, Pharaoh Setnakhte, First Month of Akhet (Season of Inundation), Day 19

Lying awake in the darkness, the boy sensed a hint of moisture—the magic of water borne on the air—and it worried him. He smelled the great river and the black Nile mud, heavy with the fragrance of jasmine and acacia blossoms. Crickets, frogs, and hunting birds of the night sang in unison, while his nurse, Tinubiti, snored on a mat by his door. A feeble breeze, the first in many hours, stirred the flame on the olive oil lamp by the balcony. Spirit shadows jumped along the painted walls. Ray lifted his head from the feather pillow on the cedar wood headrest and rolled over on his side, wondering whether it would be cooler to stay on the white linen of the bed, now damp with his sweat, or to sleep on the stone balcony. Blue moonlight cut an angled path across the floor, seeking him out, as if the moon god Khonsu beckoned him outside. He inhaled, filling his lungs, happy that he could breathe normally. Taking this as a good sign, he rose to his feet, wrapped a white linen kilt around himself, and padded out onto the balcony.

Even after two seasons of living in the golden house of Pharaoh, the majestic view still startled him. Ninety years earlier, Ramesses the Great had built his palace on an island surrounded by two channels of the Nile's eastern branch, and the water on both sides of the city glittered in the moonlight. The flowing water made him feel as if the city were a great stone boat moving up the river. Out of his view, to the south and west, canals completed the barrier around the city, bringing fresh water, sanitation, and safety. The clean white surfaces of the buildings looked blue at this hour, except where the high city walls met the massive gates made of gold, copper, and inlaid precious stones. Nearing the sixth hour of the night, the windows of the administrative buildings were dark, but the burning braziers of the temples lit their outer walls. The flames gave life to massive carved images of the great warrior-king Ramesses II defeating the tiny, but numerous, enemies of Egypt. Obelisks and statues of Ramesses dotted the city, recording his great feats of war and governance for future admirers. Closest to the gate of the Temple of Amun-Re, a 65-foot-tall figure of the great king, wearing the double crown of Upper and Lower Egypt, looked down with disdain upon the mortals who would enter the temple. Ray hoped that someone would build granite statues of him one day, although he knew there was little chance of that except in the simple tomb that he would likely build for himself when he was older. Straight below the balcony, the palace gardens bloomed with flowers and fruit trees, their beauty only partially hidden in the dim light. The image of the moon lay trapped in the still waters of the garden's sacred pools—reflections of eternity stolen from the night.

"*Pssst!*"

Ray gasped, thinking that a snake was about to strike him on the balcony. His heart almost stopped when something bounced off the side of his partially shaved head. A small stone clattered to the balcony beside his feet.

"Ray!"

Relieved that he hadn't been bitten by a cobra, Ray leaned over the balcony to look for the source of the loud whisper, and he saw two indistinct shapes in the shadows. "Who is it?"

"Pen, of course! And Bull!"

Ray looked over his shoulder to make certain that his nurse was still asleep. His friends weren't supposed to be out this late at night, and he didn't want them to get caught. He also didn't want to get himself caught, for his father could be quite severe about Ray breaking the rules, and there were many, many rules. He sometimes wondered how he could be expected to remember so many rules.

"Come down!" That was Bull's voice. Bull didn't bother to whisper because he could talk himself out of trouble. It was rare for Little Bull to be punished, because he was the second-oldest son of Pharaoh Ramesses III, co-regent of the Egyptian empire. Pentawere was third in the line of succession, and he had the gift of being able to deflect his punishments onto other people, but every once in a while his father would beat him with a rod just to remind Pen that he wasn't getting away with anything. Ray shared none of these clever skills, and he was a commoner, so he did his best to stay out of trouble in the first place. His father's job in the palace, and perhaps his own life, depended on his being a good and loyal friend to the royal children.

"I can't come," Ray whispered. "I have to go back to bed."

"Of course you can," Bull said. "All you have to do is climb down."

As his eyes adjusted to the shadows, Ray discerned the muscular shape of Bull, whose eyes glittered up at him. Pen was almost as thin as the trunk of the apple tree beside them. Both boys were fourteen years of age like Ray, so their shaved heads were shiny in the moonlight, except for a patch on the right side where their locks of youth hung down to their shoulders.

"What do you want? We're supposed to be asleep."

"It's too hot," Bull said. "We're going for a swim."

"You and the crocodiles," Ray said.

"Bull will protect us," Pen said. "The hippos and the crocodiles think Bull tastes like *cack*."

Ray tried not to laugh. Bull gave Pen a friendly punch in the side of the head.

"Come on," Pen said. "You and I have to protect the crocodiles from Bull, otherwise he'll eat them."

Ray sighed and looked over his shoulder again. The nurse still snored, and he was still too hot to sleep. Maybe no one would notice if he only went out for a little while.

"Okay," Ray whispered, stepping off the balcony into the curving branches of a big acacia tree. As he made his way under the broad canopy and down the trunk, snapping only one small branch when he snagged his kilt, it occurred to him that the city gates were closed for the night.

"How are we going to get to the river?"

"Bull knows a way," Pen said.

"The soldiers won't let us through the gates."

"I'm smarter than they are," Bull said, leading them across the garden. "That's why they're soldiers, and I'm a prince."

"Maybe I should go back," Ray said, slowing down. Bull probably was smarter than the soldiers, but the soldiers had spears and swords and other things for killing people, and they were good at their jobs, and Ray didn't want them to mistake him for an intruder sneaking around the palace.

"Maybe you should be quiet and follow us," Bull said. "Otherwise, we'll tell everyone that this was your idea."

Ray looked at his feet and sighed. He was trapped, and he knew it.

"You need a cool swim," Pen said, tapping Ray on the head with his palm. "You think too much, so your head overheats."

Resigned to his fate, Ray followed them through the sweet-smelling apple orchard. Night birds screeched, and the bugs were louder here. Following the line of an irrigation trench that fed the sacred pools beside the Temple of Amun-Re, Ray was surprised when Bull took off his loincloth and stepped down into the shallow water with a soft splash. The water gurgled past his thighs when he stopped behind the temple where the trench met the base of the city wall. Using one hand for balance on the shallow bank, Pen dropped his kilt, slid into the water a few feet behind Bull, and beckoned to Ray.

Ray looked down at the flowing water. It seemed shallow, but he couldn't be sure in the dim light. No one had ever taught him to swim like the other two boys, who were both staring at him now. This really seemed like a bad idea. On the other hand, if they were going to swim here, it seemed safer than wading out into the dark Nile on the other side of the city walls.

Pen grabbed Ray's ankle. "Come on! Don't be an old woman!"

"Wait!" Ray stumbled into the water, making a loud splash.

"Quiet," Bull whispered. "We're near the wall and we don't want to attract the guards."

They waited a moment, sitting low in the water, before they decided that no one had heard the splash. Ray felt the cool current flowing across his skin, raising goosebumps, and it was a great relief from the hot desert air. His feet sank into the rich black mud and he wriggled his toes. He didn't even get upset when he realized that he still wore his kilt; he simply removed it and lobbed it onto a nearby bush. With his eyes closed, he settled back against the bank keeping everything but his head under the water.

"What are you doing?" Bull asked.

Ray opened his eyes. The other two boys looked puzzled.

"I'm cooling off."

"You're sitting in the mud in an irrigation ditch," Pen said.

"The river's through here," Bull said, pointing at the base of the wall where the water flowed under an arch that was only one hand-span above the surface. To illustrate his point, he bent forward and dove under the arch.

Ray gasped and shook his head. "I can't go under there."

"It's not far," Pen said. "We tried it last night. Just hold your breath and go under the wall. Bull is on the other side already."

"I can't swim."

"You don't need to swim. Just hold your breath and walk forward like a hippo." Pen suddenly looked over Ray's shoulder and his eyes got wider. "I hear something. Let's go before they catch us!"

Pen grabbed Ray's arm and hauled him under the arch. Water went up Ray's nose, but he managed to keep it out of his mouth. He kept his eyes open, but he couldn't see anything. His scalp scraped against stone while Pen dragged him forward. He couldn't go back, he was certain that he'd drown, and the worst part was that his father would be angry when they found Ray's body floating down the river. If he were lucky, maybe something would eat him before anyone found his body. On the other hand, if his body disappeared, it could not be beautified by the sem-priests to ensure his immortality in the afterlife. He was doomed.

His face broke the surface of the water again.

"You are *such* an old woman," Bull said, sitting on the bank above them as Ray spluttered with water streaming out of his nose. "There's a whole world out here for you to explore, but what do you do? You spend all your time reading the words of dead men. Your life will be over before you realize that you never left your bedroom."

Bull liked to point out Ray's shortcomings, but he also understood that it was Bull's way of trying to help him.

"I'll make a note of that," Ray said, sitting down on the bank.

Pen skipped a flat rock down the ditch toward the river. It stopped and sank when it hit the water weeds.

Ray ducked his head and glanced around. "Pen?"

"What?"

"I thought you were worried about noise. You heard a guard on the other side of the wall."

Pen snorted. "Scaring you was the only way to get you here."

Ray sighed and looked out at the sparkling waters of the broad river, where bats darted for insects above blue and white lotus flowers floating on the water. The Nile was near its seasonal peak when the waters rose to cover the land and deposit fresh black silt where crops would grow in abundance. The annual flood also increased the range of the crocodiles and hippos that lay hidden beneath the surface, and he knew that two servants doing laundry in the river here had been taken by hippos over the last few days. The priests of Hapi, goddess of the Nile, were the only people allowed to eat hippo meat, and this protection allowed the beasts to multiply and attack people without penalty whenever they wished. The priests of Sobek protected the crocodiles. Ray often wondered why people, other than the temple priests, seemed to have so few rights in the natural world, but his father said that was the way of things and he had to accept it. The only exceptions were for the royal family—when the proper offerings had been made at the temples, a one-day permit would be issued for a hunting party. Ray gazed at the strong current flowing past beyond the thick beds of papyrus, hoping that Pen and Bull would come to their senses and let them all go back to bed. Failing that, he'd try to convince them that the water here in the irrigation ditch was cool enough, or maybe he could talk them into swimming in the adjacent lagoon. The only problem with that plan was that they were likely to make Ray enter the lagoon first, as one of his implied tasks as a "royal friend" was to act as a decoy to protect the princes. Life was never easy for a royal friend.

"I fear that Ray has been hypnotized by Hapi," Bull said, standing to survey their route to the river. "His tongue has gone silent, and his eyes see only the waters of the east."

"I see only my meeting with Osiris in the near future," Ray said, "for the current is strong, and I am but a simple boy who lacks your great mastery of the water."

Pen smiled. "Nicely said. However, you'll never learn how to swim unless someone teaches you."

Ray shook his head. "If Hapi had meant for us to swim, she would have given us the ability to live in water, which is only for drinking, bathing, boating, fishing, and watering the fields."

"You speak like your father," Pen said.

"My father is wise. That's why the Living God made him our tutor."

"Your father will never be anything more than he is because he never takes any chances. He avoids new experiences. Where's the wisdom in that?"

Ray frowned. Why would his father take chances? Hapu always said that gambling was for fools. And he had certainly taken enough risks to get Ray into the Great King's golden house for a better education. Even before he made his son co-regent, Pharaoh Setnakhte had sought out the most educated man in Egypt to teach his children, but Scribe Hapu said he wouldn't take the job unless Ray could be educated alongside the royal offspring. He remembered Vizier To's surprised expression when Hapu made this request in the front room of their modest mud-brick home in Thebes, but Pharaoh had agreed to the arrangement in the end. This put Ray in the precarious position of being a royal friend, along with all the hazards that came with the position, but he did appreciate access to the palace's wonderful library. Pen wouldn't be able to understand his father's idea of risk. He shook his head—risk without thought was simply gambling, and his father only gambled when the odds favored his family.

Still, Ray knew it would be better to keep these thoughts to himself. "We're fortunate that my father is nothing more than what he is, otherwise he wouldn't be available to teach us."

"While you stand there and talk all night, I'm going for a swim," Bull said, stepping down into the ditch and through a clear space in between the papyrus beds. A moment later, he dove into the river. The graceful maneuver barely made a splash in the swift current.

"There, he went first," Pen said. "Nothing to worry about. Now, you go."

Making one final effort to escape, Ray gave him a weak smile. "You haven't told me how to swim. Perhaps you should show me first."

Pen rolled his eyes, then moved as if to step past Ray between the reeds. While Ray took a deep breath in relief, Pen grabbed his arm and they both tumbled into the river.

Out of control, Ray bounced and rolled underwater, bumping his head and legs against the reeds. His lungs heaved in protest as he flailed his limbs, hoping to catch something so he could pull himself out. Then a big hand closed on his right arm and lifted, and his feet found the muddy bottom.

"You're not doing it right," Bull said, towering over him where he stood in the shallow water. "You have to float and move your arms. Or you can just stand up—it's shallow here."

Bull let go of his arm, and Ray stood in a crouch, gasping and fighting for balance in the cool water that swirled around his legs. His feet sank into the mud. The slight breeze on the river chilled his wet body, and he now wished he were back in his hot bed.

"Maybe I should go back," Ray suggested. "I can try this again after I've thought about your instructions."

Bull laughed, but it was a kind laugh, and Ray appreciated him for it.

He almost fell over again when something heavy brushed against his leg. The rough surface scratched his skin as it moved past. Thinking it was Pen playing a joke on him from behind, he turned against the current, but Pen was nowhere to be seen.

"Get out!" Bull yelled at Ray, waving his arms just before the crocodile broke the surface and slammed its long snout into Bull's chest. Bull stepped aside and punched at the eyes on top of its head, but his blow landed without harm against its scaly hide. It scratched his chest with its long claws while it turned and darted behind him. From nose to tail, it was a little taller than Bull, so it was a young one, maybe six years old. The last thing Ray saw before it vanished beneath the surface was the sparkle of jewelry attached to the top of its head, which meant that it had escaped from one of the pools in the Temple of Sobek.

When it reappeared behind Bull, the crocodile's mouth opened wide, displaying its cone-shaped teeth. Without thinking, Ray stumbled forward to help his friend, who had just started to turn toward the splash, but it took less than a heartbeat before the teeth bit into Bull's left arm and pulled him under the water.

Spluttering, Ray lost his footing in the mud and was swept off his feet by the current. With his eyes open under the water in the moonlight, he saw the dark shape of the crocodile trying to wedge Bull under a big rock so that he would drown. Since it couldn't chew, it would leave Bull's body under the rock until it started to rot, at which point it could eat his tender flesh at its leisure. While Ray drifted closer, unable to control his course in the river, Bull struggled and kicked up clouds of mud. Remembering to hold his breath, Ray grabbed at the mud and tried to turn his body so that his legs were together and pointed downstream, figuring he would hit the crocodile with his feet. He heard his heart pounding in his ears, but all he could think about was saving his friend.

The crocodile saw Ray's clumsy approach and turned to face him with a graceful motion of its tail. Wedged under the rock now, Bull still appeared to be struggling, but the twisting of his limbs could have been caused by the current. Ray tasted copper in his mouth and realized that he'd bitten his tongue—not that it would matter in a few seconds. His lungs screamed for air.

A thundering splash above the crocodile startled everyone. At first, Ray thought it might be another crocodile, and then he realized that it must be Pentawere jumping in from the bank. Pen was on the crocodile's back with his arms wrapped around its neck when Ray's right foot smacked it in the eye. He tried to grab the creature to help Pen, but the current carried him past until he grabbed one of Bull's legs. His weight combined with the power of the current to wrench Bull free of the boulder. Pen was occupied with the crocodile, so Ray knew he had simply made it possible to drown himself with his unconscious friend.

Stunned when his head and neck smacked into the reeds in a papyrus bed, Ray lost precious seconds before he plunged his free hand into the reeds. His feet found the mud and he rose into a crouch, gasping for air, supporting Bull against his legs to lift his head out of the water. Bull's eyes were closed and his chest remained still.

Fishing along the river when he was younger, Ray had watched as one of the priests from the House of Life restored the breath to a woman rescued from the water. With this image in mind, he pulled Bull farther up onto the slippery bank, hoping there weren't any more crocodiles or hippos hidden among the reeds. He rolled Bull onto his stomach with his head pointed down the slope of the bank. Ignoring the blood streaming from Bull's head and his left arm, Ray pressed both hands down on his friend's back. Bull's wet skin felt cold and it looked blue, although that could be caused by the moonlight. Ray pressed down again on Bull's back, bouncing up and down, uncertain of the technique that the priest had used to revive the woman. He had never been close enough to hear any magic words or prayers that the priest had used to bring her back to life.

"Bull! Come back, Bull!" If he screamed loud enough, Bull's spirit might hear him.

At the periphery of his vision, Ray sensed someone else approaching, but he didn't have time to think about it. Bull suddenly coughed and vomited into the mud, returning the river water to its source. Ray rubbed the prince's back while he continued to heave and gasp for air. His skin began to warm.

"By the blood of Horus," Pen spluttered.

Ray turned to see Pen stooping over them. He had several bleeding cuts and scratches on his body, and he was breathing hard, but otherwise seemed as if he'd just been out for a rough swim in the river.

"I thought he was dead," Pen said, kneeling down in the mud beside them. His eyes were wide when he turned to whisper at Ray. "You brought him back to life."

Pharaoh's personal physician, Seini, had been trained at the House of Life in Abydos, which was known for the high quality of its teachings in medicine and healing magic. Summoned from his bed in the palace three hours before sunrise, Seini wore no wig on his bald head nor golden collars of office around his neck. Dressed in a rumpled white tunic, carrying a small reed box that contained the tools of his trade, he puffed into Bull's bedroom with a red face and droopy eyes.

Pen had slung Bull over his shoulder like a dead gazelle and carried him all the way back from the river, trading off only briefly with Ray, who was quickly winded from the exertion. Bull slept during most of the trip, waking on occasion to have a coughing fit or to vomit more water down the backs of Pen's legs. Once they reached the palace, two guards had carried Bull the rest of the way to his bedroom, their footsteps and whispers echoing through the blue corridors inlaid with lapis lazuli and turquoise, dazzling even in the dim light of the olive oil lamps. Once they reached Bull's room, his nurse was sent to fetch Seini and Bull's mother, Chief Queen Isis. Bull remained asleep on his back after the guards placed him on the bed with great care.

Seini loomed over the bed and motioned for one of the servants to bring the oil lamps closer. With a suspicious look in his eyes, Seini questioned Pen and Ray about Bull's condition. He then set his tool case on a low table and bent over so that his ear was close to Bull's mouth. He listened to Bull's breathing, and Ray could tell that it sounded raspy. Moving lower, Seini placed the side of his head against Bull's bruised and bleeding chest, then grunted and stood up.

"He can be treated," Seini said, taking linen bandages from his tool case.

Ray sighed with relief. If Bull survived, his own life might be spared from Pharaoh's wrath, and his father might be able to keep his position in the royal household.

Seini looked at the nurse while he wrapped bandages around Bull's crocodile-damaged arm. "Bring me honey, cream, milk, carob, colocynth, and date kernels."

When the nurse left, Seini told another servant to bring seven bricks heated over fire.

Ray's back was to the bedroom doorway, so the sudden scent of perfumed oils surprised him. When he turned, he was amazed at how fast Queen Isis had been able to rouse herself from sleep and appear here fully dressed in a pleated white gown and gilded sandals, her lips and eyebrows painted with an artist's precision. Distracted by her beauty and her scent, Ray barely remembered to bow and extend his arms, palms up, to show his respect. Her two attendants remained outside in the hallway as Isis stepped forward and touched the top of Ray's head, allowing him to rise. This was a good sign, as he was sure that the queen already knew what had happened to her son, and who had been with him when he nearly drowned. She walked around to the other side of Bull's bed and watched in silence as the physician continued his work.

With a flickering candle in his hand, Seini peered into Bull's face and thumbed open each of the prince's eyes, turning his head aside when Bull gurgled and coughed.

"We'll know tomorrow if the water he inhaled has affected his thinking. His other wounds are minor. However, I need to treat his cough and make it easier for him to breathe so that he can sleep better."

Isis stroked her son's forehead and spoke in a calm voice. "Know this, Seini. I have already lost one son to Osiris this past year, and I will not lose another one under your care. I wish you success in treating young Ramesses, for if he dies, you will accompany him on his final journey to the west. You will watch him rise to the heavens to become a star. Then your heart will be weighed before Osiris, your failures will become known, and you will be eaten by the Devourer of Souls."

The cold eyes of the queen rose to meet Seini's attentive gaze, prompting him to bow and extend his arms. "I understand, my lady. I will do all that I can, and I will pray to Imhotep to heal your son."

Ray shivered. If the royal physician would not be allowed eternal life due to his failure, how could Ray fare any better? Isis's youngest son had died of a strange illness two seasons before Ray had started living in the palace, but he had been warned never to mention his death to her because it would cause her distress.

The nurse returned with the supplies Seini had requested. With a stone grinding bowl from his tool case, he crushed the carob and colocynth grains with the date kernels. This powder was then combined in another stone bowl with the cream, milk, and honey, forming a thick paste. By the time he was done, the servant had returned carrying a tray with seven mud bricks that had been heated over a fire. Ray recognized this as the same mixture Seini prepared whenever he had breathing problems during the night; on those occasions, Seini would burn the mixture on the bricks and cover the fumes with a clay jar that had a hole in its bottom. Ray would then inhale the fumes through a hollow reed inserted in the hole. He didn't know how Seini would get the unconscious Bull to inhale the fumes.

After placing a jar over the smoking mixture on one of the bricks, Seini inserted a long reed in the hole and placed the other end in Bull's mouth. By holding the mouth closed, and pinching Bull's nose shut, he managed to make the boy inhale the fumes. Ray nodded with approval. Seini had the nurse assume the task of holding Bull's mouth and nose shut so that he could raise his arms and look toward the ceiling.

"There is a shouting in the southern sky in darkness," Seini said in his deep voice. "There is an uproar in the northern sky. The Hall of Pillars falls into the waters of the Great River. The crew of the Sun God bends its oars, and their heads fall into the water. Who leads hither what he finds? I lead forth what I find! I lift up your necks and fasten what has been cut from you. I lead you forth to drive away the God of Fevers and all possible deadly arts!"

Seini had never prayed to Imhotep to intercede with Ray's breathing problems, but he understood that Bull's problem was more serious, requiring stronger healing magic. To ensure a successful treatment, some sort of sacrifice would likely be made later that morning when Seini visited the local Temple of Amun-Re. At least, he assumed that Amun-Re would be the correct god for this task—Sekhmet might be more appropriate, but

Ray didn't know for sure because he didn't really understand the ways of physicians or temple priests. Perhaps he could ask his father after he was finished beating Ray for endangering the life of the prince.

Isis's expression hardened into a mask when she caught sight of someone new coming through the doorway. Revealing no emotion in the rest of her face, Ray was startled by the hatred in her cold eyes. Guessing who it must be, Ray turned and bowed.

Queen Teya wore a transparent flowing gown that displayed the beauty of her perfect almond skin. She wore no jewelry except for three gold rings, but the long black hair of her wig was styled in precise braids and tight curls. Her eyes were rimmed with black kohl, while her eyelids sparkled with powdered green malachite. She returned Queen Isis's stare without blinking as she walked quickly across the floor on bare feet to hug Pentawere from behind. In a few more seasons, he would be as tall as his mother, who was known for her height among the women of the harem. Pentawere barely noticed her, continuing to stare at Bull on the bed.

Ray's father had explained that both queens held the title of "Great King's Wife," but Isis held the higher rank as "Chief Royal Wife." Isis was a noblewoman who had known Ramesses III since they were children. Second in importance, Teya held the rank of "Principal Royal Wife," although she still had a higher status than the lesser wives and the women of the royal harem. Ray didn't understand why Isis and Teya disliked each other so much, as Pen was second heir to the throne if Bull should die, and Ramesses treated Isis and Teya almost equally. Although the ailing Pharaoh Setnakhte had three other sons in addition to his eldest son, Ramesses, they were no longer in the line of succession since Ramesses had been appointed co-regent.

Teya turned Pen's face so that he would look at her. "You are all right?"

"Yes, mother."

Teya nodded at Isis. "And Bull? How is he?"

"The *prince* will survive," Isis said, stroking his forehead and refusing to look at Teya any more. "He is strong like his namesake."

"I'm told he is fortunate that my son was there to rescue him from the crocodile."

Isis's eyes glittered at Ray. "I believe Ray also deserves our thanks."

"That one can't even swim," Teya said with a snort. "I'm sure my son had to rescue Ray as well."

Pen smiled at Ray. "It's not his fault, mother. He tried to help Bull by distracting the crocodile. That gave me time to wrestle with the great beast and drive it away."

Teya patted Pen on the shoulder. "You see? Without any thought of his own safety, my son rescued Bull and the other one. He deserves your deepest gratitude."

Ray wished that Teya would refer to him by name. His father, Hapu, said that Teya treated people this way because of her beauty, which made people want to do things for her. She used her appearance and her pleasing voice to manipulate and to harm, and Hapu had warned him to avoid her as much as possible. She mostly kept to her own apartments and the harem within the palace, so Ray only saw her when Pen was around to protect him. She didn't appear to like or dislike Ray—he had the impression that she just didn't care, as if he were a piece of furniture, or a floor she could walk on without thinking about it.

Isis studied Pen's face for a moment, and then gave him a slight bow. "I thank you for helping my son. You're a good friend to him."

Pen bowed in return, and Teya looked satisfied. She took Pen by the hand and led him toward the door. "My boy needs his rest. If Bull is called for his final journey into the west, and Sesi does not return from battle, Pentawere must be prepared to take his place at Pharaoh's side."

With a heavy sigh, Isis rolled her eyes and looked at Ray. "Thank you for your help, Ray. Your father has raised you well. Now, you also should get some sleep, as the night has been long and tomorrow may be difficult."

"I'd like to stay," Ray said, gesturing at the sleeping form of Bull, who continued to inhale the healing smoke through the reed. Muttering to himself beside the bed, Seini made notes on a scrap of papyrus.

"You'll be notified if anything changes," Isis said. "And I'm sorry to say so, but I suggest that you pray and make a sacrifice for my son, as your own fate is entwined with his. May the gods protect you both."

Ray swallowed. He knew what that meant.

Khait bowed her head and closed her eyes as the bucket of water splashed over her. She waited a moment, relishing the feel of the cool water trickling down her skin in the dry air, and then felt delicate hands scrubbing her with wet natron from head to toe. Blinking the water from her eyes, she looked up at the dim pre-dawn light filtering through the windows cut into the stone just below the ceiling. She was careful not to move on the small bathing slab, knowing the wet stone surface was slippery from the scented oils of women in the harem who were washed here daily, and she didn't want to fall. There were only a few other women with their servants in the harem's bathing room at this early hour, and they looked like beautiful wet statues on their pedestals. Her body servant, Kemisi, massaged the coarse natron crystals into her muscles, making her skin tingle all over. Kemisi was also naked, and Khait opened her eyes to admire her servant's strong muscles as she worked her way down to Khait's feet, which had gradually become smoother and softer like the feet of the other harem women who never had to toil outside.

Khait had joined the harem almost a year ago, and her feet had been tougher then. Being the daughter of a noble—the important Panhayboni, Overseer of Cattle on all of Pharaoh's lands—Khait had never worked in dirt, but until she was sixteen she had enjoyed the freedom of playing and going barefoot most of the time. After she joined the harem, she learned that this was a sign of low status that would no longer be tolerated in an adult woman from a noble family in the royal household. Now, she wore delicate leather or reed sandals all the time. Her feet received regular scrubbings with castor oil and natron before being massaged with honey and olive oil. She had also learned to stay out of the sun as much as possible to avoid darkening her light brown skin. There were a lot of rules in the golden house of Pharaoh.

Kemisi dumped two more buckets of water over Khait, using her hands to make sure the natron was scrubbed away, then rinsed her hands in another bucket before she picked up a white linen towel and began drying Khait's short black hair. Her life was so much better since her father had convinced Queen Teya to admit Khait to the harem. Her skills as a weaver of fine royal linen, and as a dressmaker, had earned her a following among the nobility of Heliopolis ever since she was ten years old. There were four grades of linen. Royal linen was the finest cloth of all, and her weaving made the cloth so transparent that it looked like a white mist when made into clothing. When Queen Teya had learned of Khait's reputation, after receiving many fine gifts from Panhayboni that included some of her woven linen, she had wasted no time in summoning Khait to the harem in Piramesses—the longest journey she had ever taken on the Great River.

Her father had not told the queen that Khait knew how to read, write, and work with numbers, fearing that she would seem too odd for the golden house. Women were not accepted at scribe school in the House of Life, and her father had only taught her these things in case she failed to gain her place in noble society. If she had not been admitted to the harem, where her needs would be satisfied for the rest of her life, she would have helped Panhayboni's Chief Steward and Senior Scribe with management of the family estate in Heliopolis. This would have been a job for Panhayboni's oldest son, but his wife, Afrikaisi, had only borne him two daughters before dying during her third pregnancy when Khait was eight years old. Devastated by the loss of his wife, Panhayboni had buried himself in his work and never remarried.

Kemisi finished working olive oil into Khait's hair and pulled a sheath dress over her head. She beckoned toward the alcoves along the sides of the room where two relaxed women sighed with pleasure while oil was worked into their muscles by their servants. "Do you wish a massage this morning, mistress?"

Khait shook her head. "Not today. Queen Teya will be waiting for me. I'm finishing her new dress for the festival tomorrow."

Kemisi bowed and smiled as she quickly toweled herself off. "Will you teach me to weave when you return? You know I'm good with my hands."

Khait smiled. Kemisi came from a common family somewhere nearby in the Delta and might never have the chance to wear fine linen. She had often asked if she could learn to weave, but it took long hours of practice to properly spin thread from flax and become proficient with the vertical loom, and she had too many other duties in the harem. At thirty years of age, she was also a little too old for such an apprenticeship, and her eyes would quickly weaken from the fine work.

Khait didn't want to see her face when told her no once again. She stepped into her sandals and turned to walk back to her room in the harem so that Kemisi could paint her face, put on her wig, and dress her for the meeting with Queen Teya. "I need your hands for other things, Kemisi."

"I understand, mistress."

Khait made a mental note to give Kemisi enough fine, second-grade linen to make herself a new dress.

The summons had come just before sunrise. The nurse, Tinubiti, gave Ray's shoulder a gentle shake. When he opened his eyes, he saw lines of worry in the normally smooth face that hovered over him. She said that Ray would have an audience with Pharaoh Setnakhte before the appointments of the day prevented such an unscheduled interruption of the affairs of state. Ray knew he should be honored to be singled out in this way, but he dreaded the conversation and what might happen to him as a result of his foolhardy adventure the previous night. He sat up in the bed and rubbed his eyes, wishing he could sleep for a few more hours before he had to defend himself in front of Pharaoh.

Tinubiti helped him into a clean white kilt and placed a broad collar of blue turquoise and copper over his neck. Despite the counterweight on the back of his neck, the collar hung low over his bare chest. It was a heavy thing, and he didn't like wearing it, but it was a pretty gift from his father, and one had to keep up appearances in the palace. Tinubiti had already laid out the pair of sandals that Ray customarily wore on formal occasions, and now she knelt to slip them onto his feet. His stomach grumbled.

"Do I have time to eat something?"

She bowed her head. "It's best not to make the living god wait for you, my master. He awoke early and demanded to see you before his morning sacrifice at the temple."

"Perhaps *I'll* be the sacrifice."

"Don't say that. It's not wise to joke about the gods."

"It may not be a joke."

When she stood, he saw the look of alarm in her eyes. "Why are you so worried, Tinubiti? I was the one who sneaked out last night."

"I was the one who slept all night while you were gone. You were in my care and I failed to properly watch over you. You're still young, and you're expected to make mistakes, but I have seen twenty-six flood seasons, so I'm supposed to know better. If anyone is sacrificed this day, it will be me."

Ray took her hand and looked up into her face. "No harm will come to you."

"I am nothing, my master. Don't be concerned for me." She forced herself to smile. "Besides, if harm comes to you first, how could you help me?"

Two soldiers, armed with curved *khepesh* swords and spears tipped in gleaming copper, escorted Ray through the cool blue turquoise and lapis lazuli corridors of the palace. A few bald priests in white robes and sandals, accompanied by scurrying servants in short kilts, were the only other people he saw at that early hour. The lamps were still lit, but the gray glow in the pre-dawn sky had already begun to brighten the windows that looked out onto the palace gardens.

The public throne room was intended to strike awe into visitors, and it had the same effect on Ray. White limestone columns supported the high ceiling. The thick walls were decorated with brightly colored tiles showing scenes of bound captives, humble vassals paying tribute to Pharaoh, and lions eating prisoners. The floor tiles were covered with representations of the many enemies of Egypt, past and present, so that Pharaoh could walk on them during his daily business. The air had a pleasant smell of incense. Only two lamps were lit in this large chamber, placed on either side of a doorway that led into a more intimate audience room that glowed with light. As the two nearby thrones on the raised platform were empty, Ray realized that the smaller chamber would be their destination. His stomach fluttered, and he was glad that he hadn't eaten before his audience with the living god who ruled the Two Lands.

Pharaoh Setnakhte sat on a throne of ebony and gold, its feet carved to resemble the paws of a lion. Following the precedent set by his own ancestor, Ramesses the Great, Pharaoh kept an actual old lion named Shenti on the floor beside the throne, motionless except for the tail flicking at the air. Shenti had been raised alongside Ramesses III, and it was rumored that the 56-year-old Pharaoh treated both of them as his sons. The lion's eyes snapped open at the sound of Ray's footsteps, prompting a chill to run down his spine despite the warmth of the air. The guards hung back at the doorway while Ray proceeded forward to stop a respectable distance from the throne, then knelt and bowed low, arms outstretched as his forehead touched the floor.

"You may rise, Ramose, son of Hapu."

Setnakhte was the king's birth name. When combined with his second epithet, *meramunre*, his birth name meant, "Victorious is Set, Beloved of Amun-Re." Four years earlier, when he had taken his place on the throne, tradition prompted him to take a throne name, which was Userkhaure Setepenre, meaning "Powerful are the Manifestations of Re, Chosen by Re." Except for a brief introduction when Ray had first come to the palace, he had never been in the same room with Pharaoh, and he didn't like being there now. Bad things could happen to throne room visitors, or so he had heard. He wished Hapu were there, as the calm presence of his father could minimize any urge Pharaoh might have to execute Ray right on the spot.

Ray stood and tried to look subservient while memorizing every detail of Pharaoh's face. There was a definite resemblance to the depictions of Ramesses the Great on the city walls, although some claimed that they weren't related. The proud face and angular lines of the jaw had been softened by time. He knew from Pen's comments that Pharaoh had aged considerably after only four years of ruling their great land of Kemet. As Setnakhte grew more concerned about his health in the last few months, he had appointed Ramesses III as co-regent so that the younger man could continue the fight against the regional warlords who had sprung up during the chaos years to challenge the power of the golden house.

Rather than wear the heavy double-crown of Upper and Lower Egypt for this informal visit, Pharaoh wore only the striped cloth *nemes* over his head, and the hanging folds of the fabric helped to cover the deep wrinkles in his neck that were visible behind the traditional false beard tightly bound beneath his chin. The white linen robe fell in neat, pleated folds from the heavy *usekh* collar of gold inlaid with semi-precious stones of green jasper, symbolizing resurrection and joy; red carnelian, the color of blood and life energy; and blue lapis lazuli representing the protective sky.

A small feast of bread, roast goose, smoked meats, fruit, and milk had been placed before Pharaoh on a low table made of cedar wood and ivory. Ray's stomach grumbled as Pepi, a tiny little man who served as one of Pharaoh's personal assistants, brought a small bowl of Pharaoh's favorite dates and popped one into his mouth before setting the bowl on the table.

Setnakhte rubbed Pepi's bald head, then saw that Ray looked confused. "My food is always tested before I eat it. There is a long tradition of Egyptian kings killed by poisoned foods, and I don't intend to maintain that particular custom. So it always is with the successful, *neh*?"

"Such concerns are far beyond me, my lord."

"So you may think, but every man has enemies, and you will have your share. Hear what I tell you. You should be on your guard against all who are subordinate to you, of whose plotting one is not aware. Trust not a brother, know not a friend, and make no intimates, for it is useless. When you lie down, guard your heart yourself, for in times of trouble no man has supporters."

"I will remember this, great lord, but I don't understand. Is this meant to imply that I can't be trusted? I would give my life before I would ever harm you or anyone else in your household."

Setnakhte raised one eyebrow. "You are young, Ray, and you were not raised among the schemers of a royal house. It may be that you are more trustworthy than anyone."

"Then you understand that I didn't try to harm Little Bull?"

"I understand that you rescued him from the river and returned him to life. This is a valuable skill. Have you considered becoming a physician in the House of Life?"

"No," Ray said. "I want to be a scribe like my father."

"A worthy ambition; a scribe can be many things. And Hapu is a good man. Just remember that you have choices, and that the gods may have need of your services some day."

"I was happy to help Bull, but the gods wanted him to live. I'm not a healer."

"You are an instrument of the gods, as we all are. You may not think you're a healer, but I never thought I would be Pharaoh—the great Amun-Re revealed his plan to me only a few years ago. But you are young, and there is still time for you to learn your way."

Pepi had finished munching on each of the delicacies prepared for Pharaoh. He bowed low with arms extended, then turned and retreated to the shadows along the wall. Pharaoh leaned forward and his hand hovered over the bowl of dates before plucking one out so fast that Ray almost didn't see the movement.

Still bent forward over the bowl, Pharaoh looked up at Ray and smiled before holding out his closed fist. "Take this date from my hand."

Ray hesitated only for a moment before he reached forward. Pharaoh opened his hand to reveal an empty palm.

"This is opportunity, young man. When an opportunity appears, you must strike swiftly without thinking. There are more dates where that came from, but this will not always be true." He opened his other fist to reveal the date in his palm. "Look at that. The date has not been eaten because it was hidden in a safe place."

Ray accepted the date when Pharaoh dropped it into his hand. "Thank you, my lord." Before Pharaoh changed his mind, Ray popped it into his mouth. The date pit had been removed by the royal servants of the kitchen.

Pharaoh chose another date and held it up for a moment before biting it in half. "A bowl is not a safe place for a date, even though it looks like all the others. One might think that a single date would find safety in numbers, but a god might pluck it from the crowd and eat it at any time."

"Yes, my lord." He began to wonder if Pharaoh had been drinking too much wine at this early hour.

Setnakhte leaned back on his throne and tipped his head while chewing. "You may think the old Pharaoh has gone mad, speaking of dates as if they were something precious to be safely hidden away."

"No, my lord."

"Ah. Hapu says you're a smart one, and his evaluation may be more than a father's pride. Why do you think I speak of dates in this way?"

Not wanting to sound simple, Ray tried to come up with a good reason. He felt a trickle of sweat tracing a course from his forehead to the end of his nose. This appeared to be some kind of a test, and he didn't want to fail. Pharaoh's judgment could be harsh.

"The dates represent people. The princes of the royal house, perhaps?"

Pharaoh tore off a hunk of bread from the loaf and bit into it. The smell of fresh bread drifted past Ray's damp nose.

"The princes may not be hidden from view. They're public figures, and their absence would be noticed. In a world of schemers, this also makes them targets, of course, but we do whatever we can to protect them. On the other hand, there is always the possibility that all of them will be eaten at once. What then? Who would rule the empire?"

It was clear that Pharaoh wanted an answer. As hard as it was to follow this line of conversation, Ray made his best guess as to the proper answer. "The hidden date?"

Setnakhte laughed and slapped his knee. "Excellent!"

Ray bowed his head and breathed a sigh of relief. "Thank you, Great One."

"Eat, Ray." Pharaoh handed him the rest of the bread loaf. "Eat and know that Pharaoh's eye is upon you."

Pepi approached from the shadows and cleared his throat. Pharaoh waved him away.

"Our time for this morning is over, but we will speak again," Pharaoh said, rising from his throne. He picked up the bowl of dates. "I want you to ponder the meaning of hidden dates before our next meeting, Ray. For now, I must attend to the tedious business of the day, for the ruler of the Two Lands has no control over his own time. Nothing moves without being set in motion by the living god."

As Pepi gestured for Ray to follow him to a side exit, the living god Setnakhte limped toward the main throne room munching on his bowl of dates.

Striding with purpose, Pepi led Ray through a section of the palace that he had never seen before, its light-colored walls painted with relaxing floral motifs and river scenes of water birds and fish. Ray noticed that the painted scenes showed no crocodiles, hippos, or their unsuspecting victims being killed in the Great River. If these same scenes had been painted in the throne room, dismembered bodies would probably be strewn everywhere along the river banks to impress foreign visitors or wide-eyed country people summoned before Pharaoh.

Pepi glanced sideways at Ray as they walked. "Don't let your head get big just because you had an audience with the living god."

"I was honored by his summons."

"Of course. What I'm saying is that he was curious about you and that's all. Don't expect to speak with him again."

"I am at his pleasure. If he wishes to speak with me, I will obey. If not, I expect no more."

Pepi nodded. "It's wise to know your place. You'll do well to remember that."

"My thanks for your assistance," Ray said, wondering why the little man seemed to be threatening him.

"There is one more who's curious about you, just as an unusual bug is often studied before it gets stepped on. Be respectful, and remember that you're in the presence of a favored queen, otherwise you also may find a great royal foot coming down upon you."

Getting stepped on seemed like a natural concern for someone of Pepi's size, but Ray wasn't worried.

Pepi turned through a doorway bordered with brightly painted lotus blossoms, nodded at a guard in the small bedroom on the other side, and finally led Ray out into the filtered sunlight of a small, private garden. A rectangular pond, where small fish darted beneath white lotus blossoms and orange poppies, was surrounded by a walkway bordered with trees and flowers planted in neat rows. Palm, fig, and willow trees provided plenty of shade and shelter for chittering birds. Yellow daisies and red roses were the only flowers that Ray recognized, but there were many more in shades of blue. After his senses had recovered from the shock of seeing so much color in the charming little garden, Ray's stomach grumbled when he saw a smaller imitation of Pharaoh's morning feast laid out on a low table.

He caught the smells of roast goose and gazelle, and it made his mouth water. Bread, fish, red grapes, and pomegranates were arranged in an artistic fashion on golden plates. In the shadows along the walls, servants waited for their master and a blind harpist began strumming his instrument.

Pepi turned and bowed. Sensing someone behind him, Ray also turned and bowed. Queen Isis swept into the room, her face, hair, and dress made up as perfectly as they had been in the middle of the night when she had visited her son's bedside.

Her graceful, soft hand rested on Ray's head and lingered there a moment like a bird. He maintained his bow with forearms extended.

"Your head has a pleasing shape," Isis said, rubbing his scalp. "No bumps."

Ray wasn't sure how to answer, so he just nodded.

"Pharaoh awaits me at court," Pepi said, starting to rise.

Isis slapped her other hand against the top of Pepi's head. "Remember your place, worm."

"Sorry, mistress. Sorry," Pepi said, bowing lower.

Isis gave him a dismissive wave. "Get out. Your master needs your back for his footstool."

Pepi extended his arms and backed toward the door. "Yes, mistress. Thank you, mistress."

Isis placed her hand under Ray's chin and raised his head so that he could stand. Her dark eyes sparkled with reflections from the pond. He felt as if he were looking into the infinite abyss, but the mysterious darkness there welcomed him as a friend. When he realized he was staring, he forced himself to look away, and she lightened his heart with a delicate laugh.

"This has been quite a day for you. You helped save my son's life, then Pharaoh spoke to you, and now you're offered a nobleman's morning meal."

Ray glanced at the food. Was she serious, or was this another of Pharaoh's tricks? His normal breakfast was bread, although it was a good quality of bread, and maybe a little bit of roast ox or fried fish when he was lucky. He was never hungry, but they didn't usually feed him the elaborate meals that Bull and Pen received. Seeing the question in his eyes, Isis took his hand and led him to the feast.

"Eat and be happy," she said, selecting a few grapes.

Ray hesitated, then took some bread and a few grapes. "You are generous, my queen. May you live a long life of prosperity and good health."

Isis smiled and broke off a chunk of the dark bread for herself. "Hapu has raised you well. Have you suffered any ill effects from your adventure last night?"

"Only my sorrow at Bull's condition."

"My son will be fine. He's very strong, and I spoke with him just before I came here. He wanted me to thank you for helping him, and I wanted to thank you by providing a good meal."

"You are very kind." Suspicion about her motives still lingered in his mind, but he also knew he could be reacting that way because people within the palace kept telling him that he should.

"What did the Great One speak to you about?"

"Dates, mostly."

"An important event coming up?"

"No, I mean actual dates from the palm trees. He compared them to people."

She raised one eyebrow. "Pharaoh is old and sick. His mind wanders, and that's why he needs my husband to take his place. However, Sesi can't be two places at once, and he still has battles to fight to restore peace to the country. Chancellor Bay did much damage behind the backs of the last two pharaohs—now that he's gone, the warlords in the towns must be punished for their defiance of the living god."

Ray noted how she used the nickname, *Sesi*, for Ramesses III, and he wondered if the co-regent minded her casual use of this name among those outside the family.

Hapu had taught Ray and his other pupils about the traitorous Chancellor Bay, and how he stole power from the royal house of Pharaoh Siptah, but Bay was no longer a threat—he had been hunted down and sent to a permanent death so that his spirit would not bring disorder to the domain of Osiris. After the young Pharaoh Siptah died at sixteen, and his stepmother, Twosret, assumed the throne as Pharaoh, there were rumors that Bay and Twosret had conspired together. The Syrian chief Kharu, who had been hiding Bay, managed to escape with his warriors to terrorize many Egyptian towns. Without Bay's support, Twosret couldn't control the empire, and civil wars brought chaos to the land until Setnakhte deposed her from the throne.

"Did Pharaoh say anything of my husband? I've tried getting information out of Queen Tiymerenese, but the old crocodile refuses to tell me anything. She protects Setnakhte's secrets as if they were her own, and she has plenty of them, I can assure you of that."

Ray bit into a savory piece of goose meat. Grease dribbled down his chin. The goose had been prepared in the Theban style, and the spices startled his tongue. "Pharaoh said nothing of your husband."

She studied his eyes. "You wouldn't be another one who hides his secrets?"

Ray stopped chewing, aware that he might be in danger. "No, mistress. I would hide nothing from you."

Her face relaxed. When her smile returned, he started eating again.

"Ray, I'm sure you've heard the rumors about Kharu. They say my husband destroyed Kharu's army last month, catching them before they could run away with the gold and silver they had stolen from the temples. If that's true, the people will understand the extent of my husband's power.

Setnakhte will have to step down, and Ramesses III will be accepted as the new Pharaoh. Are you sure you didn't hear anything about this while you were with Pharaoh? Maybe you overheard a conversation along the way?"

"No, mistress. I'm sorry."

"All right," she said with a heavy sigh. "Horus knows why, but Pharaoh has taken an interest in you. Perhaps if you spend more time with him, he'll speak more freely in your presence."

He nodded, unsure if this was a test, and bit into more of the bread.

Isis looked over his shoulder and frowned. "Tentopet! Why are you skulking about in the garden?"

Ray's muscles tensed. He brushed the crumbs away from his mouth and turned toward the greenery, where the daughter of Ramesses III stepped out onto the path from behind a willow tree. She was about the same age as Ray. Her face was framed by the long black curls of the wig that hung down to her shoulders, and she wore a white linen gown belted with a gold cord. Her delicate feet, in gold-painted sandals, didn't make a sound as she walked toward them on the pathway.

"Please excuse my daughter," Isis said. "She has the manners of a goat."

Remembering the bread stuck in his throat, Ray coughed, swallowed, and coughed again. With encouraging words, Isis rubbed his back with her warm hand, and Tentopet rushed forward with a look of concern, placing a light hand on his forearm. He felt better already, but pretended to cough a bit more because he didn't want to interrupt what the women were doing. He closed his eyes, feeling his skin tingle.

Tentopet poured water into a goblet at the table and handed it to him. "Drink."

The water tasted sweet and cool. He stood up straighter, and Tentopet smiled. He noticed that she had gold flecks in her deep brown eyes, set off against the glittering green malachite powder painted on her eyelids. "Thank you, my lady."

Tentopet glanced at Isis and giggled. "You act as if we've never met, Ray."

Confused by the roaring in his head, Ray blushed. He saw Tentopet every morning when Hapu was teaching, but she had never spoken to him before. He didn't think she had ever noticed him. He knew this because he spent much of his time staring at her when she wasn't looking.

"I'm sorry if I offend, Tentopet."

She lifted the empty goblet from his hand. Her golden fingers were as smooth as the finest linen. "You do not. I'm glad that you've come to visit us."

Watching the interaction between the two of them, a hint of a smile appeared on Isis's face. "That's better, but it still doesn't excuse my daughter for listening to our conversation. It's hard enough to get a private moment within these walls."

Tentopet gave Isis a slight bow. "I fell asleep in the garden. The shade was pleasant, and the scent of the flowers was so strong, I guess I was overcome."

"Clever girl," Isis said. "Your lies sound so much more sophisticated these days. You've learned much from your teacher."

"I have many teachers," Tentopet said, smiling at her. "And I learn from all of them."

Ray thought that sounded like something his father would have said.

Isis turned her attention back to Ray. "If you've finished with your meal, perhaps you'll escort my daughter. I believe Hapu is waiting for all of you at the zoo this morning."

Ray licked his lips and eyed the table of food, then saw Tentopet watching him with a curious stare. Unnerved, he stammered out his reply. "I will. Yes. I'm happy to escort her. Of course. Thank you, mistress."

Ray bowed low with his arms outstretched, then backed away and followed Tentopet out of the room. The skirt of her white gown swirled around the faint outline of her legs, and he was happy to follow her flowery scent that hung in the air. When they reached the doorway into the corridor, he remembered where he was and turned suddenly to thank Queen Isis for the meal. Although she raised her hand to cover her mouth, he saw her stifling a laugh.

The narrow valley lay quiet in the fading moonlight; a remarkable silence considering the forces gathered there among the shadows. It was a night for spirits of the dead to walk the desert sands, whispering among themselves, watching as preparations were made for battle, studying the dreamers who would soon be joining them. Here and there, a glint of moonlight on spear or shield betrayed the position of a Tjehenu soldier camped on the valley floor, unaware of the Egyptian soldiers roosting like hawks among the rocks above them.

Didu, Standard-Bearer on Pharaoh's Right Hand, sat close beside Ramesses III, co-regent and Lord of the Two Lands, whose hawk-eyed gaze pierced the darkness to study landmarks, enemy positions, and anything else they could use to their advantage in the coming battle. Estimates had the number of Libu and Meshwesh soldiers at almost 18,000—a near match for the four divisions of Pharaoh's army—and Didu felt that the living god could see every one of them, despite the darkness. Didu had seen Pharaoh's trance many times, and he knew that the orders to follow would bring yet another victory for Pharaoh and for the great Amun-Re, who clearly favored his golden son, Ramesses. Pharaoh was also guided by Montu, god of war—mighty of sword and slayer of the country's enemies—who would appear to Pharaoh before major battles in his guise of an armed, falcon-headed man wearing a solar crown. Yes, the Tjehenu were only another army of barbarians among many that had tried to attain the wealth and resources of the land of Kemet through force, and they would soon join their predecessors in the afterlife. The civil wars were over, the living god Ramesses had brought peace to the Two Lands and, after this final battle, the army would return home to Pi-Ramesses laden with the gold, cattle, and slaves they had earned. Didu himself wore a necklace of gold flies presented to him by Pharaoh, who had also given him fertile land along the Nile, and his share of the slaves. Didu had no wife, having devoted the last five years of his life to the Pharaoh Division after leaving his father's farm near Thebes, so perhaps it was time to find one. Having experienced more of the world and what it offered, he didn't want to return to farming, but he didn't have the education of a scribe; however, he knew there would be work in Pi-Ramesses for a strong man with leadership abilities and Pharaoh's endorsement. Perhaps Vizier To would help him find an appropriate position. The small fortune Didu had earned in Pharaoh's service would give him time to find a suitable home and make a wise decision. Of course, they had to return home first. Didu had no fear of death in the coming battle because he would be with Pharaoh and the gods would protect him, but this was the army, and delays could multiply like rats.

Pharaoh's dark eyes glittered when he studied his own forces arrayed along the cliffs. This army would follow him anywhere—a hot desert wind driving soldiers forward like grains of sand too numerous to count; a cloud that would smother the enemy and sting their skin. In the open desert on the other side of the hill, the *tent-htor*—the chariot force—waited in the darkness near the Sherden mercenary infantry, ready to sweep onto the valley floor when the golden boat of Amun-Re rose above the eastern horizon. Ramesses wore his special armor—a coat of overlapping metal plates inlaid with semi-precious blue and green stones—that protected him from his neck to his thighs. Didu had seen arrows bounce off the armor as if they were feathers. When the light of the sun-disk was on Pharaoh at the front of his army, the shiny metal would blind any enemies who dared look upon him, and it would be the last thing they would ever see.

When dawn touched the distant mountain peaks with flame, a silent signal passed from Ramesses III to Chief General Hori and on to the lesser officers and archers nestled among the rocks. Nebamun, Standard-Bearer on Pharaoh's Left Hand, held the bulbous blue leather crown—the *khepresh* war helmet adorned with the golden *uraeus* cobra that protected the royal family—in his beefy hands. Ramesses formally accepted the helmet from him with care, placing it securely on his head, the cobra on his brow prepared to strike. Didu then handed Pharaoh his enormous composite bow, finely crafted of horn, sinews, and wood. A leather sling held arrows tipped with bronze points. With their hands free now, Didu and Nebamun raised their standards—long poles bearing the flowing yellow silk flags of the sun with the golden ram's head of Amun-Re mounted on the top.

A sound like distant thunder told them that the chariots were on their way. Pharaoh pointed at a large tent that had become visible with the sunrise, and the startled Tjehenu chief—Meryey, son of Ded—stumbled out of the tent, his robe in disarray. This was the first time they had actually seen Meryey at a battle, as he preferred to command his army from the rear, positioned on horseback with his senior generals at the head of the long line of ox-drawn carts that carried the women and children. His presence in the camp reassured Didu that they had, indeed, surprised him. Pharaoh rose quickly, set his left foot up on a boulder to steady himself, drew his bow, and released his first shot. The deadly arrow of the sun-god arced high above the camp and plunged into the chest of a Libu general standing beside Meryey. Before the general hit the ground, Ramesses let loose a second arrow that found its way straight into Meryey's right shoulder, disabling his right arm and spinning him around before two soldiers grabbed him and pulled him back into the relative safety of the tent. At that range, unable to see his attacker, it must have seemed to Meryey that the arrows had fallen straight out of the sky as omens from the gods.

With a deafening cheer, over two thousand archers stood up among the rocks and sent death into the air above the Tjehenu camp. Volley followed volley, and the bearded bodies of startled Libu and Meshwesh soldiers littered the camp below. When the chariot force approached from the east with a massive dust cloud rising behind it, Ramesses took a golden axe from Nebamun and charged down the rock face toward the action. Didu still held Pharaoh's sickle-shaped sword, which Ramesses wouldn't need until he was in the enemy camp. It was all Didu and Nebamun could do to keep up with Pharaoh as he hopped barefoot from boulder to boulder toward the golden war chariot and white horses they had hidden behind an outcropping of rock. Arrows shrieked through the air while the archers continued their attack. When the chariots came close enough, they would send their own flights of arrows into the chaos, then the volleys from the cliffs would stop and Pharaoh's archers would descend to the valley floor with their long spears, stabbing anything in their path.

Pharaoh's chariot driver, Maty, had been killed in battle two days earlier. Didu was acquainted with Pharaoh's two war horses and had been a good chariot driver before his promotion, so he had temporarily been entrusted with the task of driving the fast golden chariot. He knew that being so close to Pharaoh in battle could shorten his lifespan considerably, but Didu also felt the protective aura of his lord and the gods that would see to Pharaoh's survival. Following his master, Didu stepped up onto the springy leather surface of the chariot floor, placed the standard of Amun-Re in its holder, picked up his shield, and grasped the reins. Strapped to the side of the light wood chariot were two quivers of arrows and twelve short spears with shiny bronze points, some meant for throwing and a few meant for stabbing. They would head straight for the tent of Meryey, of course, while Pharaoh unleashed his arrows along the way, one after another, hitting most of his targets as he usually did. Despite extensive practice, shooting arrows accurately from the bouncing chariot moving at full speed was a skill that Didu had never managed to learn, so he had always been the shield-bearing driver and Nebamun had been the archer. With a final glance over his shoulder, Didu nodded at Nebamun, who would follow in a second chariot when General Hori caught up with him. He hoped he would see his old friend again. Nebamun was a skilled warrior, but he would not be traveling under Pharaoh's protection.

The Tjehenu camp boiled in chaos, and no one wanted to interfere with the shining figure of death racing toward them on the war chariot, picking off targets along the way. From the corner of his eye, Didu saw the thundering chariot force break across the eastern flank of the Tjehenu army like an enormous sandstorm, smashing over the rough lines of defenders who had managed to organize themselves just in time to die. Emerging from the dust cloud behind the chariots, the Sherden mercenaries, big men in horned helmets with shields on their backs, ran into the mob with their long swords as soon as the arrows stopped flying.

When the chariot approached the striped red and white tent of Meryey, Pharaoh dismounted at a run, wielding his spear and axe, before Didu realized what was happening. Fearing for his lord's safety, Didu reined in the horse, grabbed the standard of Amun-Re with his left hand while holding the sickle-shaped sword of Pharaoh in his right, and ran into the large tent. Inside, he saw four broken arrows on the floor beside Pharaoh, a Libu general with a spear in his chest, and three more generals lying in a spreading pool of blood on the ground. Cushions, tables, and weapons lay scattered in the sand. Ramesses turned quickly with his axe raised, then relaxed when he recognized Didu, who found himself shaking after having been speared by the angry red light in his lord's eyes.

"Meryey has escaped," Pharaoh said, pointing at the bloody robe the Libyan chief had been wearing when struck by his arrow. "We must find him quickly—the cobra's head can still bite after being severed from its body. Take Nebamun and organize a search."

But it was already too late. That evening, while the hands of dead Libu and Meshwesh soldiers were being removed for an official count by the scribes, Didu and Nebamun heard rumors that Meryey had dressed up like a woman and escaped among the fleeing camp followers, aided by a sandstorm, allowing him to evade an intensive search.

The Tjehenu army was destroyed, with almost 12,000 dead and over 6,000 taken captive as slaves, but Pharaoh considered this battle a failure. The cobra's head could still bite.

TWO

1184 BCE—Royal City of Pi-Rameses

Year 4 of His Majesty, King of Upper and Lower Egypt, Chosen by Re, Beloved of Amun, Pharaoh Setnakhte, First Month of Akhet (Season of Inundation), Day 20

Queen Teya allowed Khait to hold the pleated white dress while she stepped into it and Khait worked it up her graceful body. The spaced gold threads that ran the length of the dress sparkled in the light. Khait was painted and appropriately dressed for the audience with her royal highness, so she had to be careful of her own clothing as well as the queen's dress. She tipped her head back to keep the long and narrow braided strands of her black wig from snagging on the dress as she tugged it up under the queen's breasts, checking the temporary stitches in the side hem along the way. She had once pulled a dress over the queen's head and angered her when the stitches snapped away and the dress fell to the floor. The beating that followed had been quick, leaving only a few bruises, but Khait always took extra care after that not to let it happen again. She liked the comfort and security of living in the golden house, and did not wish to do anything that might jeopardize her future in the harem.

"I want it tighter," said the queen, tugging at the fabric. Her proud right breast was exposed, and a single strap suspended the garment from her left shoulder. The high waist would be decorated with a sash of red cloth with tails that hung down to the queen's knees.

"Yes, Highness, but we must be careful not to make it too tight so that you can take it off and put it on again."

Queen Teya raised an eyebrow and stared at her. "It only has to go on me once for the festival. You can stitch me into it this afternoon."

"As you wish, Highness." Khait barely avoided snorting, which would be very dangerous. Knowing the queen's reputation, she'd be surprised if the dress she had spent so much care making for her would survive the first few hours of the festival.

As Khait made some adjustments, the queen continued to study her. "I'm told you are now Overseer of Weaving for the golden house. I know we have many weavers, but you are the best at making royal linen with your loom, so do not think you will be able to stop making linen for me."

"Of course, Highness." Khait couldn't actually count the huge number of weavers in the harem, but only a few of them had the strength to use the vertical loom. That was why so many men were now employed as weavers for the golden house, but they lived elsewhere in the city.

Queen Teya bent over to pluck a grape from the bowl of fruit on the small table beside her. Khait paused and gritted her teeth, hoping she wouldn't pop any of the temporary stitches. Straightening, she placed the grape in her mouth. Crisis averted, Khait returned to her adjustments of the dress.

"You will also continue to be my dressmaker. Whenever I summon you, I expect you to come to me without delay."

"I am always at your command, Highness." As if she had a choice.

"Do not forget it." The queen looked her over some more, making her feel like a piece of meat, or perhaps a foreign slave. "You have an attractive face, girl, but you are too fat. You should never expect to attract the attention of Pharaoh."

"I would never dream of such a great moment," Khait said, starting to hem the bottom of the dress. The queen told her she was fat almost every time she saw her. It seemed to make the queen feel better. Khait had no idea why because she would kill to have the queen's thin body with the kinds of curves in the right places that gave her power over men. Khait didn't have that power, and she wasn't sure she wanted it because it led to complications, but she sometimes thought being a little thinner would make her life easier.

"Ridiculous. All women of the harem want to attract his attention, but only a handful of us are attractive enough, skilled enough, and able to speak knowledgeably on matters of interest to the Great One. It is only due to your father's great service and loyalty to me that you were allowed to join the harem in the first place."

And his many bribes, Khait thought.

"While you're down there, you should kiss my feet to demonstrate how much you appreciate being of service to me."

Khait sighed inwardly and pressed her lips to each of the queen's feet. As she did so, she became aware of someone standing behind her in silence, but returned to hemming the dress.

"Pentawere! Stop staring at the girl. You can have any woman you want. You don't need this one."

"Mother, I make my own choices about such things."

"No, you do not. You are a prince, and you will be Pharaoh one day. A prince does not consort with the help."

"That's not likely. Amana and Bull would have to die before I could ever become Pharaoh."

"Things change. People die. There are so many different ways to die—accidents, sickness, battle, suicide. The gods are unpredictable, and they like to have their fun."

The queen looked down and pushed on Khait's forehead with the toes of her right foot, forcing her back on her heels. "You're done now, girl. Get out."

"Yes, Highness, but I will need to take the dress with me to make it ready for you."

The queen glared at her, but tugged the dress down and wriggled out of it, dropping it on Khait's head. Khait bowed and backed away. Having forgotten that Pentawere was standing there, she bumped into his legs and gasped.

"Apologies, prince."

"My pleasure," Pentawere said, helping her up.

"Get out," said the queen. Khait could never understand how the woman looked so intimidating when she was naked, but she was a master at it. Khait hurriedly bent and backed out through the doorway. However, once she was in the adjoining audience room, she saw it was empty so she paused by the doorway and listened.

"You seem displeased with me, mother."

Even though she couldn't see them now, Khait felt the tension in the air.

"You had an opportunity last night and you failed. Have I taught you nothing?"

Khait wasn't sure what the queen was referring to, but she would wait a moment to see if she could learn anything useful. As her father always said, one needed to gain advantages at court, as long as one didn't get killed in the process.

"I don't know what you mean, mother."

"Don't be a fool. I haven't raised a fool, have I?"

Khait heard footsteps approaching in the distance. Before anyone could see her, she turned and walked toward the exit. Advantage would have to wait.

Itennu, second assistant to Merubaste—Lector Priest and Assistant to the High Priest of the Temple of Amun-Re—remained silent and kneeling on the hard sand outside the god's golden sanctuary, wishing he could take the pressure off of his aching knees, trying to remember that this task was considered an honor among the student members of the priesthood. Roused from a peaceful sleep well before dawn, it was his turn to perform the rites and greet the sunrise with Merubaste and Bakenkhons—the *Hem-netjer tepey*—Overseer of the Priests of All the Gods and High Priest of Amun-Re. The old high priest arrived last. After having been awakened at his home on the eastern side of the temple's sacred lake, student priests had escorted Bakenkhons to the House of Morning, where he had been ceremonially purified with natron salts and water from the lake. The lake's waters represented Nun, the Primeval Water from which all life had been created, so the high priest had been reborn by this ritual. Like Itennu and the other priests who served on the permanent staff of the temple, Bakenkhons had been shaved of all of his body hair, including his eyebrows, to represent purity. He was then dressed in pleated white robes of fine linen, white sandals made of papyrus reeds, adorned with a golden collar studded with stones of blue faience, and then given a light meal before entering the House of the God.

The great stone blocks of the walls jumped with living shadows from the burning braziers on their tall stands. The fires provided enough light to perform rituals, but not enough to destroy the mystery of the shadowy chamber. The sweet smell of myrrh incense filled the air, its smoke drifting through the yellow-gold light of the braziers, almost strong enough to taste. The incense burned in a small pot shaped to look like a cupped palm at the end of a forearm. Until Itennu learned his way through the massive temple complex, an older priest had been assigned to lead him to this sacred inner sanctum. The common people would never see this place, for they had their own Chapel of the Hearing Ear outside the main temple where they made offerings to the god to hear their petitions.

Before Itennu arrived, attendants with containers of water from the temple lake had refilled the drinking cups arrayed among the flower garlands on the altar before the shrine. These same attendants were now ferrying food from the temple kitchens to the altar so that the god would have something to eat when the sun-disk rose above the horizon and the world was reborn. The smell of roast meat and warm bread wafted through the room, making Itennu's mouth water. The last trays of fruit, vegetables, beer, and wine were brought and the attendants scurried away, their jobs finished for now. Itennu's stomach gurgled.

Itennu glanced up at the sound of a tiny bell. The first rays of sunlight touched the high windows, splashing the white walls with a golden glow. Immediately, Itennu and the others began chanting the morning greeting to the shrine: "Awake in peace, great god."

Merubaste stepped forward and unbolted the door of the shrine, bowing as he swung it open. Inside sat the glittering figure of the god Amun-Re, seated on a golden throne, almost three feet tall and wearing his traditional crown topped with two tall plumes. The statue also wore colorful clothing and his ornaments of office. In a scene etched and painted into the stone at the back of the shrine, Pharaoh Amenhotep III, wearing the Blue Crown of Ceremonies, prayed and made eternal offerings to Amun-Re, whose shrine he had built. The sunlight from a tiny window high above gave the god's image a special radiance.

Bakenkhons stepped forward and said, "It is Pharaoh who has sent me to see the god." Only Pharaoh was officially allowed to approach Amun-Re, but the high priest performed his daily duties in Pharaoh's place after explaining himself first. His primary focus was to serve all of the god's needs so that the god would care for the people of the Two Lands. If the gods were pleased, they would continue to push back the forces of chaos to keep the world in balance.

Chanting softly, Bakenkhons knelt and held out a small statue of the goddess Maat, symbolizing the proper order established at the creation of the world. "Praise be to Amun-Re, the Bull in Annu, the chief of all the gods, the beautiful god, the beloved one, the giver of life. Homage to thee, O Amun-Re, lord of the thrones of the Two Lands, who art chief in thy fields, whose steps are long, who art lord of the South, who art lord of the Matchau peoples, and prince of Punt, and king of heaven, and first-born god of earth, and establisher of creation. Thou art chief of all the gods, creator of men and women, maker of animals, and lord of all things that exist."

While Bakenkhons continued the long chant that would allow the great god to assume his earthly shape once more, Itennu and Merubaste entered the shrine to remove the clothing and ointment provided for the god the previous day. They purified the shrine with water and incense, then painted the god's eyelids with green and black paint, anointed the entire body with scented oils, and dressed it with jewelry and fresh clothing in the colors of white, blue, green, and red. Each color had its significance: the white and red cloths protected the god from his enemies, the blue hid his face, and the green ensured his health. Finally, he was presented with his symbols of power: the scepter, crook, flail, and a gold collar inset with stones of blue lapis-lazuli and green malachite.

Bakenkhons chanted the offering prayer listing the food arrayed on the altar for the god's breakfast. The god wouldn't physically consume the offerings—he would merely absorb the food's essence, which he could then share with the lesser deities in the other temple shrines as he wished. Itennu didn't want to be reminded about the food when he was so hungry, so he concentrated on the last of the morning preparations. Merubaste burned more incense while Itennu spread cleansing natron salt mixed with resin on the floor. When Bakenkhons was done chanting, he backed away so that Itennu could use a broom to brush their footprints from the sand. To stimulate the god's other senses, musicians and dancers moved into the chamber to provide entertainment while the god was eating. While the male musicians shook sistrums, rattles, and slapped small drums, female dancers clad only in leather thongs performed the graceful acrobatic movements of the ritual dance. When Pharaoh arrived a bit later, a special bull would be sacrificed to the god, and the morning rituals would be complete.

"You've done well," Bakenkhons said, placing his hand on Itennu's shoulder. "The steps are not difficult, but many of your fellow students have trouble remembering them."

Itennu nodded. "I am but a humble servant of the great god."

"Do you know the words to the greeting and the incarnation chants?"

Itennu glanced away. He knew most of the long chants, but he hadn't expected a test. "Some of them."

Merubaste shook his head. "We don't expect students his age to know the incarnation chant, Overseer."

"This one may have the memory for it," Bakenkhons said, peering intently into Itennu's face. "You must practice the chants. Today, however, you will sacrifice the bull when Pharaoh arrives."

"Oh?" Itennu tried not to smile so that he could maintain a serious priestly demeanor. "I mean, yes, of course."

"Iabi will not be pleased," Merubaste said, narrowing his eyes at Itennu.

Itennu knew that Iabi had been making Pharaoh's bull sacrifice every day for many years. He was old and weak, but that didn't mean that Itennu wanted to anger him by taking his place in the ritual that he had now performed for three successive rulers.

Bakenkhons dusted the sand from his white robes. "Iabi can remain in his bed this morning. I want Itennu to make the sacrifice, after which he can accompany me for the day. I'll need his help to prepare for the feast this evening."

Taking a loaf of bread from the altar, Bakenkhons turned and strode from the room. Itennu thought the well-fed high priest could have waited for his proportionately large ration of the food offerings to be distributed later that morning, but perhaps that was one of the privileges of being the overseer of the priesthood—and the second most powerful man in the Two Lands. Itennu started to collect the rest of the food so that he could return it to the kitchen for distribution.

"Take care," Merubaste growled. "The hawk that rises too near the sun-disk may set his wings on fire."

Itennu nodded, not knowing how else he could respond. The high priest had taken special notice of him, and it now occurred to him that such attention could make his life more difficult.

Itennu felt light-headed, but his senses were unusually sharp. The brilliant sunlight of early afternoon dazzled him when he stepped out of the temple with the high priest.

"Pharaoh Setnakhte appreciated your work," Bakenkhons said, shading his eyes with one hand as he looked out across the temple's sacred lake. A tame flock of geese—the sacred geese of Amun-Re—floated across the lake's surface like the boats of the gods. Some of the geese perched on the steps leading down into the shallow lake, their heads disappearing when they rooted for snacks in the mud.

Itennu suspected that his first meeting with Pharaoh was the cause of his dizziness. Either that or he was still shocked by the rush of warm blood over his body when he had killed the bull, followed by a bath in cool water drawn from the healing waters of the lake. Itennu had sensed some resentment from the other student purification priests who had drawn his bath and acted as his attendants during the ritual, but he also saw the look of respect in their eyes. Neither they, nor Itennu, could determine how he had merited this special task, but they felt the power of the ritual, and they watched as both Pharaoh and Bakenkhons clearly admired Itennu's efforts.

"I'm not as skilled with the knife as Iabi," Itennu said. "And I didn't know all the words of the offering chant."

"Nonsense," Bakenkhons said, continuing to study the geese. "Someone new needs to learn the ritual—Iabi is old and will soon be setting off on his journey into the west. And it didn't matter that you missed some of the words—it's all about the performance, enthusiasm, and your purity of spirit. That's what Pharaoh appreciated."

"I appreciate the opportunity." Itennu smiled. He wished he could tell his father about this wonderful day. He would have been pleased that all of his sacrifices, extra donations to the temple granaries, and carefully placed bribes to the right priests had brought Itennu the success that he desired for his son.

"And there will be more," Bakenkhons said, leading him toward the homes of the senior priests along the eastern edge of the stone-lined pool. "How long have you been with us at the temple now?"

"My father brought me here when I was ten. I'm fourteen now."

"You say you're not skilled with a knife. Where did you grow up?"

"On a farm about half a day on the river from here. We grew grain."

"Then you were only being modest about your use of the knife. A pleasing trait for a young priest." Bakenkhons swept his arm toward the glittering waters of the sacred pool. "Have you ever seen the golden boat on the lake at night?"

"What golden boat is that?"

"Ah," Bakenkhons said with a smile. "On certain nights, a golden barge emerges from the waters of the lake, as resplendent as in days of yore. The pharaoh who steers it is pure gold, and his sailors are made of silver. When the moon shines, the barge sails, leaving behind a long wake of glittering precious stones. At times, it comes to the dock as well; if some brave soul with a heart thrice bound in bronze comes forth to dare the great adventure, he climbs aboard the phantom ship, then returns to his home laden with fabulous treasure. But, everyone knows that if he makes the slightest sound—the merest sigh—the phantom barge, the gold king, and the silver sailors will sink immediately below the waters of the lake, engulfing the foolhardy one forever."

Itennu's eyes were wide. "I want to see that!"

Bakenkhons shrugged. "Alas, the appearances of the mysterious boat are rare these days. I, myself, have only seen it once in the last few years, and that was when the young Ramesses III helped Pharaoh Setnakhte end the civil war."

"I'll watch for it every night."

"Then perhaps you'll see it. You, of all people, may have that chance. Praise be to Amun-Re, the beloved one, the giver of life."

Sensing that he was supposed to respond, Itennu nodded. "Praise be to Amun-Re."

Although Itennu's experience of fancy homes was limited, it was clear that Bakenkhons lived in the largest house he'd ever seen, with a cellar; an enclosed courtyard with a pond; a main floor with the kitchen at the back, an office, a household shrine, and the public rooms; a second floor with sleeping spaces and extra rooms; and a rooftop that looked out over the sacred lake. On the inside, the mud brick walls were smoothed to a creamy texture that allowed many detailed scenes of gods and life along the Nile to have been painted there. Bakenkhons guided Itennu on a tour of the house himself as he went from room to room checking on the servants and their preparations for the important Festival of Drunkenness to be held there that night. Itennu was told that his first task would be to help mix the special beer for the evening—a blend of the usual porridge-like beer along with pomegranates, mint, figs, and honey. A second, larger vat held red beer, a beer colored with red ochre that would be drunk on the first night of the festival to appease the lion-headed goddess Sekhmet—the aggressive aspect of the goddess Mut. Timed to start twenty days after the start of the year's first big flood that renewed the farmlands with the waters of the Nile, this festival marked the start of the new year with singing, dancing, and drinking. While drunkenness was generally frowned upon except for ritual purposes, the celebrants would drink until they passed out, hoping for visions of Sekhmet, whose visiting statue had been brought to the high priest's home from Thebes the previous day. During the celebration, sober attendants would remain ready to take care of the guests. The Temple of Mut in Thebes would be the focal point of this festival, but most of the local people would not be able to travel that far along the Nile for the occasion.

Oshairana, the beer priestess from the Temple of Mut, was a stout woman with thick arms and a fierce expression who quickly evaluated Itennu's skills and decided he would be best used to stir the thick brew in the vats. This turned out to be tiring work that dragged on through the early afternoon. Itennu thought it would be easier to be an oarsman on one of Pharaoh's fighting ships, so he was happy when Bakenkhons returned and assigned him a new task. He was to go to Pharaoh's great house and find out how many members of the royal household would be attending the festivities that evening. Glad of the excuse to leave, he bid farewell to Oshairana and the giant serving spoon that had become his tormentor.

Careful not to step on any of the flowers strewn on the ground that were being woven into garlands by a long row of seated women, Itennu was almost out of the courtyard before he caught sight of the brilliant colors being painted on a small section of the home's back wall beside a closed bronze door. The painter had traced the outlines of a woman with the head of a lion—the goddess Sekhmet—on a grid of lines, and was now filling in the spaces of the figure with a rainbow of gold, blue, red, pink, and white. The figure was more lifelike than most of the painted images Itennu had seen inside the temple, or anywhere else for that matter. Awed by the young painter's talent, he inadvertently stepped on a small bowl of blue paint that washed over his feet and splashed across the sand. It looked like he was standing in a shaft of glowing moonlight.

"I'm sorry for my clumsiness," Itennu said with a slight bow, wondering how he'd get the paint off of his feet before he went to the palace.

The painter looked down at the spilled paint sinking into the thirsty sand and sighed. "Of course it had to be the blue. I should never have left it on the ground near the pathway where any unthinking fool could step on it."

"I humbly apologize."

Itennu noticed spots of various bright colors of paint on the young man's arms and in his unusually long black hair. He appeared to be in his early twenties, with a strong face and an athletic appearance. The painter continued to stare at the spilled moonlight. "The blue is the hardest to make. I brought it with me from Thebes."

"Perhaps I could help you make more."

"Perhaps you could go drown yourself in the lake," the painter said through gritted teeth.

The painter seemed to be getting angrier. Itennu thought it might be better if he could distract him. "That's a beautiful painting."

The painter glanced at his work. "No thanks to you."

"Your hand is moved by the gods. What's your name?"

The painter closed his eyes and took a deep breath to control himself. "Neferabu."

"And you're from Thebes? I've heard of a sculptor there by that name. Your father?"

"I was a sculptor, from a family of sculptors who have worked in the royal tombs for generations."

"And now you're a painter as well. How wonderful."

Neferabu glared at him. "It's a punishment. I didn't sculpt the rock in the traditional way. The poses and angles of my subjects were *incorrect*. But if I *paint* something the foreman doesn't like, they can always paint over it the next day."

"Oh. Well. You're still an excellent painter. My name is Itennu."

"Good for you."

"Can you use some of the paint on my feet?"

Neferabu looked down, then quickly bent and daubed up some of the paint from Itennu's feet with his brush. "This may be enough," he grumbled.

"Itennu!"

Itennu jumped when he heard the voice of Bakenkhons booming from the house.

The bulky figure of the high priest appeared in the rear doorway. "Stop painting your feet. Must I give you a different task and send someone else to Pharaoh's great house?"

"I'm on my way," Itennu said, jogging out of the courtyard.

Neferabu called after Itennu's retreating back. "Don't hurry back, Blue Foot!"

"The large beast with the short tail in back and the long tail in front. Who knows what it's called?"

Hapu looked at the four students with his eyebrows raised. He was dressed in his customary white robe and gold collar that he used when teaching, and his fine leather sandals creaked whenever he took a step. He stood with his back to a large pit lush with vines, exotic trees, flowers, and a pool large enough to allow the animal to swim. Ray, Tentopet, and Pentawere stood facing Hapu where they all had a good view of the creature. Ray thought it felt strange not to have Bull there with them in class, but they had been joined by Bull's younger brother, the stocky Amanakhopshaf. A few days earlier, Amana had returned from war-chariot training with the Ptah division, where he had been sent into his first battle against a tribal warlord after Ramesses III had noted his ability as an archer. A short distance from the rest of the group, Amana sat on a rock and stared at some of the birds behind the rope nets of their large cages. Ray knew from past experience that Amana had little patience for his lessons, and would start to twitch after being seated in class for a short time.

"Come on, someone must know what the creature is called," Hapu said, glowering at Ray.

"Elephant," Ray said, glancing at the hairless beast with the huge ears. He'd seen the elephant once before, but he was surprised that nobody else seemed to know the answer.

"Good lad," Hapu said. "And where is the elephant from?"

"It was brought here from Nubia as a gift to Pharaoh."

Hapu pointed at another creature studying them from the high branches of a nearby tree that rose from the same pit. Others were lurking nearby, but Ray couldn't see them. "And that baboon? Where is it from?"

"Thebes," Pen said. "Pharaoh Hatshepsut had the original baboons brought to Egypt along with the live myrrh and frankincense trees from the Land of Punt."

The other students glanced at Pen, surprised that he had spoken the name of the ancient woman who had worn the beard of pharaoh and built her vast mortuary temple in the Great Place at Thebes. Although she had ruled almost 300 years earlier, her name was still rarely spoken, and then only in hushed tones. Her monuments were all over Egypt, although her name had been removed from most of them by her son, Thutmose III, when he assumed the throne of the Two Lands.

"Correct," Hapu said, raising his arm to sweep it across the zoo that surrounded them. "The history of this place and its creatures reflects the history of the pharaohs. Trading routes and gifts from distant lands have given us the unusual beasts we see here, and all are evidence of Pharaoh's power. The great armored rhinoceros was captured and brought here for Pharaoh's pleasure, as were the giraffes, cheetahs, and lions. The gods demonstrate that the natural world must bow to Pharaoh's will, just as the empires of our enemies must bow in the end. Animals are as people in that they exist for Pharaoh's pleasure—for his life, prosperity, and health."

"As it shall ever be," Amana said, tossing a small stone at a baboon. The baboon skittered away to a distant branch.

"Forever is a long time," Ray said. He realized his mistake when the other students, the blood of the royal house, looked at him as if he were a talking baboon.

Hapu cleared his throat, as he often did when one of his students said something that lacked any sign of reasoning. "The pharaohs have ruled this land for over two thousand years, Ray. Their pyramids and monuments will outlast all who walk this land, and the empire will endure as the gods have decreed. Only a simple person would doubt this most basic truth."

"Only a simple person," Amana said. He tossed a stone at Ray, but it bounced off his chest without causing any harm.

"My father," Ray said. "Have you not also said that the barbarians are always watching from beyond our borders? Isn't it possible that the barbarians outside the Two Lands might outnumber the civilized people within?"

"Pharaoh, the living god, protects us from the barbarians. His armies are his hands, keeping them away."

Ray nodded. "Yes, but there have been times when foreigners invaded and threw the country into turmoil for years. Pharaoh couldn't stop them."

Hapu sighed, and Ray saw that his patience was wearing thin. "There have been short periods of chaos, and pharaohs who displeased the gods, but the next pharaoh always rises up to restore peace and balance to the world."

Amana threw another stone at Ray. "He *is* simple."

Hapu gestured at the great house of Pharaoh. "Pharaoh Setnakhte is a good example of this. When the land was in desolation and Egypt had drifted away from trusting in the great god, Amun-Re extended his hand and chose Setnakhte out of the multitude. He became like his father, Set, who flexed his arms in order to snatch Egypt back from those who had violated her; his might was all-encompassing in protecting her. The criminals he dealt with were seized with fear in their hearts, and they fled like tits and sparrows with a falcon after them. They abandoned the gold, silver, and bronze of Egypt, which they would have given to the Asiatics to bring about a quick victory for them, for the chief men of Egypt were ineffectual and disastrous conspirators. Then, finally, every god and every goddess manifested their oracle to Setnakhte, the living god, proclaiming a bloody victory through him and pronouncing at break of light that he was the rightful and honorable ruler of the Two Lands. Through his own son, Ramesses III, Pharaoh continues to restore Maat—peace and balance—to the world."

"I see," Ray said with a nod, having heard the story of Setnakhte before. "Peace and balance through revolt and war."

Pen smiled. "The strong always survive, and Pharaoh will always be the strongest."

"And our *gods* are the strongest," Tentopet added. "They are the oldest, the most powerful, and none can defeat them."

Ray saw that they had settled the issue among themselves, so there wasn't any point in trying to argue them out of it. He shrugged. "You're right, of course. I'm a fool."

Expecting it now, Ray dodged the next stone that Amana threw.

Hapu led his students down the main path through the palace grounds. Despite the growing heat of late morning, the path was somewhat cooler once they left the close white walls of the temples and administrative buildings, and they were now shaded by olive trees and vines that arched overhead. Colorful flowers grew in the space between the road and the adjacent canal that reflected the dark blue sky. This was one of Pharaoh's holy roads, where the light traffic was limited to high government officials and prominent temple priests, few of whom would venture outside when Amun-Re's golden sun-boat was high in the sky. As they walked, Hapu drilled his students in the fine points of government structure and administration; a topic that would have put some of them to sleep had they been sitting still. Even so, Amana's eyes were glazed over, and he walked as if asleep. As for Pen, he gave a quick response to many of Hapu's questions, but Ray always felt that he was holding back, as if he were giving the others a chance to look good in Hapu's eyes.

When they reached the sandy training ground where the soldiers of the city garrison performed their weekly drills, they were met by a big man whose torso looked like a pyramid turned upside-down. Ray had seen prosperous stonecutters with this shape, gained from carrying heavy blocks of stone as they plied their trade. His black hair was cut short in the military style under his striped head cloth. A quilted shirt without sleeves protected his light brown skin from the relentless sunlight, and a white kilt hung from his waist. He wore a collar of rank around his neck, but it was the glittering gold fly that dangled beneath it—a battle decoration from Pharaoh—that immediately caught the eye. This was not uncommon for one of the faithful Sherden mercenaries that Pharaoh had hired from Libya—or Tjehenu as it was also known—as they were the most trusted of the soldiers, forming the loyal core of the army and the royal bodyguard. The Sherden appreciated strength, and many of them felt that the Libu and other chiefs of their homeland would never win a war against Egypt, although some remained there out of loyalty. A short khepesh scimitar hung from his waist in a curved leather sheath, and he stood straight with the end of his copper-tipped spear planted in the sand. More spears, swords, clubs, shields, bows, and arrows hung in equipment racks a short distance away. Ray felt exhausted just looking at so many tools of death.

Hapu nodded at the soldier, then turned to face his students. "Pasai will oversee your exercises today. He's very experienced in the ways of war, and Pharaoh selected him personally for this honor. May the gods protect you."

Ray watched his father retire to the edge of the training field to lie down in the shade of an olive tree. Satisfied that Pasai would take care of his students, Hapu promptly closed his eyes and started snoring. Hapu had no interest whatsoever in training them for the business of war, but he urged them to pay attention to their trainers so that they would know how to defend themselves from attacks of all kinds. Pasai was the newest in a long line of instructors; they never lasted more than a few seasons—perhaps out of fear that they might lose their lives by accidentally harming the children of the royal household.

They stood in a loose clump waiting for instructions while Pasai studied them with the expressionless face of a sphinx. Pen took a step closer to their trainer and smiled. "So, Pasai, what sort of torture have you scheduled for us today?"

Pasai hefted his spear and lowered its shiny tip toward Ray.

Surprised, Ray looked over his shoulder to make certain nobody stood behind him. The trainers normally ignored him until the end of the session because he was of lower rank and looked too weak to hold a weapon for very long. He took two steps to the right and the spear tip followed his movement. "What do you want me to do?"

The spear tip swung toward the equipment racks, then back to Ray.

"Not very talkative, are you?" Ray asked as he walked over and picked up a shield of battered wood. Startled, he jumped back when the spear tip *thunked* into the shield. Pasai seemed to have the magic skill of moving faster than the eye could follow because he now stood in a casual crouch only a few steps away from Ray. He heard the other students gasp.

Jumping behind the equipment rack, Ray grabbed a short sword. When he turned back to face Pasai, the man was gone. The tiny hairs stood up on the back of his neck. Although he didn't hear or see any indication of what would happen next, he spun around and raised his shield just in time to stop the spear point from plunging into his flesh. The spear moved again, and he saw his short sword spinning through the air toward the other students, who scattered to avoid it. A glance at his father showed that he was still sleeping peacefully beneath the tree.

With his heart pounding, Ray ducked in time to avoid the other end of the spear that *swooshed* past his head. Stumbling, he flopped on the sand, then rolled to avoid the foot that would have come down on his back. The side of the equipment rack stopped his rolling motion. Crouching, he raised his shield to block Pasai's kick. The impact knocked him against the equipment rack again, and a club thumped into the sand by his head. Grabbing the club, he swung it in an awkward arc to slam it into Pasai's left foot. Pasai grunted, tripped on Ray's ankle, and fell with his full weight on top of Ray's shield, squashing the boy flat. Dazed by the impact, his mouth full of sand, it took a moment for Ray to realize what a mistake he'd just made. If Pasai was unconscious, or simply angry, Ray would suffocate under the shield with his face buried in the earth.

Pasai grunted and rolled off, releasing the enormous pressure that pinned Ray to the soil. Coughing, Ray felt a strong hand grasp his wrist to haul him to his feet. Clearing the sand from his eyes, he was surprised to see Pasai grinning at him just before he slapped Ray once on the back, knocking him forward.

"You surprised me," Pasai rumbled. "Excellent."

Ray managed a half-smile while stifling a cough.

"Oh, yes, Ray is a fearsome warrior," Amana said, clapping his hands together as he walked closer. "No unprotected foot is safe from his mighty blows."

"And no unprotected butt is safe from my mighty foot," Pasai said, turning with a fierce expression to face Amana.

"You wouldn't dare," Amana said, taking two steps back.

"I've given my word to Pharaoh that I will train all of you in the killing arts. In his great wisdom, he has given me permission to harm you as necessary. I will train you hard, and you will perform as if your life depends on it, because it does." He gestured at the equipment rack. "These weapons are real; their edges and points are sharp. I will try to hurt you with them, and I expect you to treat me as your worst enemy, even though in truth I am your closest friend. In this way, you'll come to know the intensity of the fight, and you may even survive a real attack. A powerful enemy will teach you more about yourself than you could ever learn from years of drills and practice. Any questions?"

"Am I done for the day?" Ray asked, still breathing hard, bent over to rest his hands on his knees. He didn't want to show his weakness in front of Pasai, but his evil spirits had returned to steal his breath away.

Hapu sat up under the tree with his eyes on his son. "You're done. Come with me."

As Ray staggered away, Pasai pointed his spear at Amana. "You're next, Prince."

Ray knew he couldn't have made it back to his room by himself. Hapu helped him walk, taking a break every few steps to let his son catch his breath. Whenever these spirits tormented Ray, they made it impossible for him to inhale more than a sip of air at a time. And they were unpredictable. Sometimes, the spirits would free him after a short time and his breathing would return to normal. He hoped this was one of those times.

When they got closer to the palace, Hapu was panting from the exertions of bearing so much of his son's weight, but a white-robed priest of Amun-Re took up part of the burden. The young priest's feet and sandals were painted blue, and Ray assumed this had some religious significance in connection with the Festival of Drunkenness—possibly something to do with the grapes used to make juice and wine.

In time, Ray was back in the cooler shadows of his bedroom, gently being lowered onto the clean linen sheets. Hapu then scurried away to find Seini, the court physician, not wanting to trust this task to one of the slaves.

The young priest of Amun-Re closed his eyes, chanted a prayer, and made strange gestures in the air over Ray's bed.

"Thank you," Ray whispered. "What's your name?"

"Itennu," the priest said. Then he smiled and left.

Tinubiti, the nurse, already knew what the physician would say. She set about gathering the clay pot, the hollow reed, the bricks, a stone grinding bowl, and other materials she would need to create the same smoking mixture that Seini had assembled to treat Bull's breathing problems after he almost drowned in the river. A servant was sent off to heat bricks. While Ray waited, he rolled over on his side as Seini had shown him, believing that this posture would make it easier for him to breathe, but it remained a fight to draw air into his body and push it out again. Slipping his fingers under the waistband of his kilt, he withdrew the small figure of gold and blue lapis from its pouch. The standing figure was Thoth, whose human body was topped with the head of an ibis, but the artist who carved the image had wisely blunted the long bird beak so that it wouldn't hook on skin or clothing. In his thoughts, Ray called upon the strength and wisdom of Thoth to help him survive.

Tinubiti ground grains and date kernels with the carob. After this powder was mixed with the honey and cream to form a paste, Ray would breathe the smoke of the heated mixture to chase the evil spirits out of his body. He hoped this attack would be over soon, but there had been times when his breath eluded him for days, leaving him weak and near death before life-giving air flowed back into his body. He focused on the simple rhythm, in and out, in and out, that should have been an unconscious act, but was now the most important part of his world—in and out, in and out.

A shadow fell across Ray's closed eyes. Expecting the physician, knowing at least half an hour had passed, he was surprised to find Queen Isis hovering over him. Frowning, she sat down on the edge of his bed and stroked his forehead with her soft hand.

"Be still, little man. You must purify your body to chase out the evil spirits. Pray to Imhotep to help you. Pray to Amun-Re and Thoth to support you."

Ray nodded, unconvinced that the gods would help him, but willing to try because Isis had asked him to do so. Her touch on his forehead was soothing.

Isis smiled. "Don't worry. This isn't your time to leave us. The oracles say you're destined for greater things in this world."

"Oracles?" Ray whispered.

Isis put a finger to his lips to keep him quiet. She then rubbed his back while Tinubiti placed a hot brick smeared with the smoking mixture by his bed. Isis took the end of the reed that protruded from the hole in the smoke pot and inserted it between his lips. When he inhaled the smoke, he realized that the hand rubbing his back was already making him feel better. She began a soft chant that he remembered his mother singing to him when he was a child—a comforting story about talking animals that protected sleeping children.

When Seini arrived with Hapu following along behind him, the sour expression on the physician's face made it clear that he'd been interrupted by Hapu while doing something much more important. When he stopped suddenly, Hapu almost stumbled into the physician's back.

"You've given him the smoke of purification?"

Isis turned to look at Seini with one eyebrow raised. "Tinubiti has many talents. Perhaps she should be the royal physician. She's certainly easier to locate."

Remembering himself, Seini bent at the waist with his arms outstretched. "Yes, my queen."

Tinubiti blushed and bowed her head, closing jars and putting away the smoking supplies. Seini glared at her and moved around Isis so that he could inspect the materials on the hot brick. He sniffed twice. "Too much honey, not enough carob. However, it should be sufficient. If he needs more, I'll make it myself and do it correctly."

"Of course," Tinubiti said.

Seini looked at Hapu. "You carried him back here yourself? Did his lips ever turn blue? Was he ever unconscious?"

"He remained alert. His face looked normal," Hapu said. "Fortunately, a young priest came along to help me bring him back from the training field."

Isis smiled. "Itennu?"

Hapu nodded. "You know him?"

"Bakenkhons sent him to speak with me about the festival. He seemed concerned about Ray's health, which is how I knew to come here. An admirable young man."

"I found him so," Hapu said.

"We will keep an eye on the boy. We can always use friends within the priesthood of Amun-Re."

Seini frowned and cleared his throat before bending over to stare into Ray's eyes.

"In addition to the physicians, of course," Isis said. She smiled at Seini. Ray noticed that the grumpy physician softened when she smiled, and he realized she was using feminine magic.

"Will Ray be able to attend the festival?" Hapu asked.

"If his body cooperates with me," Seini said, peering down Ray's throat, which was now raw from the smoke. "I will apply all of my arts to heal him."

Isis patted Ray's chest and stood up to leave. "See that you do."

Khait couldn't help but admire the dress she had made for Queen Isis. As she smoothed the beaded linen over the queen's lithe and strong body, displayed so well through the transparent white cloth, she felt privileged to be this powerful woman's trusted servant. Queen Isis was the Chief Royal Wife of Pharaoh Ramesses III and mother of the prince—the Hawk-in-the-Nest—who would one day rule the Two Lands. As Principal Royal Wife, Queen Teya was a distant second in rank to the powerful woman who now stood before Khait with a smile that filled the room with light. The queen's bedroom, decorated with bright wall paintings of the Great River, its flowers, and its wildlife in brilliant hues of blue, green, and yellow, all paled in comparison to the queen in her new dress.

"You have outdone yourself, Khait. This is beautiful work," said the queen, lifting her arms to examine the winged sleeves of pleated linen, suggestive of a graceful bird about to take flight. The beads of blue faience and green turquoise formed a pattern like a fishing net that clung to the queen's body from the two straps over her shoulders all the way down to the fringe at the bottom hem. The fringe itself was made of over one hundred hollow shells with tiny stones inside that made the shells rattle when the queen moved her legs.

The queen stood on her toes and twirled in place. "What a lovely sound. And the beads sparkle as they catch the light. All eyes will be on me. I only wish Sesi were here to see this."

"May I ask when the Great One will return, Majesty?"

Queen Isis sighed. "Only Pharaoh knows that. He will return when the Two Lands are once again safe from foreign invaders. All I know is that it will be long after tonight's festival."

"You miss him."

"He is my life and my reason for being. I always miss him when he's away, and I always spend as much time as I can with him when he is here."

"I hope to have that someday," Khait said, adjusting the high waist where the thin gold belt would be cinched below the queen's breasts.

The queen smiled at her. "You will. You are fortunate not to have been married off to the son of some distant king, far away from this beautiful land. The men of the court may not be the best choices for you, for wealth does not always indicate good character or wisdom, but you will meet someone. Perhaps someone you don't expect. That is part of the fun and mystery of being young and alive."

Khait always felt special just being in the presence of Queen Isis. She radiated hope and love, just like the goddess Isis. If Khait had ever met her own mother, a good woman who died giving birth to her, she hoped she would have been like this special queen.

As the queen pulled gold and silver bracelets from her jewelry box and studied them alongside the beads of her dress, the bedroom door opened and Tentopet poked her head in. The plaited strands of her black wig were strung with sparkling red and blue gems. "Mother, someone is here with a message." She smiled when she saw what the queen was wearing. "What a beautiful dress! Khait is a magician."

"I agree. Khait is one of our greatest treasures, and we must find a way to reward her."

Khait bowed. "Thank you, your Majesty." Although the queen didn't mind when she spoke less formally in private, she was careful to show proper respect when others were present. She lifted a heavy gold collar studded with gems and settled it around the queen's neck with the gold counterweight, shaped like an ankh, dangling between her shoulder blades.

"Send in the messenger, Tentopet."

The door opened the rest of the way. Tentopet was also dressed for the festival, but the messenger was what caught Khait's eye. It was Ray. She didn't know him well, but he was an attractive young man. He looked nervous, and that made him more attractive in her eyes.

The queen raised her eyebrows and smiled. "You're feeling better, Ray?"

He cleared his throat. "I am, your Highness. The physician's smoke often helps me."

"And the gods favor you. They protect you."

"Perhaps," he said with a shrug.

"You have a message for me?"

"Yes, I'm sorry." He licked his lips. "Queen Teya sent me to get Khait."

Queen Isis chuckled. "She can wait. Khait is helping me dress."

"And it's a nice dress, Highness. Very pretty," he said, glancing at Tentopet, and then looking at the blue stone floor.

Tentopet walked over to the queen and picked up the jewelry box. "I can help you. I'm all ready for the evening."

Khait looked at the queen, who nodded. "You may go with Ray, Khait. Thank you for your magnificent work."

"It is my pleasure to serve you, Highness. Thank you."

Khait and Ray bowed low, their arms extended, and backed out of the queen's bedroom. Khait smiled at him as they started across the queen's empty audience chamber. "I heard you were sick, Ray. I'm glad you're better. It was very brave of you to rescue the prince."

"He would have done the same for me."

He was humble, and she liked that, too. "Didn't she look wonderful? She makes me so happy when I make dresses for her."

Ray hesitated. "Yes. Tentopet looked wonderful."

"I meant the queen."

"Oh, yes. Yes. The queen also."

Khait tried to look at his eyes as they walked, but he looked away. "You're attracted to Tentopet, aren't you?"

"What?"

"I saw you watching her. And I've seen it before."

"I'm not sure what—"

Khait laughed. “She’s a princess, you know. You’re a commoner. You don’t have a chance.”

“I would never—“

“Don’t bother to deny it. Men are simple and transparent to women.”

“I don’t think—“

“Tentopet is beautiful, but you should look for a companion who is not above your station. Someone who would make a good wife and bear you healthy children.”

“I’m not looking for—“

“You’re what, fourteen or fifteen years old now? You need to start thinking about settling down and raising a family.”

“Why am I—“

Khait raised her hand to stop him as they approached the guard outside Queen Teya’s audience room. “I’m glad we had this little talk, but I have to go. The queen will beat me if she thinks I’ve taken too long to get here.”

Khait nodded at the guard as she entered the audience room, smiling to herself. If Ray went to the festival that evening, she would hunt him down and leave him speechless once more.

Still confused by his conversation with Khait, whom he didn’t really know that well, Ray returned to his room to prepare for the evening. Placing his best clothes on the bed, Tinubiti informed him that Bull was still recovering from the Nile's invasion of his body, which made him sad. He hoped that Seini's rituals would be enough to heal his friend—he clearly wouldn't be able to attend the festival at the home of Bakenkhons with Ray and Pen that evening, but there would soon be other happy occasions that Bull could enjoy.

The preparations for the short journey to the Temple of Amun-Re had been going on for hours. Whenever a pharaoh went out in public, it was traditional for the living god to glow like the sun to inspire everyone who saw him. Selected officials, noblemen, wives, princesses, and women-of-the-following would accompany Pharaoh Setnakhte in a lengthy train of processional chariots and covered litters so that Pharaoh could make a suitably dramatic arrival at the home of the High Priest of Amun-Re. Escorted by his father, Ray would be allowed to attend the first part of the festivities, after which he and the rest of the royal children who would not be playing a part in that evening's ritual would then return to the golden house of Pharaoh.

Ray put on his pleated white robe of fine linen and ran his hands over the smooth fabric. It wasn't as nice or transparent as royal linen, but was the nicest he had ever worn. As Tinubiti slid white sandals of papyrus reed onto his feet, Hapu entered the room with a gold collar. Blue stones of lapis lazuli dotted the shiny metal, and the counterweight was a figure of Thoth with his two eyes made of sparkling red gemstones.

Ray was surprised when Hapu secured the heavy object around his neck. "You must have made a good impression on Queen Isis, my son. This collar she sent for you is quite a gift."

Ray glanced down at the collar, running a finger along its smooth edge. "It's a fine thing. And she knows I favor Thoth. She is very generous, although I don't understand why."

"Perhaps because you saved the life of her son."

Ray didn't believe that, but he didn't want to disagree with his father, who seemed to have forgiven him for his stupidity in going to the river in the middle of the night. "Perhaps. I know I was surprised when they invited me to the festival."

"You've done well," Hapu said, turning Ray to face him. His expression was serious. "However, you must be careful this evening. Don't drink too much of the red beer, for it loosens the tongue and makes the head spin. You must keep your wits about you. This is a serious occasion. You'll be in the presence of both Pharaoh and High Priest Bakenkhons, the two most powerful people in the Two Lands, which means you'll be sitting in the lap of danger. Remain quiet and observant. Don't behave like a servant or a priest, but you should also be careful not to act like one of the royal family, despite what your friends may do. Watch the festivities, show gratitude to the goddess and learn what you can, then return to your bed before the hour gets too late. You are still too young to participate in the overnight activities. Do you understand all that?"

His father seemed to take pleasure in scaring him. "I think so. Maybe I should just stay here?"

Hapu shook his head. "You can't turn down an invitation of this kind. You're a *Royal Friend*, and that title carries certain responsibilities along with the privileges. Pharaoh Setnakhte—may he live a long, prosperous, and healthy life—requested your presence himself."

Ray's eyes widened. "I'm honored."

"Stay with me in the procession. We'll be walking at the back of the line behind the carriages of the ladies of the court and the lords of the bedchamber. It will be dusty, but we don't have far to walk."

Ray and Hapu arrived in the forecourt of the palace in time to see Pharaoh Setnakhte step into his golden chariot and take the reins of the two horses, which were arrayed in blue and white fabrics and feathered head-dresses. Pharaoh's pleated robe of gold cloth glittered in the sunlight, and he wore the tall double crown of the Two Lands. The Sherden bodyguard would run ahead of his chariot, keeping the path clear, while others ran on both sides of his horses. The chariots in line behind him held Pen and Amana, followed by the radiant Queens Isis and Teya, and then Tentopet with the other princesses. Behind them, fifteen Women-of-the-Following preceded the court ladies and noblemen. Ray spotted Khait, elaborately dressed like the rest of the harem women, walking well ahead of her noble father, Panhayboni, the important Overseer of Cattle. It was quite a colorful crowd. As the royal procession started moving, Ray wondered if Bakenkhons had a large enough house to hold all of them.

Walking off to one side to avoid some of the dust, Ray turned to Hapu. "It seems that we should be going to one of the temples to see Sekhmet instead of someone's home."

Hapu winked at him. "Priests move in mysterious ways. One might expect to see the traveling Sekhmet housed in the Temple of Ptah, her consort, since she has no temple of her own here. She normally resides in the Temple of Mut in Thebes. However, Bakenkhons says that the goddess Sekhmet may only visit briefly with the gods in this city, and that it would be too dangerous to keep her in the temple during the festival."

"Too dangerous?"

"She is the warrior goddess; the violent aspect of Mut, Hathor, Bastet, and Isis. The royal family likes her because she represents the power of kings, but she must be appeased during her annual festival, else we might all be destroyed by her fury."

"They say that's why we drink the beer."

"Sekhmet would have destroyed all human life. Re, the sun god, tricked her into drinking great quantities of red beer, telling her that it was blood. Sekhmet passed out and was transformed into the kinder, gentler Hathor—so humanity was saved. We honor her by drinking the red beer on the first day of her festival."

The house of Bakenkhons seemed spacious enough to handle quite a large crowd of worshippers. Ray knew that the priests were powerful and wealthy, but this high priest apparently wanted everyone to know it. The food, wine, and the barley for the beer probably all came from offerings delivered to the Temple of Amun-Re, which meant that the high priest would get the largest share after the gods were done with the food each day.

Ray and Hapu remained at their assigned places in line as Pharaoh Setnakhte stepped down from his chariot, now carrying the crook and flail—symbols of his office—in each of his hands with his arms folded across his chest. Although he was old, he managed to stand straight and proud in the stiff posture required of him in public. Only the nobles, high-ranking priests, and high civil office holders would be allowed in the presence of Pharaoh and his family during the festival, but even they expected their living god—the good god who ruled the Two Lands—to put on a show for his people. His presence at the festival ceremonies would also ensure that Sekhmet acknowledged their offerings, for the great Amun-Re spoke and ruled through Pharaoh.

The small crowd outside the house got down on their knees, pressed their foreheads to the ground, and stretched their arms toward Pharaoh; a human tunnel forming a clear path to the front door where Bakenkhons waited. Ray saw a look pass between Pharaoh and the High Priest that reminded him of two cobras meeting on a path in the desert, carefully evaluating each other as they decided whether or not to strike. The moment passed, then Bakenkhons bowed low to welcome Pharaoh to his home. Pharaoh allowed him to rise and followed him through the portal.

"Did you see that?" Ray whispered to his father.

"I saw," Hapu said. "There is an uneasy balance of power between the two of them. With each passing flood, the priesthood grows stronger. There's even a rumor that Bakenkhons would prefer that the living god never leave his golden house, except when required for ceremonial occasions."

"Couldn't Pharaoh just replace him if he becomes a problem?"

"Another would rise to take his place. There is no shortage of priests. Such is the nature of things."

Among the last people trying to enter the house, Ray and Hapu found it impossible to get through the crowd in the front entry, so servants directed them around to the rear courtyard, where garlands of red and white flowers were hung everywhere, adding their color and sweet scent to the warm air. There were only a few people in the spacious courtyard, and one young priest smiled before approaching them. When he got closer, Ray recognized him as the priest who had helped Hapu carry him back to his room.

"Ray! Hapu! How nice that you could join us. You're feeling better?"

"I am. Thank you," Ray said.

Hapu frowned for a moment, then remembered and placed his hand on the priest's shoulder. "Itennu, was it?"

"That's right. Come and join us. I'll get you some beer."

The bald head of a priest poked out of the rear doorway to the house. "Itennu!"

Itennu shrugged at Ray and Hapu. "I'm sorry. My master calls me. I suggest that you find jars of beer, then step over near the painted wall of Sekhmet. The temporary shrine is right next to it, and you'll have a great view when Pharaoh and the High Priest come out of the house for the ceremony."

"Thank you again," Ray said.

As Itennu spoke, he happened to spot the painting of Sekhmet with its brilliant colors and realistic appearance. He shuddered. "The painting looks much too real, as if the lion-headed goddess lives within it."

"This must be a special place," Hapu said. "Sekhmet is with us."

Itennu smiled and started toward the house, then suddenly turned. "I almost forgot. Queen Isis has summoned you, Hapu. Please follow me."

Hapu placed his hand on Ray's shoulder and looked into his eyes. "Stay here. Enjoy yourself. And if you don't see me before then, return to your bed at the fifth hour of night."

A few minutes after Hapu left, Ray heard the muffled sound of a harp inside the house, its gentle sounds competing with tambourines, ivory rattles, and the jingling of sistra. Clouds of incense poured from the rear door to the house as if it were on fire with scent. A female servant with light skin and blue eyes brought Ray a jar of beer while he walked toward the outdoor shrine as Itennu had suggested. The beer was red and as thick as porridge. In the shade of the palm trees and acacias that dotted the courtyard, the painting of Sekhmet glowed with a light of its own, capturing the eye and unwilling to let the viewer go—Ray had to force himself to look away. Flowered garlands were hung everywhere around the shrine, and the golden statue that held Sekhmet's essence seemed pleased by the array of food and drink on her altar. Small braziers burned on both sides of the shrine, filling the air with the exotic scent of myrrh.

Gradually, the music got louder as the celebration within the house moved toward the rear door. The dancers were the first to emerge; numerous young women wearing only leather thongs and colorful beaded collars, their bodies smoothly weaving while they encircled the shrine and danced for the goddess. They were accompanied by female musicians, each one jingling a bow-shaped sistrum, shaking a white rattle, or thumping a tambourine. Once the musicians had stationed themselves out of the way, and the dancers had spread out around the courtyard, a hush fell over the crowd. A special priestess—the *meret singer* who played the role of Meret, the goddess of rejoicing—walked backwards out of the rear door, her eyes on Pharaoh inside the house, while clapping her hands in time with her chant: "He comes who brings! He comes who brings!"

Pharaoh emerged with Bakenkhons just behind him, their arms raised wide, chanting as they approached the shrine. Close beside them, Itennu carried two bowls of incense on chains, and the smoke swirled up around the two men. Once they were outside, a crowd of nobles filed out of the house and gathered around Sekhmet's shrine. Servants passed among them, passing out fresh jugs of red beer. Ray noticed that several people weren't very drunk yet, and they also found themselves marveling at the lifelike painting of the goddess.

Except for Pharaoh and Bakenkhons, everyone kneeled and raised their arms as Bakenkhons began the ceremonial hymn to Sekhmet:

All hail, jubilation to You, O Golden One,

Sole ruler, Uraeus of the Supreme Lord Himself!

Mysterious One who gives birth to the Divine Entities,

Forms the animals, models them as She pleases, fashions men.

O Mother! Luminous One who thrusts back the darkness,

Who illuminates every human creature with Her rays.

Hail, Great One of many Names,

You from whom the Divine Entities come forth in this Your Name of Mut-Aset!

You who cause the throat to breathe,

Daughter of Ra, whom He spat forth from His mouth in this Your Name of Tefnut!

O Nit, who appeared in Your barge in this Your Name of Mut!

O Venerable Mother, You who subdues Your adversaries in this Your name Nekhbet!

O You-Who-Knows-How-To-Make-Right-Use-of-the-Heart,

You who triumphs over Your enemies in this Your Name of Sekhmet!

It is the Golden One, the Lady of Drunkenness, of Music, of Dance,

Of Frankincense, of the Crown, of Young Women,

Whom men acclaim because they love Her!

It is the Gold of the Divine Entities, who comes forth at Her season,

The month of Epipi, the Day of the New Moon, at the Festival of "She is Delivered."

Heaven makes merry, the earth is full of gladness, the city of Pi-Ramesses rejoices!

By the time the first cycle of chanting was finished, Ray had finished his third jug of beer. Hapu had not returned. He found himself seated on the hard sand, his head spinning, wondering if he might actually hear the voice of Sekhmet as she watched him from her shrine, her lioness eyes glittering in the firelight as full darkness descended over the land. However, he found that he was easily distracted by the young dancers moving through the crowd, their skin shining with dampness from the heat, their bodies moving sinuously like cobras hypnotizing their prey. He had noticed that Pen and Amana, kneeling a short distance behind Pharaoh and Bakenkhons, received much of the attention from the dancers, but there were two who seemed to have taken a liking to Ray. As servants continued to distribute red beer to the thirsty crowd, Ray noticed that many of the celebrants had gradually slumped from their knees into sitting positions, onto their sides, or against each other, and some of them were singing or mumbling variations of the hymn to Sekhmet that they had just heard. Remarkably, most of the servants bringing the beer appeared to be sober, as did several of the priests hovering at the edges of the crowd in their white robes, having been given the task of keeping the worshippers from harming themselves during the festival.

Beside Sekhmet's altar, Tentopet and a dozen of the other young women from the harem began to sing chants in time with the music, their dresses flowing around them in the gentle breeze. Khait was also among them, smiling as she sang. Ray had not seen many of these ritual performances, but he was always amazed at how beautiful their voices sounded when singing together, as if songbirds were gathered to greet the golden boat of the dawn. This was music to entertain the gods, and Sekhmet must surely be pleased by the performance. He could also pick out Tentopet's voice from those of the other performers, for she made the most beautiful sounds that he could imagine. Intimidated by the power of her song, he saw that the other singers gradually moved away from her, as did the closest members of the audience, many of whom were frowning. He knew they were probably whispering about Tentopet's performance, and some went so far as to raise their eyes to the sky—perhaps thinking that the gods would show some sign of their pleasure.

Ray's eyes drifted back to the lifelike painting of Sekhmet on the side of her shrine, now brightly lit by flaming braziers to push back the darkness. The colors looked brighter now, and her lion head made slight movements; the reflective cat eyes judging what they saw in the courtyard. The goddess seemed to have fully inhabited the painting, favoring it over the cold statue seated on its throne inside the shrine. When the eyes turned to look at Ray, he felt as if she were about to speak when he was interrupted by another dancer gyrating in front of him, close enough that he noticed the pleasant smell of the perfumed oils on her skin and hair. He looked up and also saw an alert intelligence glimmering behind her kohl-rimmed eyes, although those eyes had a disturbing similarity to those of Sekhmet.

The earth moved and Ray landed on his back. The dancer smiled and moved away, leaving him looking up at the tiny lights spinning high overhead. Then he gasped when a large object blotted out the sky, but it turned out to be the bulbous head of Itennu smiling down at him.

"Feeling okay, Ray?"

"I'm not sure. The world is revolving around me, Sekhmet is watching me from her painting, and I keep being distracted by the dancers."

Itennu nodded and helped him sit up again. "Then you are worshipping the goddess, and she will be pleased. However, your father has sent me to remind you that it's getting close to the fifth hour of night, and you should return to the golden house of Pharaoh. The High Priest is hosting the Pharaoh and Queen Isis inside, so your father will remain with them for the evening."

Ray knew this was a great honor for his father. He would have to ask him about it in the morning.

Another voice interrupted them. "Enjoying yourself, Blue Foot? Who is this turtle on his back?"

Itennu spoke to the young man who had joined them. "This is Ray, son of Hapu, friend to Pharaoh and dweller in the golden house."

"Did you knock Ray down?"

"I did not," Itennu said, stiffening. He looked at Ray. "This is Neferabu, the one who painted Sekhmet on the shrine wall."

Ray rotated his wobbly head as Neferabu sat beside him. "Your painting. It's—"

"Amazing," Neferabu said with a nod. "Yes, I know. It's all a matter of having learned to see the curves and shapes of real figures cut from the rock, as a sculptor does, combined with the use of color and shadow that the expert painter employs. I'm sure you've noticed that most of the paintings you see are flat and have no life, which is fine if they're going to be buried out of sight in a tomb with the owner, but a painting made for public viewing needs to have a life of its own."

"It's magic," Ray mumbled.

"Yes, I suppose it is. My work obviously pleases Sekhmet, who has already spoken to me once this evening."

"She spoke to you?"

"From the painting, yes. The gods respect my work, even if no one else does. Bakenkhons also congratulated me—he may be old, but he has a good eye for quality. Imagine what I could have done if I'd only had more blue paint."

Itennu cleared his throat. "I'm sorry, Neferabu. I—"

"Forget it." He looked at someone in the crowd and smiled. "Now, if you'll excuse me, there's a young woman over there who wants to learn the intimate secrets of a master painter."

Ray started to turn his head to look, but Neferabu blocked his view. "Don't look. I don't want to scare her off."

"There are secrets you can teach her?" Itennu asked.

Neferabu smiled and stood up straight, lifting a jug of beer from a passing servant. "Yes, in a manner of speaking." He raised his jug in salute to Ray. "Enjoy yourself, boy. Before the night is out, I plan to travel through the marshes."

Ray frowned at Itennu. "He's going to travel through the marshes at night? Is that part of the festival?"

Itennu sighed and helped Ray stand up. "I think your father should be the one to explain that to you tomorrow. In the meantime, you should be on your way home. I have to return to my master."

The world was spinning again, making Ray question his decision to stand up. "I don't think I can find my way back. Can you take me to my father?"

"Itennu!"

"Sorry, I have to go. My master calls," Itennu said, jogging into the house.

Ray bumped into a soft figure standing directly behind him. After a careful turn, he saw Khait standing very close and smiling at him. She held two jars of beer in her hand and offered one to Ray. “Enjoying the festival, Ray?”

“I find it confusing.”

Khait took his right hand and wrapped it around one of the beer jars, her hand lingering on his arm. “This is for you. Do you mind if I hold onto you for a moment? I’m a little dizzy.”

“Okay. Thank you for the beer, but—“

“I like your gold collar,” she said, pressing her face close to look at it in the dim light. She was close enough that he could smell the scent of myrrh in her hair, along with the fragrant oils on her warm body. He inhaled her scent, feeling dizzier than he had before. She seemed much nicer now than she had earlier in the day, and he noticed he was breathing fast. Keeping her face close, and pressing her body against his, she lifted her eyes. “It’s very pretty. Do you think I’m pretty, Ray?”

Ray found it hard to form words for some reason. Probably because of the beer. "Well, um, yes, I—"

Off-balance, Khait suddenly jerked sideways. A meaty hand was on her arm, and it belonged to her father, Panhayboni. Everything about him always seemed unusually large and round—a look more often favored by prosperous merchants and priests rather than administrators of the royal court. His angry eyes were small and piggy in his round face. "Take your hands off my daughter, boy! Who do you think you are? You are nothing but dust!"

Ray tried to think of something to say, but he couldn't figure out what was going on. "I'm sorry? I'm not sure—"

Khait tried to twist out of her father's grip. "He didn't do anything!"

"Insolent pup!" Still holding his daughter's arm in a tight grip, he used his other hand to give Ray's chest a hard shove. Stumbling backwards, he sat down hard, his head still spinning. Panhayboni turned and walked away, dragging Khait along behind him.

The crowd that had formed around the disturbance began to drift away. Ray considered the merits of staying on the ground, which seemed to be the safest place for him, but he knew he should find his way back to the palace and his bed. Maybe one of the helper priests would notice him if he stood up. Thinking this over, he tried brushing some of the dirt from his white robes, but there was enough light to see that it was pointless.

Ray felt a soft hand stroking his neck. He thought it might be one of the dancers, but he was afraid to look up because he didn't want to startle her away and she might be able to help him. He inhaled her flowery perfume as it wrapped itself around him.

"I can take you home," the woman said from behind him. She sounded drunk, but her low voice was as soft as her hand. "Come with me, and I'll make you feel much better."

Ray smiled. Maybe she could stop the spinning in his head. He turned to look at her and his smile disappeared. Sultry eyes rimmed in black kohl stared back at him, her fluttering eyelids sparkling with powdered green malachite in the firelight. The scented wax cone on top of her black wig had melted to release its strong perfume. She wore a filmy white gown that fluttered in the lightest breezes, tied around the high waist with a red sash, with her right breast exposed. She was short, but she stood proud and straight like a queen. Queen Teya.

The queen bent and placed her hand on the side of his face. "Such a good looking boy. Fragile on the outside, but with an inner strength that's very appealing. And so smart."

Ray didn't know if someone in the crowd bumped against her or if she simply stumbled, but she suddenly lurched forward and he caught her in his arms to keep her from falling. Unfortunately, as dizzy as he was, he fell backwards and she landed on top of him. She didn't weigh very much, but the impact knocked the wind out of him, or maybe it was her breast in his face that took his breath away.

A moment later, Teya was lifted to her feet by Pen and Amana. As she rose into the air, her red sash belt, which had caught under Ray's elbow, pulled loose and drifted down over his chest. Pen grabbed the sash and shoved it at his mother. When Pen turned toward Ray again, he thought his friend was going to help him up, but he just left Ray on his back as he scowled. "What are you doing?"

"Nothing," Ray sputtered. "She fell. I tried to catch her."

"Men have been killed for less," Pen hissed. "Do not forget yourself in the royal presence."

Ray thought Pen seemed a little drunk as well, which might explain his odd behavior.

"I'm sorry, Pen. It was an accident."

"Here," Amana said, stepping around behind Ray. "Let me help you up."

Amana awkwardly raised him to a crouched position, then placed his foot on Ray's rump and kicked him forward onto his face.

"Stop it," Teya said, stepping between Amana and Ray, who was lying on his face in the sand. "He was helping me, you fools!"

The crowd had re-formed to watch Ray's antics—he was clearly part of the entertainment—but they parted to let Tentopet push through. Ray knew it was her, even though he only saw her delicate feet at first. She wore a gold anklet that he recognized, and had the best-looking feet that he could remember, now glowing in her golden sandals. She rolled him over on his back and brushed the sand from his face. Her look of concern made his heart melt.

"Wonderful," Teya said, staring daggers at Tentopet. "Fine. The pup will be tended by the kitten. You deal with him, then."

Teya turned and left, escorted by Pen and Amana. When Ray saw them leave, he sighed with relief, then thanked Tentopet for helping him and complimented her on her song.

"You've had too much to drink," Tentopet said.

"I wanted to see Sekhmet."

Tentopet glanced in the direction of the departing Teya. "I think she just left."

THREE

1184 BCE—Western Desert

Year 4 of His Majesty, King of Upper and Lower Egypt, Chosen by Re, Beloved of Amun, Pharaoh Setnakhte, First Month of Akhet (Season of Inundation), Day 21

Two days after the battle with Meryey, chief of the Tjehenu tribes, a small hunting party left the main Egyptian camp, passing through a gap in the wall of shields that helped protect them from surprises during the night. Meryey was still missing, and three of the four divisions of Pharaoh's army had stayed behind to sort out the new captives, finish counting the dead, obtain supplies for the return trip to Pi-Ramesses, and record the valuables taken from the Libu and Meshwesh soldiers. Having spotted plenty of wild game in the area, Pharaoh was anxious to do some hunting before the day's march began. Accompanying Ramesses III on foot were his standard bearers—Didu and Nebamun—along with Chief General Hori and a dozen favored officers from the Pharaoh Division, many of whom bore noble titles long before they had joined Pharaoh on this campaign to stop the incursions along the Libyan border. Notably absent was the revered General Imhotep, whose family had served many pharaohs since the time of Ramesses the Great. Imhotep had suffered multiple breaks of his right leg during the recent battle, and there were rumors that Pharaoh had reluctantly asked Imhotep to retire from the army due to his age.

As the lowest-ranking members of the hunting party when they weren't carrying their standards, Didu and Neb walked at the back of the group armed only with their spears, knives, and lassos—long ropes with stone balls at the end. They had scouted the area before dawn by chariot, and had discovered a large herd of antelope grazing near a small oasis at the base of steep cliffs a short distance from the camp. When the hunt was over, water carriers would be sent out to the oasis to fill more jugs and skins for the journey. Keeping thousands of soldiers alive in the desert required enormous amounts of water.

Didu glanced over his shoulder at the camp now receding into the distance, dusty with the activity of soldiers rising to eat breakfast, break camp, and prepare for another long march.

"Anxious to get back?" Neb asked, still staring straight ahead at the backs of the officers ahead of them.

"These hunting trips make me nervous. We're still in hostile territory, and Pharaoh needs protection."

"That's why he's got us. And the gods watch over him."

"Yes, well, we could have brought a few more reliable veterans along in case of trouble."

Neb snorted. "You worry too much. The only thing likely to attack us out here are the mosquitoes hanging around the oasis."

Didu sighed. "Meryey is still free, and we know that some of his Meshwesh warriors escaped."

"Meryey ran away dressed like a woman. I doubt we'll be hearing from him again."

"Perhaps." Didu studied the steep, eroded cliffs pocked with dark caves and deep shadows where the sunlight would not penetrate until mid-morning. Many things could hide up there, just as Pharaoh had hidden a thousand archers in the dark cliffs above Meryey's camp two days earlier.

"I've got better things to think about," Neb said, "like what I'm going to do with all of my new wealth. Have you thought about your plans?"

"Not so much."

"Going to stay in the army?"

Although Didu couldn't imagine Nebamun as anything other than a soldier, his own ambition motivated him to think about a better life. He wouldn't miss the constant dust that followed the army wherever it went, the threat of death, the tiresome military drills, the bad food, and the endless marches across burning sands to foreign lands. As a civilian, he wouldn't mind traveling to see the ancient pyramids built during the Old Empire, or the hills of Nubia where it was said that gold was as plentiful as grains of sand, or maybe even the exotic Land of Punt, but he really just wanted to return to civilization, settle down, and become a wealthy bureaucrat.

"I haven't thought about it much," Didu said. "How about you?"

Neb shrugged. "It's all I know how to do, really. I've thought about starting a small slave trading business with my gold and the Libu captives that Pharaoh gave me, but I haven't decided yet."

Didu nodded, keeping his eyes on the cliffs. "Plenty of wealthy slave traders. Good business if your slaves don't get sick, or break a leg, or run off, or try to kill you before you've trained them. Supply can be a problem of course, since you need wars to get new captives."

"You're cheerful in the morning, as always."

Approaching the herd of antelope, Pharaoh held up his hand for silence. Collecting the loose coils of a lasso in his left hand, he hefted the ball hanging from the end of the rope and allowed it to dangle from his right hand. Soldiers assigned to hunt these antelope for the army's meals would use bows and arrows to quickly kill as many as possible, but this was only done out of necessity. Pharaoh's hunt would be done with style, disdaining fancier weapons for the traditional lasso to demonstrate his skill.

Ten minutes later, Pharaoh had ventured ahead of the group to get within range of a big male antelope. Wanting to give it a chance to escape, he yelled once. The startled antelope turned and ran, but Pharaoh swung the heavy ball in a circle and released it. The weight of the ball pulled the rope along behind it, sailing through the air in a graceful arc before the rope wound itself around the front legs of the antelope. Pharaoh pulled hard on the rope once, dropping the antelope on its side, then ran forward to wrap its hind legs before it could get up. The rest of the hunting party started forward to help carry it back to camp.

Didu looked up at the cliffs again and saw the sparkle of sunlight on polished metal.

"Neb. Did you see that? Up in the rocks."

Neb's head snapped around in time to see a second glint. "Spear point?"

"Or arrowhead."

"Are they in range?"

"Depends on their bows." An arrow *snicked* into the sand near Didu's feet and he nodded. "They're in range."

Didu and Neb ran forward together, yelling and pointing up at the cliffs as they passed the officers in the hunting party. Crouched over the antelope, Pharaoh looked up in surprise when he heard their footsteps pounding toward him.

"Great One!" Didu yelled. "Ambush!"

Pharaoh stood up straight. His keen eyes immediately spotted the volley of arrows that had just been launched. He looked at Didu and Neb and pointed at the antelope. "Help me pick it up!"

With Didu and Neb at each end of the animal, and Pharaoh in the middle, they hefted it onto their shoulders as arrows hissed into the soft sand around them. Three arrows *thumped* into the antelope's side. Pharaoh reached over and plucked one of the arrows free so he could study the feathers used for the tail fletching. "Meshwesh."

The rest of the hunting party had joined them. While the rest of the group crowded around Pharaoh to protect him from the next volley, Chief General Hori plucked an arrow out of his shoulder and flung it to the ground. "Meryey sends his greetings, my lord!"

Pharaoh snorted. "Meryey runs from danger. This is the work of a Meshwesh chief."

More arrows landed among them. Didu saw one coming toward Pharaoh and knocked it aside with his spear. Pharaoh stomped on the arrow with his right foot, snapping it in two, and smiled at Didu.

Burdened by the heavy antelope, the group began to run back toward the camp while angling out and away from the archers on the cliffs. The next flight of arrows fell short. Movement among the cliffs indicated that their attackers were ready to come after them on the ground. Pharaoh's hunting party had only gone about half the distance back to camp.

Chief General Hori stopped and planted the end of his spear in the sand. "That's far enough! The great river will dry up before I run from Meshwesh! They'll either join their comrades as our slaves, or I'll personally see that they join their friends in the underworld!"

Didu looked at Neb and rolled his eyes. Hori had always been strong on strategy, but weak on tactics. Right now, they needed a strong tactician. He also hoped that one of the camp sentries would notice the large group of Meshwesh warriors running toward them from the cliffs.

"Who will see to Pharaoh's safety?" Neb asked. "There aren't enough of us to protect him out here. We have to get the living god back to camp."

Pharaoh drew his short sword. "The gods will protect me."

Several of the officers volunteered to run back to the camp to seek help, but Hori looked them over and only chose the fastest one among them, a young nobleman named Djadao. Leaving his spear and lasso with the defenders, Djadao sprinted away.

It didn't take long for the Meshwesh to catch up to the hunting party. When it looked like some of the attackers were stopping to launch more arrows, Pharaoh startled everyone by leaving the safety of the antelope shield to lead the hunting party in a charge. With his sword in one hand and his long spear in the other, he shaded his eyes to study the Meshwesh soldiers, then ran forward and yelled, "Behold! We have found Mesher, Great Chief of the Meshwesh! Montu has delivered our enemy to us! Death to those who know not the power of Amun-Re! May Horus and Sekhmet carry us into battle!"

Yes, they were outnumbered by four to one, but Didu marveled at how Ramesses III could inspire his men against such odds. Like the rest of them who had heard Pharaoh's call to battle, Didu defied all logic by running toward the Meshwesh.

The Meshwesh soldiers stopped cold, frowning in confusion. Those who were preparing to shoot arrows dropped their bows and scrambled to get their spears or swords ready to defend themselves against the roaring Egyptians racing toward them. They all had the same curious hair styles where the left sides of their heads were shaved bald. Most of them didn't use armor and wore only loincloths, but their upper torsos were painted red, and many of them had spiral tattoos on their arms and chests. Mesher stood in front of the group with a huge scar that ran diagonally across his dark face until it vanished into his black beard. Unaffected by his sprint across the sand, he waited patiently with a widening grin on his face, gripping a heavy battle axe in his right hand. Didu assumed that Mesher and his group had fought in the previous battle alongside Meryey's troops, but he had been smart enough to escape with his survivors before they could be captured. Before the big battle, Pharaoh had warned his generals that Mesher was smart enough to make his warriors the greatest threat to the Egyptian army, so part of the chariot force had been assigned to hunt for him—without success. Now, Pharaoh's luck had delivered Mesher to them, but the bulk of his army was still in camp. Didu could only hope that the priests had done their jobs, praying and sacrificing enough to the appropriate gods to keep them safe on this bright morning.

Holding a spear in his left hand and his short sword in his right, Pharaoh initiated the attack by running straight at the Meshwesh chief. Mesher stood his ground, then raised his battle axe just in time to block Pharaoh's descending blade. When the battle axe turned to take a swing at Pharaoh's side, it was deflected by Pharaoh's spear, the base of which was planted in the ground. Turning with the axe strike, Pharaoh used the momentum to thrust his short sword at Mesher's face. Mesher leaned back to avoid it, and Pharaoh used the big man's weight against him by slipping his leg behind Mesher and giving the big man a shove. With a surprised expression, Mesher fell and landed flat on his back.

Didu and Neb stayed together, their spears aimed low, running forward as the hunting party charged into the Meshwesh, who were already startled by Pharaoh's quick attack on their chief. After burying the point of his spear in two of the Meshwesh and using his foot to push them off the point each time, Didu saw a sword blade out of the corner of his eye, its polished surface swinging toward his neck in a flat arc that would neatly separate his head from his shoulders if he didn't avoid it in time. However, before he could duck, Neb's sword came up near his head and *clanged* against the incoming blade, deflecting it over Didu's head. With his spear on the wrong side of his body, Didu ducked and turned with his dagger, driving the point into the stomach of his Meshwesh attacker. Neb's sword completed the job when its point passed straight through the man's neck.

Didu detected a vibration beneath his feet, accompanied by thunder approaching from behind. The pace of the battle slowed and Meshwesh warriors began to sprint back toward the cliffs. Didu turned and confirmed his suspicion that the chariot force had arrived, led by Djadao, the runner they had sent back to camp. The chariots moved in two columns as straight as arrows aimed at the Meshwesh.

Expecting to see Mesher impaled on the point of Pharaoh's sword, Didu was shocked to find Pharaoh down on one knee with a bleeding gash across his left thigh. Mesher was nowhere in sight. In the dust and confusion of the retreat, it took a moment before Didu was able to spot Mesher running alongside his soldiers back to the cliffs. A smart move: If they reached the rocks before the chariots caught them, and if they avoided the arrows fired from the chariots, they'd have a good chance of escape.

Streaked with blood, most of which was not his own, General Hori helped Pharaoh to his feet. Hori looked strong enough to carry the living god all the way back to camp if necessary, but it appeared that Pharaoh could still walk. Neb used a roll of linen to wrap the leg and stop the royal blood from flowing into the sand. When Didu got closer, he saw that Pharaoh was smiling.

"A fine warrior," Pharaoh said. "Mesher and his people would make excellent soldiers in my army."

"As you say, my lord," Hori snorted. "Assuming we could train them not to run away from battle."

Pharaoh dismissed the idea with a casual wave of his hand. "Tactical retreat. They weren't equipped to fight chariots on open ground. That would be madness."

Hori wiped his bloody dagger on his kilt, leaving another streak of red. "Madness was the idea of attacking us in the first place."

"If you had a choice, would you not choose to die while attacking a king?"

"An attack on Pharaoh is suicide. The gods protect you."

"But what a fine death it would be, neh? The gods would respect a man who died in single combat against the Lord of the Two Lands."

"Personally, I'd prefer not to die at all."

Pharaoh smiled and patted Hori on the shoulder that had been punctured by the Meshwesh arrow. "We must all make the journey over the western horizon, Hori. Osiris awaits us all."

Hori glanced off into the distance where the Meshwesh had almost reached the rocks. The first chariots were close behind, beginning to launch their arrows. "Some sooner than others, I hope."

Pharaoh nodded, his thoughts turning to other matters. "We'll need to break camp quickly this morning. While we were fighting, Mesher said something that worries me."

"They're going to attack us again?"

"No. He said that Meryey sent messages ahead of us yesterday morning—by fast horse, by boat, and by bird. At least one of those messages will get through. He ordered an attack on our palace."

"Impossible. His army is in ruins behind us."

"Mesher said that Meryey is frustrated and has no honor. His assassins are already in place, just waiting for his signal."

Hori stared at Pharaoh with an incredulous expression. "Why would Mesher tell you this? He could be lying."

"He respects me. And I respect him. He doesn't approve of Meryey's actions, and he also knows it's too late for me to respond to his news."

"What could Meryey possibly hope to accomplish with a few assassins?"

Pharaoh paused and looked off into the distance where Pi-Ramesses lay far beyond the horizon. "He wants to kill my sons."

Ray opened his eyes. He felt odd, but his head was no longer spinning. A heavy silence hung in the golden house of Pharaoh. At that late hour, with most of the residents, staff, and guards off celebrating the Festival of Drunkenness, Ray heard only the quiet chirping and scuttling sounds of the night, punctuated by the occasional screech of a hunting bird swooping down on its prey. He vaguely remembered Tentopet escorting him back from the house of Bakenkhons, but the details were fuzzy in his memory. The room had a pleasant smell of incense, and the coils of smoke rose in soft curls from a dish under a shaft of moonlight that angled through the window, bathing the room in muted blue and silver.

Shifting his position on the bed, Ray's eyes widened when he felt warm skin snuggled up to his side. Turning his head, he saw the lovely face of Tentopet close enough that he could smell her sweet breath on his cheek. He stopped breathing, wondering if something horrible had happened while he was drunk—something that would end with his being impaled on a stick while Pharaoh watched. His stomach muscles tightened in anticipation. Afraid to startle Tentopet, he moved his right hand with great care until it brushed against her clothing, which she was still wearing. He lifted his head and studied what he could see of her in the moonlight, then felt relief wash over him. Nothing bad had happened, at least as far as he could tell. Although he was inexperienced with these things, he was pretty sure that the presence of clothing draped over Tentopet's delicate curves meant that he was safe from impalement by Pharaoh.

Right then and there, he swore to the gods that he would never drink the red beer again. The dizziness and loss of reason brought on by the evil brew was far too dangerous.

Now, the question remained how to deal with Tentopet. Was she also aware that nothing bad had happened in his bed? He looked around and frowned, wondering if the red beer had made him think that his room looked different now. Perhaps the smoke from the incense was too thick, tricking his eyes. Lifting his head more, he realized that he must be in Tentopet's room, tucked away in the palace's harem apartments. He felt a chill when he realized that the harem was always watched by Pharaoh's best and most trusted guards, most of whom were eunuchs and none too happy about it. He felt doomed.

On the other hand, how had Tentopet gotten him in there without the guards seeing him in the first place? Could he possibly be lucky enough to discover that they were all drunk and passed out on the floor to worship Sekhmet? What about the other women of the harem? Many of them had accompanied Pharaoh to visit Bakenkhons, but not all of them. He was certain that Pharaoh had at least 200 women in his harem, although many of them were there to manage the making of linen and clothing. He'd never visited the harem before, particularly since it would mean his death, but the locked rooms ran the length of one end of the palace. Could he sneak out without being seen?

Moving no faster than a snail in the Nile mud, Ray slid away from Tentopet and onto the floor. His head thumped along with his heart. On his hands and knees, he crept around in the dim light, seeing no one else, until he spotted a wood door covered with intricate carvings of giant Pharaoh figures surrounded by tiny females playing games with him, singing, dancing, or playing instruments. Still on his knees, he rose up enough to slide open a small spy hole and peer into the corridor beyond. The oil lamps in the corridor were burning low, but he saw three guards on their backs or curled against the wall as they slept. Soft snores echoed off the walls. Only one guard was seated upright on the floor, and he seemed to be half-asleep. Feeling optimistic now, Ray tried the door.

Locked from the outside. His head thumped harder.

"Ray?"

Ray bumped his head against the wall and almost relieved himself on the floor. Jerking his head around, he saw Tentopet sitting on the edge of the bed.

"Good evening," Ray whispered. "Forgive me my clumsiness. And my being here. And being drunk. All those things."

Tentopet smiled and kept her voice low. "Don't worry. You're safe. You were too drunk to go farther on your own, so I brought you here."

"You are good and generous. I am but dust on your feet and do not deserve such kind treatment. However, I should leave now. The guards," he said, nodding over his shoulder. "You know how they are about these things."

"Don't worry about them."

Ray swallowed. "They will kill me. If this is your will, I am most happy to please you by dying, but I would prefer not to."

She stood up and held out her hand. "Come. No need to die for me now. I know a secret. If you'll keep silent, I'll share it with you."

Ray wasn't sure he wanted to learn a new secret. People had a tendency to get secrets beaten out of them, particularly when they were caught where they didn't belong in the palace.

Tentopet took his hand, dragging him beyond the bed, through another doorway, down a short corridor, and into a large room with a clear pool of water trapped in the floor. Focused on his hand tingling in hers, he barely noticed the room.

"What is this place?" Ray asked, never having seen an indoor pond before.

She gave him an odd look while they continued walking past the still pool. "It's our bath. The servants fill it each day with fresh water."

Before he could ask another question, Tentopet stepped around a hidden section of wall and pulled him along into the stall behind it, stopping at another door. She tugged on the handle to check it. "This is where the water carriers come through."

"Locked," he said, seeing this was another door that was bolted from the outside. "I'm still trapped."

She reached into a corner of the stall and felt around under a pile of straw, then stood up with a long, thin piece of wood in her hand. "One of the women who carries water uses this. We're not supposed to know about it."

Tentopet pushed the slim piece of wood into the gap between the door and the frame, then slid it upwards. On the other side, the lock bolt thumped against the wood.

"That's it?"

She smiled. "That's it. You're free. You just have to watch out for the guards on the other side."

Ray sighed, then nudged the door open a crack and looked outside. "I don't see anyone."

"Just remember to lock it when you go out," she said, patting him on the back.

When he turned around to thank her, she was gone, and he felt oddly alone. He stepped outside, where there was just enough clearance between the wall and the thick trunk of a palm tree to fully open the door. The door creaked as he carefully closed and locked it. With one more glance around, he crept away among the plants and shadows along the wall.

Despite Ray's precautions, he still had the queasy feeling that someone had seen him.

Itennu was ready to fall asleep on his feet. He had spent the entire first night of the festival keeping the guests supplied with food and beer. As one of the attending priests at the festival, he was not allowed to drink the beer himself, but was required to keep an eye on the guests to make sure that they didn't hurt themselves as they communed with the goddess Sekhmet. Whenever Bakenkhons needed something, he called Itennu to attend him. For the last hour, Bakenkhons had been seated inside the house with Pharaoh, surrounded by the women of the royal harem, where Itennu was expected to maintain full bowls of the sticky candy made from the root sap of the marsh mallow plant. The cooks had spent the afternoon separating the marsh mallow roots from their leaves and five-petaled flowers, then boiling the root pulp with honey until the mixture thickened. The mixture was strained and cooled, forming small mounds of white foam tinged with gold. Some of the candy was offered to Sekhmet and Amun-Re, but the bulk of it was reserved for Pharaoh and his entourage. Common people were not allowed to eat the candy, but Itennu had sneaked a piece in private, allowing the sweetness to explode over his tongue for a few minutes before finally swallowing it. The eating of this treat was quickly followed by a small jar of beer to disguise any smell that the candy might leave on his breath.

Itennu was in the busy kitchen now, dodging harried servants and cooks. When he took a moment to stop and drink some water, his immediate superior in the temple, Merubaste, appeared beside him with a frown.

"You may have fooled Bakenkhons into thinking you're a hard worker, but you're not fooling me."

Itennu coughed as he swallowed the last of the water. "I've been working all day."

Merubaste sighed. "I've been watching you this evening. You stole Pharaoh's candy for yourself, you wasted time with your friends in the courtyard, and now you're hiding in the kitchen when the high priest needs your services once more."

Startled that someone had seen him eat the candy, Itennu's eyes widened. "I can explain."

"I'm not interested in your explanations. I saw you with my own eyes. I would punish you immediately, but Bakenkhons wants you to bring red beer to his private suite upstairs. Do I need to show you where it is?"

"No. He showed it to me this afternoon."

"Then go there immediately. We'll continue this discussion later."

Itennu turned to leave the kitchen, but Merubaste's heavy hand dropped onto his shoulder to stop him. "With the beer, Itennu. With the beer."

"Oh, yes. Sorry," Itennu said, grabbing three jars of beer from the serving table.

He turned and made his way through the house, past the room where Pharaoh's chin was tipped down onto his chest, his tired eyes fluttering, while the women of the harem created a breeze for him with their ostrich feather fans or picked at the food they had retrieved from the buffet table. Worried about what kind of punishment Merubaste might have in mind for him in the morning, Itennu barely noticed the unconscious drunks he stepped over on the floor or the giggling and gasping noises coming from various darkened rooms of the house.

Upstairs, not wanting to keep Bakenkhons waiting any longer than necessary, he located the personal suite of the high priest and ducked around the linen drape hanging in the doorway. There were only two oil lamps burning in the large space, and it took a moment for Itennu's eyes to adjust to the dim light. Before he could make out any details, he heard a grunting noise that made him think there might be a pig in the room.

Afraid to stumble over something in the shadows, Itennu wanted Bakenkhons to say something so he could get his bearings. "My lord?"

The grunting stopped and a dark mound moved ahead of him on what he could now see was a bed. The movement allowed the light of an oil lamp to shine on the surprised face of Queen Teya, naked and lying on her back.

Fearing that she was being attacked, Itennu stepped forward to confront the mound of fabric that spun to face him, prepared to throw the beer jars at the intruder.

The enraged face of Bakenkhons popped out of the mound that now towered over Itennu where the high priest stood on the bed. "What are you doing here, you maggot of Set?"

"Beer," Itennu stammered, taking a step back.

Bakenkhons roared and jumped to the floor in front of Itennu while Queen Teya pulled a sheet up over her head. Itennu never saw the blunt object that rose up to smash into the top of his skull, knowing only that he had been thrust into the safety of happy oblivion where he would not have to face the wrath of Bakenkhons.

Tentopet felt restless. After Ray left the harem, she stopped to take a bath, hoping that the cool waters would calm her while removing the dust and smells of the festival from her skin and hair. She still had this part of the harem to herself, but she knew that the other women would gradually start returning from the house of Bakenkhons. Time alone was a precious gift since she not only worked and studied with the other women of her rank, but slept with them as well, with up to four of the others crowded onto her bed. This was the privileged life she had been born into, and she was fortunate in being able to receive instruction from Hapu and Pasai with her brothers, but one of the luxuries she was not usually allowed was time to be alone. Thoughts tumbled through her mind like grains of sand on the wind, and she hoped that this brief period of quiet would allow her to sort them out, or at least allow them to settle down so that she could sleep.

The bath had done little to calm her, and she now found herself lying on top of the bed, still damp from her bath, staring at the goddess Nut protectively arched over her on the ceiling. White and yellow stars glittered against the deep blue of the painted night sky that surrounded Nut. The goddess should be helping her to find peace in her dreams, but she didn't help tonight. Maybe Tentopet would sleep better after all if her chattering and snoring bedmates were beside her on the bed. Until then, she would have to be alone with her thoughts—mostly of Ray, the silly young man who accompanied her brothers wherever they went. He was a commoner, of course, and far beneath her class, but at least she could speak to him as a royal friend. She enjoyed his company and wished she could be around him more, even though he trembled in her presence as the common people always did. They knew she could be a queen one day, or perhaps even a pharaoh if the conditions were right, and they feared her power despite her youth. Her mother said that Ray was simply nervous around her because of her beauty, but she knew she couldn't compare to the queens who were grown women—like Isis and Teya—full of inner strength, beauty, learning, and the confidence of knowing they had achieved their highest status in life.

"Where's the boy, Tyti?"

Tentopet recognized the low and liquid voice of Queen Teya before she turned to see her staggering toward the bed, her diaphanous white gown like a fine mist over her beautiful body. Teya stared at Tentopet through the streaked black kohl that had formed neat lines around her eyes earlier in the evening. Her eyelids still glittered from the green malachite when she blinked.

"I know what you were doing," Teya said, pointing at her stomach. "Look at you, still covered in sweat."

Tentopet brushed at the water drops still clinging to her skin. "I took a bath!"

"With the boy, I suppose. Don't lie to me, Tyti. I saw him sneaking away. And I saw how you treated him at the festival this evening."

"He was drunk. I helped him find his way."

"Oh, I bet he found his way. Straight to your bed! You're a *princess*, you little fool! You can't just give yourself to every commoner who says pretty things to you!"

Tentopet jumped to her feet. "I didn't!"

Teya folded her arms and tipped her head. "Then what was he doing here? Can you explain that?"

Tentopet hesitated, knowing what the truth would sound like, but not knowing what else to say. "He was sleeping."

Teya just tipped her head to the side and stared at her, obviously not convinced.

Frustrated, Tentopet threw her hands in the air. "He couldn't make it as far as his bedroom!"

"I see. Is that what he told you, or was it your idea to bring him into the harem?"

"Mine. I almost had to carry him in. When he felt better, he left."

"When he felt better. I see," Teya said, sitting down heavily on the end of the bed. "It pains me that you have sunk so low, Tyti. I was very fond of you. Now, you leave me no choice. You belong to Pharaoh's household, and therefore you belong to the living god himself. Both of them, in fact. Do you have any idea how serious this is?"

Tentopet shook her head and fell to her knees beside Teya, who looked away. "I didn't do anything! Why won't you believe me?"

Teya's voice was softer now. "Because I know what it means to be young and beautiful, child. I know how a man can make you feel when he wants something. I also know you aren't old enough yet to see beyond their lies, or understand how protected you are in the harem of the living god. You aren't old enough to appreciate it yet. However, I'm afraid you're going to learn, and very quickly, just how good your life was here."

"What do you mean? Please don't do anything. It wasn't my fault. Nothing happened. I was only trying to help him."

"Yes, they always just want you to *help* them, don't they? But your job was to remain faithful to the living god and to support this household. It's a great responsibility, and some women simply aren't up to the task. They feel like they're missing something. They want to be free to choose their own young men and not be hidden away here in the palace. When a woman fails in her responsibilities here, it's a bad reflection on all of us, and the wrath of Pharaoh in these matters can be great."

Tentopet was crying now. "But I didn't fail!"

Teya raised her arm and pulled Tentopet's head onto her breast. "You know I love you, child, maybe almost as much as your mother, but I can't let this go. You must be punished. If I kept this secret and other people saw Ray here, I might be executed along with you."

Teya put her other arm around Tentopet's head to help muffle her sobs. "I know it's hard, but our time in this world is always short. You've lived well until now. You've never had to work the fields or know the attentions of sweaty old men. There are many who wish they were in your place, even though they don't realize how hard it really is to be a princess."

Tentopet tried to speak, but she was sobbing too hard to form words. It seemed as if her body were dissolving onto the bed. Teya stroked her hair. "I know. I know. Life is hard. But maybe there is one thing that I can do for you."

The breath caught in Tentopet's throat as she heard the promise in Teya's smooth voice. She tried to control her sobbing. "Yes?"

"As I see it, you have three choices open to you now. You can take your own life, or Pharaoh will have it taken from you."

Tentopet nodded, ready to resume sobbing, gasping for air. She felt like she was drowning.

"Your third choice is very risky," Teya continued. "For me and for you. I would only take this risk because I love you as much as I would my own daughter if I had one. You'd have to follow my orders exactly if you want to save your own life, and possibly mine as well. You might also save the lives of the guards in the hallway who were too drunk to notice anything this evening."

Tentopet nodded, ready to agree to anything. "Yes. Whatever you wish. I understand."

Teya sighed. "It won't be easy. You may wish to take poison instead."

"Tell me. Please tell me."

"You would have to leave the palace, never to return. You would travel in disguise so that no one would recognize you as a princess. You could go wherever you choose, but it should be well away from here, possibly to Thebes or farther. Memphis and Heliopolis are too close, and too many people would recognize you there. Pharaoh will look for you, so you'll have to remain hidden when you can and forget that you were ever part of his harem. You would have to blend in with the common people and become one of them, otherwise the Medjay police will find you, or the people will cut off your nose and ears to destroy your pretty face. You must be someone else entirely, without privilege, without support. I know you're strong and that you can do this, but I don't know if you realize that, so you'll have to decide. As I said, you may wish to take your own life instead of running away. There are several good poisons you can use."

Tentopet collapsed on the bed. She knew her life was over, one way or another.

Approaching his own room, Ray nodded at a guard seated on the floor of the corridor who snorted and blinked at the sound of his footsteps. Sensing no danger, he leaned back against the wall and returned to his dreams. When Ray walked past, he smelled the beer on the guard's breath.

Tinubiti was not in Ray's room to witness his late arrival, and was probably off at the festival with everyone else. Exhausted by the evening's activities and the late hour, he kicked off his sandals and flopped onto the bed, landing on another occupant already sleeping there. Startled, Ray rolled off the bed onto the floor. Assuming it was Tinubiti taking the opportunity to sleep in a real bed instead of using her mat in the corner, he didn't want to yell at her, but he did want to get his own bed back.

"What are you doing?" Ray demanded.

"Sleeping," Bull said in a drowsy voice.

"Bull? You're okay?"

"Why are you in my room?"

He looked around to make sure he was in the right place. "Your room? This is my room, Bull."

"Who are you?"

Ray bent closer so that Bull could see his face in the dim light from the balcony. "Don't you know my voice?"

"No," Bull mumbled. "Is it time to eat?"

"Eat? Not for a few more hours."

"I like to eat."

A chill ran down Ray's spine. He didn't like the sound of Bull's voice. "I do, too. But it's not time yet. Everyone is asleep."

"I should be asleep."

"Yes, you should. In your own bed."

"I walked far. This is a big place. This room seemed nice."

Bull's voice had a dreamlike quality, making Ray wonder if his ears had been affected by the evil red beer. Perhaps everything he thought he was doing tonight was a dream.

"Are you a dream?" Ray asked.

"I don't think so. How would I know?"

"Good question." He studied his friend's face. "Why were you out walking at night?"

Bull blinked and looked around. "I don't know. I woke up in the dark. Nobody was there. I was worried, so I went for a walk."

Ray was surprised that Bull had been left alone. At the very least, one of the servants should have been assigned to watch him while everyone else was out at the festival. Under normal circumstances, one of the guards would have spotted him in the halls, but tonight they all seemed to be drunk.

Hearing an odd sound that might be running footsteps on gravel beneath the window, Ray walked over to his balcony. With the moon below the horizon, he saw only the dark outlines of palms and other trees in the silent garden. No one called to him. After a moment, he turned and saw that Bull had rolled over on his side on the bed. Ray sighed. Not wanting to wake up his friend again, he started for the door, wondering whether he should use Tinubiti's sleeping mat or go and look for one of Bull's servants. With help, he could get Bull back to his own bed before anyone returned to see that Ray still hadn't gone to bed himself. Questions would be asked, someone might remember he had left the house of Bakenkhons with Tentopet, and his life could be over if the wrong assumptions were made. Fortunately, no one had seen him in the harem.

The corridor was empty when he started toward Bull's end of the building, which wasn't far from the indoor approach to the harem apartments. Without attendants, many of the oil lamps had gone out, so his route was darker than usual. Having left his good sandals by the bed, his bare feet made no noise on the cold stone floor.

It might have been his fear of being discovered, but something didn't seem right. He shuddered from an imagined chill, even though it was a warm night.

Ray hesitated when he heard a soft groan. It seemed to be coming from Amana's room. Remembering how Amana had kicked him onto his face at the festival, he hoped Amana's stomach ached from drinking too much of the red beer. However, when he approached the doorway, he looked in and stopped dead, unable to move his legs any farther.

A smoking brazier lay on its side on the floor of the bedroom, its flame extinguished. Coals littered the floor. A feeble glow came from an oil lamp guttering in a far corner of the room, about to die when its fuel ran out, but it provided enough light for Ray to see the shine of a dark pool on the floor. Beyond the pool, the bed dripped with tiny streams cascading down from a lump on the formerly white sheets. Using the wall to steady himself, Ray willed his feet to take a few steps forward. He heard another groan, softer than before, followed by hissing and bubbling sounds.

A few steps more and he saw Amana lying across the bed on his back, gasping for air, trying to press his shaking hands against a huge cut across his throat.

Forgetting about the blood on the floor, Ray rushed forward, his feet slipping, to stop and stare at Amana and frantically wonder how he could help him. Sensing someone hovering over the bed, Amana flinched, then recognized Ray and whispered inaudibly. Ray bent over to hear better, horrified by the blood that covered the prince's body, and recoiling at the smell of vital fluids—the smell of death. Amana raised one hand and grasped Ray's arm, pulling him closer.

"Tjehenu," Amana gasped, coughing up blood. "Meryey's men. And Meshwesh. Run."

Amana's body relaxed into the bloody sheets. His hand fell away from Ray's arm and hit the bed, splattering Ray's kilt with droplets of blood. Frightened, Ray backed away, wondering where he could find help. When he heard the footsteps and whispering of two men approaching in the corridor, he glanced around for a hiding place, then hurled himself backward into the shadows along one wall. If the men were carrying lamps or torches, they'd see him immediately, but he didn't have any other place to hide.

One man carried a short sword, and the other carried a knife. They wore the robes of priests, but they both had beards, which was unusual since most priests regularly shaved their body hair as part of their purification rituals. In fact, beards were uncommon among his people, who considered them unclean. In the darkness, he saw no other details while the two men strode up to the bed, unconcerned by the blood on the floor or the dead boy on the sheets.

"You see? It's the older one," said the man with the knife. He spoke Egyptian with an odd accent.

The swordsman bent over to look at Amana's face. He spoke with a different accent. "Could be. Where are the others? We were told they'd all be in bed by now."

"We're still searching," said the other man.

While their backs were turned, Ray crept through the shadows along the wall and slipped out into the corridor. Unsure as to which way he should go, he decided to return to his own room in the hope that Bull was still safely asleep there. Now, the dim lighting was his friend, and he kept to the walls as he walked, darting from one hiding place to another. He felt exposed in the corridor. Even at this time of the night, there should have been the sounds of guards shuffling around to stay awake, or speaking in quiet voices, or even the soft rumble of snoring from the bedrooms, but tonight an eerie silence seemed to flow out of the stone walls.

Back in his own room, Ray put his back against the wall and took a few deep breaths, inhaling the shadows. To survive, he had to become a shadow; be one with the night. He knew this might be the last night he would ever experience. For a moment, he thought about the stories he'd heard of violent death, and he could imagine sharp blades slicing through his skin, the pain of having his insides cut up, the fear of watching a river of his own life's blood pouring out upon the ground, and the darkness that would cover his head forever.

Judging by the lumpy shape on the bed, Bull was still asleep. His friend, the future Pharaoh, was in grave danger. No guards would help them, nobody would guide them to safety, and he was certain that Bull couldn't defend himself right now. If Ray couldn't save him, he would die as surely as Amana. At that moment, Ray felt himself standing between the worlds of shadow and light, ready for a journey that could take him either way, and his fear faded to a sense of urgency. His purpose in life, at least for the moment, revealed itself to him.

Bull mumbled in confusion when Ray pulled him upright on the bed. He clapped his hand over Bull's mouth in case he yelled. There wasn't time for lengthy explanations.

"Listen carefully, Bull. You need to stay quiet and follow me. Can you do that?"

Bull stared at him for a moment and finally nodded. Seeing the look in his eyes, Ray realized he was talking to a child in a young man's body.

"You remember how we sneaked through the garden at night and swam out to the river?"

Bull shook his head.

"All right. No matter. Just stay with me."

Physically, Bull seemed fine as he lurched out of the bed. Watching Bull to be sure he was steady on his feet, Ray picked up his sturdiest pair of sandals. He still wore his festival clothes—the pleated white robe and gold collar—but he didn't think he had time to change. Bull wore a simple kilt that would be fine for traveling.

Ray led Bull to the balcony and they gazed out over the dark garden, watching for movement. He hesitated when he realized that Pen could also be in danger nearby, but it wouldn't be safe to use the corridor to check his bedroom, and he might not even be back from the festival. Tentopet was another matter. She might be okay in the protection of the harem with its maze of corridors and locked rooms, but if the assassins were here to kill as many of the royal family as possible, she was also in danger.

Hearing footsteps outside his bedroom doorway, Ray urged Bull to hurry and they climbed down into the relative safety of the garden. Ray froze when he heard someone sigh in the darkness.

"Finally," Pen said. "What were you doing up there all this time?"

Ray turned to see Pen leaning up against the wall. "You're here? What are you doing?"

"Waiting for you. I knew Bull would get restless and talk you into climbing down for a swim or a walk in the garden."

"I thought you were mad at me about your mother."

Pen shrugged. "Sorry. I was drunk at the time. Now, I'm only a little drunk, otherwise I would have gone to my bed."

"Then you don't know?"

"There are a lot of things I don't know."

"We're under attack. Assassins."

"What?" Pen stood up straight and blinked. "We must alert the guards!"

Ray surprised himself by lunging forward and clapping his hand over Pen's mouth. "Quiet. They'll hear you. The guards are all asleep, and they're probably better off that way."

Pen pushed his hand away. "Assassins? How do you know?"

He wondered if he could dodge any questions about Amana. "I saw them. Now, we have to go."

"We'll stay and fight," Pen said, clenching his fists. "We've got Bull, and I can go get Amana."

"Amana can't help us," Ray said, trying to come up with the best lie. If he told the truth, he wouldn't be able to stop them from doing something reckless. "I saw him. Too drunk. He's unconscious on his bed."

"I'm hungry," Bull said, staring off into the garden.

Pen looked at Bull and frowned. "You're what?"

Ray gripped Pen's arm and leaned closer to whisper. "I think he's drunk. Ever since I got back from the festival, he seems—strange."

"I can't fight them by myself," Pen said, his gaze darting around frantically.

"Fight all you want later, but we need to get Bull out of here first. I was going to take him out to the river."

"Through the irrigation ditch?"

"Yes."

Pen shook his head. "He'd have to swim underwater. If he's drunk, he might drown."

"We have to try. What we *can't* do is stand around here until someone kills us."

"Sleepy," Bull said.

Pen stared at Bull for a moment, then shook his head. "All right. We'll have to go out through the garden wall near the front gate. I didn't see anyone there when I came in a while ago."

When they crossed under the archway toward the open front gate, they saw no one in the side court on the other side. A statue of Ramesses the Great loomed over them with its back against the west wall, a stone guard—the only guard—on watch at his palace, two torches burning at his feet.

"So far, so good," Pen said, studying the shadows ahead of them.

Out of the corner of his eye, Ray had only a moment to spot the unusually large fist hurtling toward the side of his head.

Ray woke to the sound of running water. Disoriented, he rubbed his palm against the side of his throbbing head and slowly opened his eyes. The moon was low on the horizon, and its light glittered on the waters of the Nile, its image fragmented on the surface of the water. A slow and rhythmic thumping outside of his skull matched the thumping on the inside, but a gurgling noise told him someone was sailing a boat across the river. The boat bobbed beneath him. Pen was unconscious and draped over one of the benches near Bull, who was sleeping peacefully in the bottom of the boat. Ray raised his eyes, expecting to see the assassins from Amana's room, but he was startled to find that his kidnappers were actually his father and the new fight trainer. Pasai stood at the rudder in the boat's pointed stern, giving Ray a disinterested glance. Seated on one of the benches, Hapu wrung his hands and frowned at Ray.

"My son, you have much to learn."

"What do you mean?" He had whispered the question, but he immediately regretted talking so loud. The thumping in his head increased. It was almost as if he were drunk again.

"Let's put it this way," Hapu said. "Pasai carried you and Pen here like two dead gazelles slung over his shoulders. He said you didn't even see him coming."

"I saw his hand," Ray said, realizing it was a poor excuse.

"It could as easily have been a knife," Pasai grumbled, his eyes watching the river.

"Is Bull all right?"

"Yes, no thanks to you," Hapu said. "He's sleeping. He came along peacefully after Pasai knocked you out."

"Well, why did he knock us out? He's supposed to be on our side."

"You were too noisy," Pasai said. "Walking like hippos during mating season. You could have gotten us all killed."

Ray was trying to think, but his headache wasn't helping. "How did you know where to find us? How did you know about the assassins?"

Hapu looked out across the water. "I walked back from the festival with Pasai and some of the others. Pasai made us wait when he saw that the gate guards were missing."

"I saw the older one. Prince Amanakhopshaf," Pasai said, glancing at Ray. "Then I went looking for the rest of you. I heard you talking in the garden. One of the Meshwesh killers heard you as well, but he's no longer a threat."

"And we don't know what happened after we left," Hapu said. One of the servants went off to sound the alarm, and we took one of the fishing boats."

"Where is the Meshwesh army?" Ray asked.

Pasai snorted. "There is no army here. They knew they couldn't take the city. They sent assassins who attack in the night without honor. They scurry away like monkeys with stolen fruit."

They sat in silence for a while as Ray tried to make sense of it all—an impossible task. "What will we do now?"

"Keep the royal children hidden until it's safe to go back," Hapu said. "And you, of course."

Ray knew that his father would protect him, but it was reassuring to hear him say so. Would it ever be safe to go back? How could they be sure? And there was one other thought that disturbed him. "Father, how did they know that tonight would be a good time to attack us in Pharaoh's house? Did they know about the festival?"

Pasai's head snapped around and his eyes locked on Ray. "The boy asks a good question. We have many festivals. I can't believe it was luck. Not only were most of us out of the palace, but the guards were drunk. A point that will not be overlooked. Prince Amanakhopshaf was Pharaoh's son and Commander-in-Chief of the Chariotry, so the guards will pay dearly for their negligence. There may be a traitor among Pharaoh's staff, so I'll personally interrogate them when we return."

Hapu's eyes widened. "Do you have that authority?"

"Pharaoh will understand. He knows I have experience in these matters. General Hori would take charge if he were here, but he's weeks away with the army. In the meantime, this matter is beyond the guard captain." Pasai fingered the gold fly around his neck that symbolized the trust of Ramesses III. "However, before I can learn more, the future rulers of Egypt must be out of danger."

Ray rubbed his sore head. "If murderers can reach us in Pharaoh's own house, how can we be safe anywhere else?"

"That's the secret of the common people." Hapu said. "Safety in numbers and anonymity. They've never seen the royal children at close range, so they won't know who they are unless we tell them. We're going to my house in Thebes. It won't surprise anyone to see my son with me there—along with a couple of his friends."

"We're going there *tonight*?"

"No, it's too far to go without supplies, and too dangerous to travel on the river in the dark. We'll spend the night at Pasai's house."

Somehow, Ray had never pictured Pasai as someone who would own a house in town. He seemed more like the traditional military man who travels with the army and doesn't worry about worldly possessions until he retires or takes a new job in Pharaoh's service. A house seemed too domestic for a fierce warrior, especially when it was located outside the city walls and across the river away from the activity that surrounded Pharaoh.

Pen groaned and sat up in the bottom of the boat, frowning as he slowly took in his new surroundings. "Something hit me in the head."

"A lesson," Pasai said.

Pen turned to squint at Pasai. "You?"

"I am merely the instrument of your learning," Pasai said, shifting his grip on the pole as they approached the shore. "Whether or not you learn anything from the lesson is up to you."

"Are you a scribe disguised as a crocodile, Pasai? You don't talk like a soldier."

"And you don't talk like the child of a god," Pasai said. "You can't judge a man's life by the scars on his body. The scars could have come from a battlefield or from a drunken brawl among friends."

"Or from working in the fields," Hapu added.

"And you can't seem to answer a simple question," Pen said.

The boat thumped against the muddy bank. They were a short distance downriver from the town's main landing area on the west bank, its water steps still lit by two torches at this late hour.

"You missed the landing," Pen said, pointing upriver. "I guess navigation isn't one of your stronger skills."

"An army in retreat does not draw attention to itself if it wants to survive," Pasai said, hopping down to the mud to haul the boat out of the water.

"And Pharaoh's children don't scrabble around in the mud like common servants,' Pen said.

"They do if they want to live through the night," Pasai growled.

With most people still asleep at that hour, nobody was out in the narrow streets to see the five travelers making their way through the shadows between the low houses of whitewashed mud brick. The moon was high in the sky, giving them plenty of blue light to navigate their way through the maze. When Pasai suddenly turned and disappeared through the low doorway of a larger than average home just a few steps away from the local drinking establishment, they knew they had arrived at the evening's destination.

A cedar tree from the distant land of Byblos provided a natural canopy over a tiny enclosed courtyard. Twice the height of the one-story house, the tree gave off a pleasant scent in the warm air. Pasai beckoned them through the front door of the house. Subtly guiding Bull by the elbow, Ray led him through the doorway behind Pen while Hapu brought up the rear.

The front entry room was small, dominated by the shrine to the household god, Bes, who sneered at them with his arms raised above his squat body. Bes protected the home and brought the residents good luck. Up three steps, they entered the public reception room of the house where Pasai could sit at his big chair on a raised platform. That platform probably hid a trap door to a grain cellar where valuables would also be stored. Unlike the paintings that would normally adorn the whitewashed wall surfaces of such a home, Pasai had chosen to hang a variety of weapons on the walls, many of which Ray had never seen, although he recognized some of the foreign markings on the instruments of death. The weapons were all in good repair, and they were clearly not ornamental, with handles and blades worn by frequent use. A variety of small sitting stools and rolled mats neatly lined the walls, and these also appeared to have been made by foreign craftsmen. While Ray studied the room, Pasai reached up to light welcoming fires in the two braziers that loomed over the dais. The unusual braziers were broad black bowls, topped with sculpted bronze flames that rose to a point, mounted on silver floor stands ornamented with gold.

"The collection of an old soldier," Pasai said, watching Ray study a curved sword engraved with roses that hung above a shrine to the goddess Sekhmet. "I won every one of them in combat, and I keep them to remind me of the folly of war."

Pen sat down on a leather stool. "Odd thing for a soldier to say."

"An armed man carries not only a weapon, but also an opinion," Pasai said. "If you disagree with his opinion, he uses his weapon. A soldier's world is simple that way, but it usually means someone is going to die. It's not a good way to build an empire."

Hapu cleared his throat. "Yet a soldier does only what his leaders tell him to do, and there are times when they decide that war is needed to protect the country."

Pasai smiled. "I can see that you've never been in the army, Hapu. The man holding the weapon always has his own opinion. He knows that Pharaoh will always make the right decision, but he can only hope that the generals are smart enough to interpret Pharaoh's divine plans. When a soldier faces another sword, his opinion is put into action because it's too late for diplomacy."

"I'm sleepy," Bull said. He was still standing near the doorway where Ray had left him.

"Of course," Pasai said, pausing a moment to study Bull's face. "It's been a long night. I'll have my servants lay out sleeping mats for all of you in the bedrooms."

Fascinated by Pasai's unusual opinions about the army, Ray had almost forgotten about the dangerous night they had survived. "So, your point is that more diplomacy is needed to avoid wars, Pasai?"

"My point is that my students should listen to me when I tell them how to perform the dance of death," Pasai said, lifting a shiny bronze dagger from the waist of his kilt. "As you've seen, death stalks the children of Pharaoh wherever they go."

A moment later, the same dagger slammed point-first into the wall above Pen's head, vibrating from the impact. "Of course, that's just my *opinion.*"

Exhausted by the events of the previous night, Ray did not wake again until Re's golden boat sailed over the western horizon, filling the sunset sky with blood. Watching the colors in the sky shift to darker hues of red through the small windows adjacent to the ceiling, a dream about Tentopet faded from his memory, and he hoped she had survived the attack on Pharaoh's palace. In his dream, she slept peacefully on her bed, so he hoped that was true. Without any immediate means to communicate with the palace or the harem, he could do nothing but worry about her. From what Pasai had said, it didn't seem that the assassins would have waited around to kill more of them after their presence had been discovered, but who really knew what such people might do? As he thought of Amana's body lying on the blood-soaked sheets of his bed, his concern about Tentopet increased, and he felt fear in the pit of his stomach.

The air smelled of fish, bread, and beer. He heard voices and children laughing as they played a game in the street. His stomach grumbling, Ray rose from his sleeping mat and immediately noticed that Bull and Pen were both missing, so he was alone in the bedroom. Pasai and Hapu had intended to sleep in the public room toward the front of the house to keep the boys from being disturbed, and two of Pasai's servants had been posted to watch the front entrance.

Stepping out of the bedroom, Ray found himself in the small kitchen area. Its open ceiling was covered with brush to release the smoke and smells from the cooking fire while still providing shade. A ladder rose straight up along the east wall to allow access to the roof, where people would sleep on the hottest of nights, desperate for any kind of a cooling breeze. A stone table held a tub of freshly made beer as thick as porridge. A kneading-trough and a mortar for grinding were set into the floor near the clay oven, where Hapu was baking the bread. He liked to make it with his special mixture of honey, herbs, and spices such as sesame and coriander.

"Bread's almost ready," Hapu said, looking into the oven. "Pasai's cook offered to make it, but I prefer to do it. I get a finer texture when I knead it myself."

Ray glanced through the door that led to the public room with its weapon-lined walls, but nobody was out there. "Where is everyone?"

"It's been a busy day," Hapu sighed. "Pasai went off to see if he could hear any news about the events at the palace last night. I suspect we would have heard something by now if Pharaoh or one of the queens had been killed."

"What about Tentopet?"

Hapu looked at him. "Like I said, Pasai went out to see what he could learn. He hasn't returned yet. Pentawere insisted on going with him."

"You let Pen go outside?"

"He's a headstrong young man. I can only control him up to a point. If the prince wants my guidance, he'll listen to me, but he's not a common scribe that I can beat with a rod to make him obey. Pasai is the only one allowed to use weapons on the prince."

Ray nodded. "What about Bull? Did he go with them?"

"Little Bull is another matter. I'm worried about the boy. Recent events seem to have unsettled him. He kept wandering off down the street on his own, so we finally put him in the cellar to keep him safe. We put a sleeping mat down there so that he could get some rest."

"In the cellar?"

"It's quite safe, I assure you. We put Pasai's chair on top of the trap door so that he couldn't easily lift it to climb out, and one of the servants is watching the front door," Hapu said, removing the bread from the oven. He dropped two steaming loaves on the stone table. "There you go. Hot bread."

"Thank you, father." Ray tore a chunk of bread from the loaf and set it on the table to cool. "I've been thinking—"

"That's good," Hapu said with a wink as he tore off some bread for himself.

"I want to go back to the palace to check on Tentopet. If someone can take me across the river, I can go to the palace myself. I'm not one of the royal children, so I don't need to remain hidden. And if Pasai can't learn anything today about what happened, I can find out while I'm there."

Hapu pursed his lips. "It's good that you're thinking about other people, my son, but I can't allow that. It's too dangerous."

"Maybe Pasai would go with me, or at least take me across the river and see that I get there safely?"

"That's not the point. We need to keep the three of you together where we can keep you safe. It's your responsibility to stay with Bull and Pen."

"But Pen is gone with Pasai."

"Bull is still here. If anything happens, I'll need your help with him. From the way he's been acting, Bull may need a physician from the House of Life. However, we have to be careful if we do. A physician might recognize the boy. If we can wait for our return to the palace, Seini can examine him."

Ray grabbed a piece of bread and shoved it into his mouth.

"Don't worry. Bull seems physically healthy. And Pasai will get the news for us."

"How long has he been gone?"

"Most of the day," Hapu said, pouring a cup of beer for Ray, then drinking from his own. "He was also going to locate another boat and supplies for our trip to Thebes."

Swallowing a mouthful of the thick brew, Ray excused himself and entered the small room on the side of the house. A limestone slab with a hole in the middle rested on the dirt floor. It wasn't as fancy as the toilet stools in the palace that had running water in the trenches to carry away waste, but this was better than he expected at Pasai's house. As he relieved himself, he wondered how he could get a boat to take him across the river without his father knowing about it. He'd probably have to wait until Hapu and the others were asleep, but he doubted that he could sneak out without Pasai or one of the slaves noticing him. It was dark now, and he could leave before Pasai and Pen came back, but he'd have to give Hapu a good reason for his going outside.

A crash from the front of the house startled him. Alarmed, he turned and ran into the kitchen. Hapu was gone. Ray remembered the weapons in Pasai's reception room.

Running through the doorway and past the burning braziers without thinking, Ray spotted one of Pasai's servants—motionless on the floor with a knife in his chest, his blood leaking out onto the dirt floor. Hapu and another servant were jammed into the opposite doorway, pressing against the frame for leverage, fighting to keep a priest with a short sword from plunging its point into them. The priest had a long red beard, blue eyes, and spiral tattoos on the fair skin of his exposed forearms.

Ray raced forward, yanked a spear off of its wall mount, and turned to join the fight, dropping the spear point low enough that he could jam it into the priest's leg. The priest howled and jumped back, allowing Hapu to knock him down and kick him in the head. Pasai's servant also dropped to the floor, clutching at a knife embedded in his side.

Hapu looked up at Ray, then his eyes went wide as he started to speak. Ray spun around, weaponless now that the spear was lodged in his victim's leg, and saw a larger priest with a curved sword running toward him. He dove to one side, slid in the dirt, and slammed into the bottom of the floor stand that held one of the burning braziers. His attacker moved with him, turning in a crouch, then stopped suddenly when the brazier toppled over, dumping hot coals into his face just before the tip of the ornamental flame on top of the brazier buried itself in his chest. Staggering, he nearly fell on top of Ray, who rolled over in time to avoid his crushing impact.

Breathing hard now, and worried that he would have another attack from his own inner weaknesses, Ray rose to find that Hapu was struggling with a third priest in the entryway. Hapu was already streaked with blood where his attacker's dagger had slashed across his side. Ray stood and rushed forward, but there wasn't any room to get past Hapu to help him. Seeing no other spears on the wall, Ray took down one of the longer swords and tried to figure out how he could use it while Hapu was wedged into the doorway, grunting and swearing at the priest to leave while he still could.

Hefting the sword in his hand, Ray thought about the priest smoldering on the floor and remembered the layout of the back of the house. Sprinting into the kitchen, he climbed the ladder and stepped onto the flat roof. Like most of the neighboring houses, the roof of Pasai's dwelling was just higher than a grown man's head, which was probably how one of the priests had gained entry to the house. Reversing that strategy, he jumped down to the dark street, receiving a small cut on his leg when he brushed against his own sword blade. He stepped into the front courtyard, jogged through the front door, and ran the sword straight into the back of the priest who was attacking his father. The priest gasped, then spun around to face him, gurgling with surprise, his knife gripped in his twitching hand. Seeing his opportunity, Hapu fell forward with his full weight and plunged the sword farther into the man's back. The priest collapsed onto the other body with the spear stuck in its leg.

Sweating and shaking, Hapu got to his feet. "I'm getting too old for this. Are you all right?"

Ray sat on the floor and leaned back against the wall to catch his breath, waiting to see if his breath would leave him as it often did after such exertions. "Okay," he wheezed, thinking that he was, at least, better off than his victims. Assassins or not, he had just killed three men—and he didn't even know who they were. His hands began to shake. He closed his eyes.

Hapu stepped forward to look out into the street. "Where is Pasai? We need him here!"

Ray also hoped that Pasai would return soon. If any more assassins showed up this evening, he might not have enough energy to defend himself.

"Take it easy," Hapu said, resting his hand on Ray's shoulder. "You'll be okay."

"What about you? You're bleeding."

"Am I?" Hapu seemed to notice the cut in his side for the first time. "A scratch. Nothing to worry about. What we have to do now is get out of here before any more of these 'priests' show up. Or the police—if we explain this to them, they'll find out who we are."

"Where will we go?"

"To Thebes. I have friends there."

Their heads turned when they heard a thump inside the house.

"Another one?" Hapu whispered.

"Bull!" Ray groaned and rose to his feet.

"The cellar," Hapu gasped, running ahead of him.

Up on the raised platform, Hapu dragged Pasai's heavy chair to one side, revealing the trap door beneath it. Ray grabbed the handle cut into the wood and hauled the door open, revealing Bull on a steep staircase below.

Bull blinked up at them. "I'm hungry."

"This is a fool's errand," Hapu said. "It's too dangerous to sail on the river at night. I don't know what I was thinking."

Ray and Hapu leaned against the wall of a grain warehouse by the river landing, not far from where they had left the fisherman's boat they had taken the previous night. Bull sat on the ground and rocked back and forth, staring at his feet.

"You were thinking of saving us," Ray said as he watched a group of priests standing near a small cargo boat loaded with supplies. Torches burned along the bank. They were too far away to make out any details about what the priests were doing in the darkness, but they seemed to be ready to depart and were still waiting for other passengers. As Hapu said, it was a dangerous thing to sail on the dark river with its partially submerged sandbanks, reedy marshes, and hungry river creatures. A priest would have to be in a big hurry to leave the comforts of his temple and seek any kind of adventure—especially one that would involve risking his life.

On the other hand, maybe these weren't priests.

As Ray thought about it, one of the priests turned to look up the dark street in his direction. The man had a beard.

More assassins? It would explain why they wanted to travel at night. Perhaps they were waiting for the men that Ray had killed in Pasai's house.

"Did you see his beard?" Ray whispered to Hapu.

Hapu looked worried. "Yes. These are unusual priests."

"And they have a boat."

Hapu frowned at him. "So? You want to walk over there and take it away from them? Have you lost your mind?"

"We'll need a diversion, of course."

"We'll need an army, you mean."

A third voice behind them immediately got their attention. "I'll do it."

When they turned around, they saw Pen standing beside Bull.

Pen shrugged. "What? You have a better plan?"

"Where have you been?" Hapu demanded, moving closer to Pen. "Where's Pasai?"

Pen pointed across the river. "He's at the palace. He tricked me into staying here to wait for his return, but he was supposed to be back by now.

He said if he didn't come back by tonight that we should go on to Thebes under the protection of the night sky and wait for news."

"So you haven't heard anything about Tentopet or the others?" Ray whispered.

"Sadly, no," Pen said, looking at the ground. "The boat traffic between here and the palace looked normal today, so perhaps everything is fine at the palace now?'

"Then why hasn't Pasai returned?" Hapu asked.

Ray was ready to do something. They weren't learning anything by standing around. "We could go to the palace and find out for ourselves."

"Or we could do as Pasai asked," Hapu said. "I still think it's dangerous, but it would be easier to sneak away in the dark."

"Look," Ray said. "Some of them are leaving."

Two of the bearded priests turned and walked off into the town. It might have been coincidence, but they chose the most direct route to the area where Pasai's house was located. Hapu had led them to the water by an alternate route. Four priests remained by the boat, shifting around as if they were nervous or cold.

"Now's our chance," Pen said. "The boat is ours. Watch for my signal."

As quickly as he had appeared, Pen vanished into the darkness. Hapu started to yell, then thought better of it and leaned against the wall, shaking his head. "Headstrong young fool."

Several minutes passed before Ray watched a figure climb up out of the river on the far side of the boat and flop onto its deck. While he and Hapu quickly discussed a plan of action, Pen untied the two mooring lines and the boat slowly drifted away from the landing, guided by the strong current of the river.

Ray and Hapu picked up Bull by his arms and they ran toward the boat. The four priests started to catch on that something was happening to their transportation, so their attention was focused toward the river. Pen stood upright and waved when he grasped the boat's rudder.

It was awkward running with Bull at first, but he got the idea that they were in a hurry when they were about halfway to the boat. His natural physical skills began to operate by reflex, so Ray and Hapu found themselves chasing Bull down to the boat. Hearing their footsteps, two of the priests suddenly turned around, but they found themselves flat on their backs as Bull ran straight into them. While the other two priests reacted, Ray and Hapu followed Bull straight down to the water's edge and dove forward, splashing through the shallows and the mud to haul themselves into the boat as Pen raised the sail.

"Excellent!" Pen yelled. Although partially obscured by the sail, they saw him raise his arms in victory. "We have a boat!"

That was when the assassin's dagger struck home in Pen's chest.

Ray didn't see the blade hit Pen, but he heard the slap of flesh. As the sail caught the wind and rotated, he saw Pen holding the dagger's hilt at his chest, his eyes wide with fear.

Ray struggled to his feet and clambered over the cargo in the bottom of the boat to get to Pen, but he was only part of the way there when the prince staggered two steps to one side, sat down heavily on the boat's railing, coughed once, and flopped over backwards into the river.

"Pen!" Ray moved to dive over the far side of the boat, but Hapu tackled him from the side.

"I'll go!" Hapu yelled. "You're not strong enough!"

Before Hapu could dive in, they heard clumsy splashing noises and turned to see that two of the priests were trying to board the boat. They had moved farther away from the shore, slowed by water and mud, so the priests were having a hard time getting a good grip to haul themselves up. Bull took the opportunity to smash a wine jug over one of their heads. As the second priest reached for Bull, Ray picked up an oar and rammed it into the man's chest, breaking him free of the boat with a noisy splash.

Hapu prepared to dive in after Pen, but had enough sense to duck down when an arrow embedded itself in the mast by his shoulder. More arrows followed, forcing Ray to drag Bull down into the bottom of the boat.

The wind steered them toward the middle of the dark river and away from the arrows, which began to fall short and plop into the water. Ray crawled along the bottom of the boat until he reached a spot with some protection. Ready to dive in, he scanned the river for Pen, but saw nothing except the glittering reflections of the torches on the river's rippling surface.

Pen was gone.

FOUR

1184 BCE—City of Thebes

Year 4 of His Majesty, King of Upper and Lower Egypt, Chosen by Re, Beloved of Amun, Pharaoh Setnakhte, Second Month of Akhet (Season of Inundation), Day 3

Awareness slowly oozed back into Itennu's head. He didn't want to open his eyes because he knew it would hurt when he did. Lying on his back on hard dirt, he heard echoes of trickling water in a large space. His nose told him that this was an unpleasant place, for the scents of death, blood, and other bodily fluids filled the air, almost making him gag. If he hadn't spent so much time cleaning up after animal sacrifices to Amun-Re, he was sure that his last meal would be rapidly propelling itself to freedom through his mouth. On the other hand, his belly felt quite empty, and there was an odd taste on his swollen tongue. He remained still as he heard heavy footsteps approaching.

"Arise, *Wetyu* Itennu," said a deep, vibrant, and echoing voice.

Itennu opened his eyes and almost screamed. The huge head of a black jackal with tall ears, wearing a nemes headdress, loomed a short distance above his face. Anubis, god of the dead and mummification, Lord of the Necropolis and protector of tombs, stared into his soul.

"Great Anubis! Take pity on me! My time to join Osiris has not yet come! Behold, I am still alive!"

Anubis snorted. "Get up, fool, or it *will* be time for you to join Osiris."

When Itennu edged away with fear in his eyes, Anubis let out a heavy sigh, stood up straight, and removed his head.

Itennu began to breathe again. Unless this was some sort of trick that Anubis played on the recently deceased, the old man with the halo of wispy white hair circling his head did not appear to be a god. He might still be a threat, judging by the angry scowl on his sweaty face, but at least he wasn't supernatural.

"I am Setau, Overseer of the Mysteries, First Prophet of Osiris in Thebes, and your lord for as long as you serve here in the *Per-Nefer*, the House of Beauty. We are in the chambers of the *Wabet*—the Place of Purification."

"The House of Death."

"Some call it that, yes."

Itennu hesitated. "How long will I serve here, lord?"

"That depends on you and the quality of your service to the Great Osiris. There are those who stay only a short time, while others never leave. Some try to leave us without being released, but our guards always find them. Of course, you're a special case. I wouldn't normally come here to greet a new *wetyu*, but I wanted to see the young fool that Bakenkhons sent me, for you must have done something appallingly stupid to earn this privilege. What was it?"

Itennu rubbed the throbbing side of his head, trying to think. "I'm not sure, my lord."

Setau had the Anubis head under one arm, while his other arm was hidden behind his back. "Did you kill another student? Were you caught traveling in the marshes with Merubaste's wife, perhaps? He has a lot of pull with Bakenkhons, that one, and you wouldn't be the first to sleep with his wife."

Something about Setau's tone of voice put Itennu on his guard as he remembered the last thing he'd seen in the house of Bakenkhons. He remembered the queen under the high priest with great clarity. "I—don't remember, my lord. I only recall darkness, perhaps a candle, and something heavy hitting me in the head."

"Hmm," Setau said. "Forgetfulness can be a virtue. Perhaps you're not such a fool after all. If you remember later on, I'm sure you'll let me know what you saw that made Bakenkhons so angry? We don't get much gossip here, and I could use the entertainment."

"Of course, my lord."

"I have to wonder why Bakenkhons didn't just have you killed or transferred to a remote temple. And why go to the trouble to send you all this distance? You've been drugged for almost two weeks. Hard to know. I suspect he thought sending you here would be more of a torment." Setau beckoned to someone in the shadows. When he turned, Itennu saw the glint of a curved obsidian knife blade in the hand hidden behind his back. "Ay! Come here."

A short, fat man limped out of the shadows, dressed in a loincloth and hunched over as if he were a quarryman carrying a heavy stone block. Wisps of black hair, wet with perspiration, formed spirals on top of his shiny head. "Yes, lord."

Setau gestured at the limping man. "This is Ay, another *wetyu* who will teach you the mysteries. Listen to him well—he'll teach you the difference between life and death, light and dark, rich and poor. Many who have passed into the western horizon have also passed through Ay's capable hands."

Ay looked down at his hands and grunted.

Setau put his Anubis head back on. "Welcome to the House of Death."

The living god, Pharaoh Ramesses III, co-regent and Lord of the Two Lands, Beloved of Amun, Son of Re, and the most powerful ruler of the known world, had a headache. The bouncing of his golden chariot didn't help his head, but he wouldn't stop because the urgency of returning to Pi-Ramesses was his overriding concern. As the good god wished to drive the royal chariot himself that day, Didu was in a separate war chariot to his right, in which Nebamun was trying to stay awake while holding the division banner aloft on its tall pole. Being nearby, Pharaoh was still able to make requests of Didu when necessary. One of Didu's tasks that morning had been to hunt down Benanta, chief physician of the House of Life, who normally walked close behind Pharaoh but had somehow managed to drop farther back in the long column of soldiers so that he could avoid some of the dust from the chariots. Pharaoh's personal physician, Seini, had remained in Pi-Ramesses to care for the queens and the royal children while Ramesses was away with the army, so Benanta had been brought up the Nile from Thebes for the duration of the campaign.

Benanta now stood behind Pharaoh in the royal chariot, resting his hands on each side of the royal head as he spoke the healing spell in a deep voice that was loud enough for Didu to hear: "Repelled is the enemy in the skull! Cast out is the evil that is in the blood; the adversary of Horus, on every side of the mouth of Isis. This temple does not fall down! There is no enemy of the vessel therein. I am under the protection of Isis! My rescue is the son of Osiris!"

Didu noticed Pharaoh's closed eyes and pained expression as Benanta yelled the chant into his ear, then repeated it two more times. The spell sounded like nonsense to Didu, but of course he had never been educated in the healing mysteries. After Benanta left the chariot and resumed his place in the long line of soldiers, Pharaoh was joined by Pasenhor, a short man who carried a scribe's writing kit and always looked frustrated. Pasenhor was Pharaoh's Royal Scribe of Truth, charged with writing the official history of Pharaoh's battles and adventures. Pasenhor's job was complicated by the fact that he had to learn Pharaoh's version of the truth before writing a history that would explain Pharaoh's divine greatness and wisdom to the common masses. Only Pharaoh could fully understand how the gods made decisions and directed his actions, so only he could interpret events correctly. To the common soldier, the death of many in their own army, accompanied by a retreat from a battleground, would mean that they had lost a battle. Part of the truth scribe's task was to explain to them how an apparent defeat was actually a resounding success for Pharaoh and his army. With this great responsibility also came great risk, as Pasenhor's failure to interpret Pharaoh's words correctly for the official history would likely mean dismissal from his position as truth scribe, and probably his death. Fortunately, the battle with Meryey, and the ensuing ambush by Mesher, had both turned out well for Pharaoh and were unlikely to be misinterpreted. Even so, the greater significance of these actions would not be apparent until Pasenhor had posted his approved history on obelisks and tomb walls in various cities around the Egyptian empire.

Didu did not envy Pasenhor. It was much better to be a common soldier. Pharaoh told Chief General Hori what to do, Hori told the rest of his generals what to do, and they told the soldiers what to do, which usually resulted in simple orders such as "Form a line, march forward, kill the enemy." These were instructions that common soldiers could understand. They were told when to eat and when to sleep. No farming was necessary, and there was always food to eat. It wasn't great food, but there was usually enough of it. Life was good—as long as you didn't get killed. If you did, Pharaoh would see to it that the gods treated you well in the afterlife.

Now they were on their way home. Within two weeks, they'd be in Pi-Ramesses—maybe sooner if Pharaoh decided to go ahead of his troops and journey the last leg of the trip by water. A week after they returned, Didu would leave the army and his life would change. He wasn't sure if he was ready for that. Funny how leaving the army had sounded like a great idea just a short time ago. The idea of returning to the city, settling down, and living the easy life of a wealthy bureaucrat had its appeal, but how was he going to do that? He didn't know anybody who could help him, except for Pharaoh, and he'd be too busy once they were back in Pi-Ramesses. Most of the good spots in government were already taken by the sons and daughters of the elite, many of whom had inherited positions retained by their families for generations. He shook his head. Too many uncertainties. He wished someone would tell him what to do.

"A goat for your thoughts?"

Didu had almost forgotten that Nebamun was standing beside him. "What?"

"You look preoccupied. Worried that Mesher's going to pop up out of the sand ahead of us?"

"That would be foolish of him. Our entire army is right here."

"I was joking. I just wondered what you were thinking about."

"Probably the same thing as you, Neb."

Neb smiled and gave him a nudge in the ribs. "Women? You think the House of Kifi is still open?"

Didu sighed. "The House of Kifi has been open for years. I doubt that they would have closed it down while we were gone."

"Hard to say. The priests at the Temple of Sobek have been trying to shut Kifi down for years."

"And the high priestess of Kifi is one of the most powerful women in the city. She probably owns the land that the Temple of Sobek sits on."

Neb shrugged. "True enough. I still worry, though. There's a lot of change in the air."

Didu nodded. There was too much change in the air.

From her boat on the river, Tentopet looked out across horizontal bands of color ranging from blue below to blue above. Blue river, black river bank, green fields, brown cliffs—all covered with a blanket of blue sky filled with sunlight. Day by day, the bands of color remained the same, defining her world, with only the shapes on the landscape showing any change. The temples of Heliopolis, Memphis, Abydos, and the other cities she knew well drifted past like so much flotsam on the water, receding into the distance as her former life drifted away.

Tentopet was used to making the long trip up the Nile to Thebes as part of Pharaoh's entourage in the roomy royal barge, but the two weeks in the small fishing boat seemed to last forever. The fisherman had been bribed by one of Teya's most trusted slaves, Paibakamana, to get her safely to Thebes, and to keep silent about having made the trip. He didn't seem to know who she was. She never learned the fisherman's name, and she didn't want to know it because he kept looking at her and smiling, which made her nervous. Her plaited gown of fine linen and most of her jewelry had been discarded at the palace so that she could travel in disguise, so she now wore the coarse, white, linen sheath dress of a common woman. The dress had no folds or embroidery, fit close to her body, and extended from her ankles to her left shoulder, leaving her right breast and arm free for movement. She thought it was a dull costume, but her short dancing skirt was no better. She still had her long black wig and cosmetics, which Queen Teya had suggested she would need for her new trade, along with common oils, perfumes, and simpler clothing she would require to earn her keep somewhere. Trained as a singer, dancer, and musician in the harem, Teya had told her to seek out Paniwi, a famous dancer based in Thebes who ran a traveling group of performers. Using only her nickname of Tyti, and trying not to draw too much attention to her refined mannerisms, she should be able to keep her real identity a secret if Pharaoh's police, the Medjay, came looking for her. She had succeeded in passing the guards at Pharaoh's palace without raising their suspicions, even though they seemed quite nervous about something. Perhaps their strange preoccupation with priests moving through the city gates had diverted them from questioning her.

This was not the life she wanted, but she knew her royal blood and training would win out in the end, setting her apart so that her superior skills would quickly help her rise above the common people and earn their respect. She knew she'd have to be careful about showing off her skills too quickly, but the people would learn to worship her in time. It might take a few seasons, but she would acquire a nice home in the city, fill it with servants like a proper lady, and possibly entertain some men if she came across any with suitable backgrounds. With her education and some ability at writing, she might well be able to find other work beyond entertainment, but she assumed that traveling with Paniwi's troupe would help her locate those opportunities.

On previous trips, Tentopet had made her way from the royal barge through the teeming festival throngs to the Theban Temple of Amun-Re. Traveling in a protected group, she had never mixed with the common people of the city. Now, after the fisherman dropped her off at the city's main river landing, she was forced to walk alone, jostled by clumsy men and women, dodging loads of cargo hauled by donkeys and sleds, assaulted by merchants selling spices and oils from their stalls, and nearly deafened by screaming children at play in the dusty and narrow streets. And the smell! The streets smelled of dung and rot. Dogs rooted around in garbage, releasing more disgusting smells. Relief occasionally drifted past in the odors of baked bread, roasted meat, honey, beer, and wine—accented by hot oils and spices as she penetrated farther into the marketplace—but the foul smells were always there in the background to remind her how far she had fallen. She stopped in an open temple doorway when she detected a cloud of sweet incense billowing past, taking a few deep breaths for the first time since she got off the boat.

"It's a bit overwhelming, isn't it?"

Tentopet spun around to find that the speaker was a tall, exotic-looking woman in a flowing gown of fine, diaphanous linen, and a beautiful gold neck collar set with blue and green stones. Her skin was scented with perfumed oils, unlike most of the people in the street. She looked like a queen. "Were you speaking to me?"

A smile lit up the woman's delicate face. "I watched you come up the street from the river. You looked like you might need a friend. I'm Apollonia."

"Oh. Thank you." Tentopet noticed that she had a slight accent. "Are you a priestess here?"

She chuckled. "Just visiting. I have friends here. And your name?"

"Tento—umm, you can call me Tyti." She didn't want to answer any other personal questions, so she tried to deflect the conversation. "Where are you from? I don't recognize your accent."

"Ah. Very perceptive of you. I'm from Delphi in Greece."

"How wonderful! I've never met anyone from Greece."

"You'll see a few of us in Thebes. Most are traders who are here only briefly, but I've lived in Thebes for many years. And you're new to Thebes, am I right?"

"Well, I've been here for festivals, but I don't know my way around very well."

Apollonia glanced toward the street, then put her arm around Tentopet's shoulders. "Then you're lucky that you ran into me. Are you trying to find your husband?"

Tentopet was delighted that she'd found someone to help her so quickly. "Oh, no, I'm not married. I'm traveling alone. I'm looking for the Street of the Performers."

"You wish to hire someone, or do you seek a job there?"

"Employment. I sing and dance. And I play many instruments."

Apollonia looked surprised. "Is that so? How talented you are! If you're interested, I know a place where they could use someone like you. And they pay very well."

Tentopet couldn't believe her luck. "Really? I'd like to know more about that."

"Although, with your talents, and as pretty as you are, you probably have a job lined up already?"

"Oh, no," she said. Then she decided that she should be more clever about her negotiation. "Nothing carved in stone, in any case."

"Come with me, then." Apollonia smiled, took her hand, and led her back into the busy street. "I'm going there now. It's a nice place. You'll like it."

"What kind of a place is it? A drinking house?"

"Yes, there is drinking there—among other things. Have you ever heard of the House of Kifi?"

"You're in luck, lad. We just got a fresh one." Those were the words that echoed in Itennu's mind as Ay led him through a shadowy chamber where strange smells mixed with the strong scent of incense. A sloping floor gradually led down to a cooler area filled with the sound of gurgling water. After a moment, he realized that the room jutted into the Nile, and the roof continued to slope down to a stone wall about four body-lengths away. Coiled ropes tied to stout posts were driven into the river bank. Still confused by this strange day he was having, Itennu looked at Ay, who stopped by a closed door and looked back over his shoulder.

"Sometimes they have to wait a bit before we can get to them. Or they smell too ripe. So we tie a rope around them and let them soak in Mother Nile where it's cooler. Come with me."

Itennu squinted and shielded his eyes when Ay opened the door, revealing a brilliant blast of sunlight. When his eyes adjusted, he saw a white linen awning outside. A linen-wrapped body lay on a sled where two other stooped men in loincloths dropped the ropes they had just used to tow it under the awning.

"How much did you get, Bai?" Ay asked the taller man, who looked like a skeleton himself, while his unnamed friend wandered back the way they had come.

Bai handed Ay a thin slab of limestone covered in black hieratic script on its flat side. "Here's the order. They paid our Scribe of the Tomb 45 *deben* of copper, 1 ox—making 100 *deben*—3 sacks of emmer wheat, 5 braided baskets, and a goat. Family already has his tomb furniture made. Noble family. Looked very clean. When they come for pickup, the Scribe of the Tomb can charge them more for regular prayers and maintenance."

Ay glanced at the stone. "Wakhashem, Scribe of the Royal Granaries. Full soak, stuffing, wrapping, and treatment. Very nice. Decorated inner and outer coffins of tamarisk wood, mummy board, and carvings. Green and yellow orpiment paint—expensive and tasteful. They leave any jewelry?"

"Nothing," Bai said, spitting on the ground.

Ay winked at Itennu. "Bai is a collector. He likes pretty things. That's why he's here—he used to be a mayor's scribe, but he kept taking bribes. He's lucky he didn't get his nose and ears cut off when they caught him."

"Who's the new bird?" Bai asked, aiming a gap-toothed smile at Itennu.

"Itennu," Ay said. "A present from Bakenkhons."

"Ooh," Bai sniggered. "He must have been a bad boy."

Annoyed that everyone else seemed to know more about his circumstances than he did, Itennu crossed his arms and frowned. "The gods work in mysterious ways."

"Maybe not so mysterious," Bai said. He placed one foot on the corpse and rolled it off the sled. "He's all yours."

When Bai walked away, Itennu explained that the dead scribe's family had paid for a complete mummification with a fancy nested coffin, a *Book of the Dead*, a full set of canopic jars to hold his organs, and a set of carved *ushabti* figures to work for him in the afterlife. He then instructed Itennu to take the body inside.

Itennu stooped over the linen-wrapped body, then hesitated, not wanting to touch the corpse.

"Go on. He won't bite," Ay said, awkwardly dropping to one knee to pull the sheet off the man's corpse. Small white flowers fluttered to the sand when Ay removed the shroud and sniffed the air. "See, his relatives washed him and used perfumed oils on his skin, but he's starting to ripen in the heat. We'll take care of that."

Itennu was relieved to see that the man's eyes were closed in his pale face. He'd heard of people who died with their eyes open, and they would stay that way unless someone closed them soon after death. He didn't want the dead scribe watching them prepare his body for his journey to the western horizon. He saw that the underside of the corpse looked discolored and bruised where it had been lying on its back. The skin of the lower right abdomen was an ominous green color. The scribe's nude body looked pale and flabby, having lived a long and comfortable life well into his forties, and his head was bald.

With some effort, Ay lifted one of the scribe's arms. "Good. He's starting to get some of his flexibility back. They're easier to work with right after they die, or three days later, otherwise they're too stiff."

Ay picked up the corpse by the shoulders, so Itennu took the feet and they carried the man through the door into the cold storage room. Ay led the way through another nearby doorway into a chamber with a strong smell of wine. After a few moments, Itennu felt lightheaded. They stopped beside a shallow pool and set the heavy body down beside it.

"You're wondering about the smell?" Ay asked, placing the stone with the scribe's information on a low table beside the pool. "The new *wetyu* always ask. It's palm wine. Helps clean and preserve the skin. Get in."

Itennu gestured at the pool with a frown. "In there? Where the dead have been?"

"It's quite safe. I'll be right here with you."

Itennu sighed and stepped into the cool wine, knowing he'd come out of it smelling like a drunk. If he were lucky, that would be the only smell stuck to his body. He shuddered as his bare feet sank into creamy mud and whatever else might have collected at the bottom of the pool. Ay rolled the corpse in after him. "Now you want to massage the arms and legs."

"What?"

"Move the arms and legs around. Bend them. We need them to be more flexible so we can do our work, and our dead friend can't do it himself."

Itennu hoped he was dreaming. Giving a dead man a massage in a pool of palm wine seemed so unreal—along with the rest of his situation—that he could only hope he'd be waking up soon.

Khait sensed the sadness in Queen Isis as soon as she entered the queen's bedroom. Her eyes were red and puffy and she wore no wig. This was the first time Khait had seen her unpainted face. Her servants had dressed her in a simple white gown and her short black hair had been shaved off for the seventy-day period of mourning for her son. Perched on the edge of her rumpled bed, even at this late hour of the morning, she stared listlessly at an uneaten plate of bread and fruit on the small ebony table beside her. Khait approached halfway to the bed and bowed low, her arms outstretched.

Ten days had passed since the attack on the golden house, and it still felt like they were living in an armed camp. The city gates remained closed and guards were everywhere—two of them stood outside the bedroom door. The queen had lost at least one of her sons to the violence of the assassins, the Hawk-in-the-Nest was missing, and her daughter Tentopet had also disappeared. Khait had not seen Ray or his father since the Festival of Drunkenness, and there were rumors in the harem that they had run from the city during the night of the attack. She also knew that Prince Pentawere was missing, but she had not seen Queen Teya since the festival, and the harem women were saying she had confined herself to her private quarters to hide her grief.

The queen finally noticed Khait's presence and waved her hand so that Khait could stand up straight. "Khait. Thank you for coming. Would you like something to eat?"

Khait shook her head. "I have eaten. Thank you, Highness."

The queen sighed. "The Festival of Opet is eleven days away. I suppose I should have a new dress made quickly so that we can attend with Pharaoh

Setnakhte, although I have little interest in doing so. There are too many evil things happening right now, as you may be aware."

"I am aware of these things."

"Of course. I'm sure the harem is well-informed and that rumors are flying like flocks of ducks. Just remember to be careful about what you believe. Rumors are not facts."

"I'm sorry for all the loss you must be feeling, Highness."

The queen nodded once and looked up at the painted sky on the ceiling. "You are fortunate not to have family in the royal line. There are threats everywhere. Amana is on his journey to the western horizon. I fear we may learn that Bull has joined him. If so, Pentawere will become the Hawk-in-the-Nest, and Teya will gain much power as the queen mother."

Khait knew all of these things from her servant, Kemisi, and the rest of the harem, but it was disheartening to hear Queen Isis speak such words. "And have you heard any news about Tentopet, Highness?"

The queen blinked several times, then looked at the floor and cleared her throat. "No news so far. My hope is that Bull, Tentopet, and Pentawere learned about the attack and went into hiding. Pasai is also missing, so he may have gathered them together to protect them. However, if that were so, why have we not heard from them? How far would they go? Ray and Hapu may also be with them. Or they may all be dead. We know nothing!"

Khait took a step back in surprise as the queen tore at the neck of her dress. "I have prayed to Amun-Re with Bakenkhons and made many sacrifices. I have made offerings to all the local temples of the gods. I don't know what else to do! However, I have responsibilities and I can't ignore them. That would disturb *maat* even more and bring greater chaos. And so, you must make me a dress for the Festival of Opet. We will travel to Thebes as if nothing is wrong."

"Of course, Highness. I will make something beautiful for you."

"No," said the queen said, shaking her head. "Something simple. Something appropriate for mourning. And I shall need it by tomorrow."

"May I ask another question, Highness?"

The queen nodded.

"Have you had any news from the co-regent?"

"That is the only good news. He somehow learned that the palace would be attacked and tried to warn us, but it was much too late. We received his message yesterday. The army will return soon, but not before Opet. His return will calm the city. Too many people know that Pharaoh Setnakhte is ill, and my husband needs to be here to take charge."

This was news to Khait. She knew the aging pharaoh had attended the Festival of Drunkenness. He looked old and slow at the house of Bakenkhons, which was not good for a pharaoh out in public, but he had not appeared to be ill during the ceremony for the goddess Sekhmet. She did not recall seeing him since the festival, but that was not unusual since she spent most of her time in the harem and he rarely went there any more. That was now the domain of the younger pharaoh.

The queen suddenly brightened and stood, beckoning for Khait to come closer. Then she put her warm hands on Khait's bare shoulders and smiled. "I must try to focus more on the good news that I had nearly forgotten. You are very special to me, Khait; almost like my own daughter. You work hard, you teach the women of the harem to weave with the vertical loom, you make beautiful dresses for me with the linen you make yourself, and you listen like a royal friend. You deserve a reward, and I want to show you how much I appreciate your service."

Khait held her breath as the queen stared into her eyes.

"Being a priestess of Hathor is an important position that helps to maintain the balance of *maat*. Servants of the goddess have been around for almost two thousand years; even before the pyramid builders. Women from noble houses have always supplied priestesses to Hathor's temples, and they are paid well in temple grain. This month, you will become a priestess of Hathor. You will serve the goddess one month out of every four at her temple in Thebes. I am also a servant of Hathor, although I no longer perform my duties in Thebes. My mentor there was the High Priestess Shepsit, who is related to Setnakhte, and she will be the one to train you as well. This is a great honor for anyone, but especially for a woman who is not a scribe or a member of the royal family."

Khait felt stunned. She would never have suspected that she might receive such a high honor—especially one that legitimized her as part of the elite. Her father would be thrilled, and probably astonished by her good fortune. She also wanted to tell the queen that she could read and write as well as any scribe, but caution still kept her from revealing this about herself to anyone connected with the golden house. Her father had trained her well, and that included training in the art of discretion as part of the duties of a scribe.

Khait knelt and touched her forehead to the ground at the queen's feet as she held out her arms. This is a great honor, Majesty. I am not worthy. Thank you. A thousand times thank you."

The queen lifted her to her feet again. "Nonsense. You are quite worthy. Have you been to Thebes before?"

Khait felt herself bouncing on her toes with excitement at the prospect of seeing more of the world, then stopped because she realized this was improper in the queen's presence. "I have not, Majesty."

"There is much to see there," the queen said, turning away. It seemed like the air had gone out of her body as she sagged down to sit on the edge of the bed. "You will travel with us for Opet, but you will leave us there. People from many lands go to Thebes, but there is also danger in such a big city. A young woman must be careful. However, Shepsit will take good care of you once you reach the Temple of Hathor."

"I am anxious to meet her."

"You may go now. I must rest."

"Thank you again, Highness," Khait said, bowing low as she backed away.

Tired by their long trip on the eternal river, its currents swelled by the annual flood, Ray, Bull, and Hapu listened to the sounds of their small boat's progress: gurgling water, wind snapping in the sails, the creaking of wood, the cries of birds, and the buzz of flying insects. Then there were new sounds, indistinct at first, which gradually resolved into snatches of music, voices, laughing children, hammering, the slap and splash of men washing laundry, and the general hubbub of the marketplace. Steering the boat around a final bend in the broad river, while staying clear of the papyrus and weed beds lining the marshy east bank, the city of Thebes—or Waset, the great Southern City, capital of the fourth Upper Egyptian nome—loomed up before them, vast and glittering, with whitewashed mud-brick homes and apartments mixed in with enormous formal temples of stone, obelisks tipped with gleaming bronze, pylons topped with colorful pennants, and giant statues of pharaohs and gods—many of them framed by fires in golden braziers that flashed in the sunlight.

"Magnificent," Ray said, staring at the city. He remembered the old song:

What do they say to themselves,

those who are far from Thebes?

They spend the day dreaming of its name.

Ramesses the Great had built many temples in Thebes as part of his massive building program throughout the country—one of many pharaohs to do so over a thousand years, but it was also the home of the Egyptian government for so long that it had become the greatest of the royal cities in Egypt. Hundreds of temples crowded together in this one place—ranging from the great Karnak Temple of Amun-Re, king of the gods, on down to the smallest shrines dedicated to the principal gods of the Theban pantheon, providing homes for all of them. Across from Thebes on the west bank, beneath 600-foot-high cliffs that dominated the landscape for two miles, was the Great Place—the Valley of the Kings and Valley of the Queens—where previous pharaohs and their families rested for eternity. Sadly, Ray knew that the bodies of Pentawere and Amana would also rest there as soon as their bodies were made firm and forever enduring so they could greet Osiris beyond the western horizon.

Bull hung off the edge of the boat watching his reflection in the water. Every once in a while, he'd laugh at a duck quacking at them from the reeds. During the river trip, he had not seemed as affected as the rest of them by Pen's death, but Ray was pretty sure that Bull understood he'd never see his half-brother again. Two brothers lost in two days—it was a hard business being a future ruler of Egypt. Now bearing the full responsibility for protecting Bull, Hapu spent most of the trip sitting quietly beside him, lost in thought as he stared across the river, afraid to leave the prince alone for too long.

When Bull looked up from the water, he saw the huge buildings looming before them and his mouth fell open. "So big! Can we go there?"

Hapu reached over to pat Bull on the head. "That's our destination, lad. We should be safe now."

Ray turned and studied the two of them for a moment. "Hapu, how will we know when we can return to Pi-Ramesses?"

"Pasai knew we were going to Thebes. I didn't tell him exactly where we'd be, but I'm sure he'll be able to figure it out. When it's safe, he'll come and get us, or he'll send us a message. Until then, we have to blend in as well as we can and stay hidden. Bull's life might depend on it."

"That plan didn't work so well at Pasai's house. The assassins found us anyway."

"Yes," Hapu said, rubbing his face with both hands. Over the last two weeks, he seemed to have aged ten years. "I can't explain that. I can only assume that foreign spies saw us go to Pasai's house, or perhaps his slaves were bribed. Who can say? We knew we were too close to the palace to be safe. But disguising ourselves and hiding seems to be our only option now, unless you have a better idea."

Ray shook his head. "I wasn't criticizing you, father. Running is our only option. If Bull felt better, I'm sure he would come up with an excellent plan. As it is, however, we can only protect him and hope that his spirit eventually returns."

Bull didn't respond—he only stared at the city as if he were a small child fascinated by a new toy. Clearly, however, he was no longer a child. On the trip down the river, Hapu had shaved the heads of both young men, saying that it was time to remove their side-locks of youth. As men, they could keep their heads bald, wear short hair, or wear wigs. Hapu explained that this would also help to disguise them in the city of Thebes.

"There is one other thing we can do to help Bull," Hapu said. "We can seek an experienced physician. Seini means well, and Pharaoh Setnakhte likes him, but Bull requires someone who knows more than how to mend a broken leg. The Temple of Amun-Re has priests who can help. However, we risk discovery by going there."

"I could go to the temple and summon a priest," Ray suggested. "I know where it is. You could take Bull directly to your house and I'll meet you there with a physician."

"All right." Hapu removed one of his gold rings and offered it to Ray. "Take this. Don't tell anyone in the temple who we are. Don't even mention my name. Just give them this ring and they'll come."

"It will be enough?"

"A physician takes what he is offered for his services. An unusual gold ring like this one is more than most of them earn in a week. He will come."

Tentopet hadn't expected to find such an opulent private home in Thebes that wasn't owned by a high priest or an important official. Apollonia's house was an oasis in the middle of the city, bordered by the Temple of Sobek on one side and the Theban vizier's residence on the other, although that wasn't apparent once you were inside the quiet confines of her three-story mansion. The whitewashed adobe walls were painted as elaborately as the inside of a royal tomb, with large hunting scenes, fishermen working on the Nile, and colorful images of harem women dancing and bringing trays of food to their noble lord. Walls and ceilings were painted with blue lotus designs that delighted the eye.

In the large reception room at the front of the house, where chairs of cedar lined with ivory insets provided plenty of seating, a broad table was being loaded with food as if it were an altar with offerings to an important god. In a far corner, a smaller shrine to Min had its own altar covered with food, so the main table was clearly for the family, or perhaps for guests. Brass oil lamps provided plenty of light, and incense drifted through the room, filling the air with the expensive scent of myrrh.

Apollonia gestured at the table. "Are you hungry?"

Tentopet hadn't realized how hungry she really was until this moment. She moved over to the table and studied the riches arrayed before her: roast oxen and spiced duck, fish prepared with herbs, red and white wine, bread, cheeses, salad, honey cakes, and fruit such as grapes, figs, pomegranates, and dates. Cups were arranged around a bowl of thick beer. Beside the cool wine jugs, each wine cup held a blue lotus flower that would release its essence once wine was poured over it. In the palace, Tentopet had often enjoyed the special euphoria that came with drinking the lotus in wine, and she was impressed that it was offered here along with enough food for a royal feast. She modestly picked up a pomegranate and bit into it, using her other hand to catch the juice that dripped down her face.

"Eat all you want," Apollonia said, sitting down. "You've traveled a long way and need your strength."

"But the guests?" Tentopet asked, afraid to anger the lord of the house by eating too much and ruining the display.

"The slaves will bring more food. The guests will never know."

"Is this a festival day?" Tentopet asked, breaking a piece of bread from the warm loaf. There were so many festival days that it was hard to keep track of them all without a priest or a harem steward to do so.

Apollonia chuckled. "Every day is a festival day in this house. We want to make certain that all of our guests are comfortable, happy, and well fed so that they'll return in the future."

"Your lord must be very wealthy, then."

"*She* is, indeed."

Tentopet started to ask for more explanation, but they were interrupted by what appeared to be young women of the harem, giggling and chatting as they walked into the room. Tall and short, all beautiful, they had clearly come from many lands. They might have come from one of Pharaoh's other harems, such as *Mi-wer*, but fortunately, she didn't recognize any of them, and she saw no sign that any of them recognized her. Their expensive, finely-woven clothing of transparent linen, their elaborate hair styles topped with cones of scented wax, their perfumes, and their sparkling jewelry made their high status very apparent to Tentopet, who suddenly felt quite inferior in her simple outfit. She should have been wearing the same beautiful clothes, but these women would simply assume that she was a pitiful commoner from the street. She looked at Apollonia with concern lining her face. "I don't belong here."

Apollonia rested her hand on Tentopet's arm. "Of course you do, child. As long as you're with me, you will come to no harm."

Tentopet felt the eyes of the harem women studying her. They whispered amongst themselves and giggled, making her feel worse because they had to be talking about her. Then she felt a cup sliding into her hand. She looked up to see one of the harem girls, just a little older than she was, smiling down at her—probably out of pity, she assumed.

"Drink," Apollonia said. "It will calm you."

"Thank you," she said, sipping the red wine. The lotus flower tickled her nose.

The wine girl smiled and walked back to the table. Her silver and gold anklets tinkled with each step.

Remembering why she was there, Tentopet nodded at her host. "This is a beautiful place. As you said, I would enjoy working here if you think I would fit in."

"Tyti, I can tell by your manner that you were raised by a good family. I don't see any reason why you wouldn't fit in very well here."

The wine was stronger than Tentopet had expected. She had only sipped about half of it, but her eyelids were heavy and it was getting harder for her to concentrate. She set the cup down and took a deep breath. "If you wish me to sing or dance for someone to demonstrate my skills, I should probably do it soon, if that's okay. I'm very tired."

Apollonia stroked Tentopet's cheek. "Your skin is feverish. We should find you a bed."

"You're very kind, Apollonia. I can't believe my luck in meeting you as soon as I arrived in Thebes. Thank you." She was glad that she remembered to thank her before her head got any fuzzier.

"No need to thank me, Tyti. Your work here will be all of the thanks I need, and I'm the one who feels lucky to have found you," she said, summoning two women to Tentopet's side. "Now, go and rest. When you wake, we'll test your skills."

Ray struggled through the noisy crowds of the marketplace, dodging the shoppers, merchants, and small children who all seemed to be focused on slowing him down. As Hapu had warned him, the more time he spent in public, the more likely he was to be spotted by anyone who might be looking for them, so he was anxious to complete his errand and bring a physician to Hapu's house to examine Bull.

Having lived within the confines of Pi-Ramesses for an extended period, he had forgotten the smells, the noise, and the rough activities of some of the people he saw on the streets of Thebes. Outside the temples, the poor, the sick, and the dying clustered around the entrances seeking help. The royal city of Pi-Ramesses was always clean and beautiful, filled with fragrant plants and incense, and the people were always well-behaved—except on rare occasions. He glanced toward the river, visible in gaps between the buildings, wishing he'd been able to use the direct water entrance to the Karnak temple complex, where the boats of the priests and the royal family would dock to give passengers unmolested access to the temples. Instead, they had docked at the city's main landing, leaving him to hike in the heat for twenty minutes, watched by the unblinking eyes of two long rows of sphinxes lining both sides of the road.

Entering the Karnak temple complex through the broad gates of the main pylon, Ray saw dozens of sick and injured people waiting for admission to the various temple entrances within the complex. Most would gain entry by the end of the day, and all were treated equally, but the wealthy wouldn't have to wait in line.

For those who were waiting, there were many distractions. Sem-priests from the House of Beauty sold papyrus and stone copies of brightly colored hieroglyphic instructions that could be provided to the deceased to guide them through their journeys to the underworld. Presumably, the stone copies of these Texts of the Dead would last longer, so they fetched a higher price than the papyrus versions.

When one of the sem-priests caught Ray's eye, his face barely visible under his white hood, he gestured at his merchandise. "Remember the instruction of wise Hardjedef! Make good your dwelling in the graveyard! Make worthy your station in the West! Given that death humbles us, given that life exalts us, the House of Death is for life! Come see our fine work, young master! You can live like a king for eternity!"

Ray shook his head and walked on past the sem-priest. He wasn't interesting in shopping for tomb supplies at the moment. He planned to avoid dying for a long time.

Young priests from the *Per-Ankh*, the House of Life, sold instant remedies for common ailments to those who didn't need to visit a physician—or those who lost patience after standing in line for too long. These remedies included the popular honey-and-herb poultices that were applied to the teeth and gums to soothe pain. Roaming merchants sold food and jugs of water to people standing in the longest lines. Near the entrances to the major public shrines, sacrificial animals ranging from birds to goats were sold to visitors anxious to make a good impression on their chosen gods. Ray ignored all of these distractions, heading straight into the Precinct of Amun-Re, where he found a large crowd in the vast reception hall with its many decorated pillars. The bright colors and the vast size of the hall made him feel as small as a grain of sand on Pharaoh's heel.

After standing in line for over an hour, not one of the thirty people ahead of him had moved toward the entrance. He felt fortunate not to require emergency attention; otherwise he might die before entering the House of Life. He studied the great statues and colorful historical paintings that adorned the walls, showing Ramesses the Great and other pharaohs towering over their foes, crushing hostile foreigners under their heels, shooting arrows at cowering enemies with great armies behind them, and accepting the adulation of the grateful public and the gods during festival processions. He studied each painting carefully, from left to right, one after the other, until he had almost memorized them all, and then he started again at the far left, wondering if the golden sun-boat would descend into the west before he was able to speak to a physician.

"Excuse me, brother. You wait for healer?"

Ray assumed the voice was directed at someone else in his line, but when he turned his head, he saw a nervous little man with bug eyes staring up at him. He looked like he might be a priest, but his pleated white gown was filthy and torn. Judging by his appearance, he looked like a foreigner, and he spoke with an odd accent.

"Yes, I'm waiting for a physician," Ray said.

"*Hoo*! Long line, eh?"

"Yes."

"Hot. *Hoo*! Very hot here, even in shade."

Ray just nodded, wondering what the man might want, other than idle conversation.

"You get to front of line like this, you also need healer for sore feet. *Hoo*, yes!" He gestured at the crowd. "Many people. Busy people. Not enough healers."

"So it seems."

"That your ring?" he asked, pointing at Hapu's overly large gold ring dangling from one of Ray's thumbs.

Ray licked his lips and glanced around for possible help if the little man attacked him.

"Not to worry," the man said with a crooked smile punctured by missing teeth. He held up one of his little hands. "Nice ring, but too big. Healer would like, though. I take you?"

Confused, Ray shook his head.

"I take you quick. No more line. You get fixed and go home. *Hoo*!" He emphasized this statement by swinging his arms in a sweeping motion.

The little man grasped Ray's arm and started to pull him out of the line, but Ray pulled back, stopping him in his tracks. "Let me go. I don't have anything for you."

"You have ring. Healer pay me in grain after."

Ray understood now. He remembered hearing about servants who worked for busy physicians by scanning the crowd for those most likely to pay well. The wealthy never stood in these lines at all and would be served first, but the temple priests didn't want to lose profitable "donations" from the second-tier patients ready to pay for their services. Once the spotters had identified the good ones in the crowd, everyone else would be served last, which might mean coming back the next day, or the day after, depending on how busy they were.

"Fine," Ray said with a sigh, allowing the little man to pull him out of the line.

When Ray arrived at the little stall inside the reception hall—one of many in a row along three of the walls—the physician was just finishing with his previous patient. He looked like a living skeleton wearing the pleated white robes of a priest, so Ray couldn't even guess at his age. Muttering a prayer, the physician wrote something on a slip of papyrus, dropped it in a cup of steaming tea, and made the old man drink it. The patient, who looked muscular and healthy despite at least forty years on this earth, didn't appear to have anything wrong with him, but Ray knew from experience that many ailments were only visible to the trained eyes of a professional.

When it was Ray's turn, the little man made him sit on the low stone table in the stall, then plucked the ring from his finger and handed it to the physician. He held it close to his eyes, bit it with one of his remaining front teeth, examined it again, smiled, and patted the little man on the head. "You have a good eye, Merikare. Get back to work." Then he placed the ring in a wall niche that held a variety of silver rings, turquoise jewelry, green malachite hair clips, and other tokens of affection from his patients that day.

As the little man scurried away, the physician suddenly bent over and held his ear against Ray's chest.

"I'm not here about me," Ray said.

The physician ignored him. "I am Khaemope. You need not fear me, for I am very skilled at my art."

"But—"

"Silence!" he barked, keeping his head on Ray's chest. He had the voice of a man who was used to people following his orders.

Startled, Ray shut up for a moment. Khaemope stood up straight and grasped Ray's wrists, holding his arms out from his sides.

"Your heart speaks clearly. Your skin is not flushed or hot. You are healed," he stated, dropping Ray's arms and looking beyond him to see if any other patients were waiting. "Go with Amun-Re's blessing."

"I need you to see my—cousin," Ray said, rubbing his wrists. "Not me."

Khaemope eyed him skeptically, then picked up the gold ring from the wall niche, studied it carefully, and returned it to the pile of gifts. "Where is your cousin?"

"He's in the city. It's not far. Next to the Temple of Thoth."

"I have other patients," he said, watching for Merikare's return. "I can't leave now."

Ray felt desperate. He knew his father wouldn't be pleased if he couldn't perform the simple task of getting a physician to come to his house. "I pray that you can help my cousin, for we have all heard of the great Khaemope and the miracles that he can perform with his healing arts."

Khaemope agreed to visit Hapu's house that evening. After giving the physician careful directions and reminding him of what a nice ring he had donated for his cousin, Ray left the temple and set off into the oppressive heat of early afternoon in Thebes.

Tentopet was dreaming of her long trip on the river when she opened her eyes and realized that Apollonia was shaking her. "Wake up, girl. It's getting dark. Time for your audition."

Blinking, Tentopet sat up. On the clean white sheet beside her, she saw a transparent gown of the finest linen beside a layered wig, a perfumed wax cone to place on top of the wig, and an array of jewelry. After leaving the palace, Tentopet had assumed that she'd never see such clothing again.

"Gifts for the new girl," Apollonia explained. "We want you to look nice."

"Oh. I have my own clothes," she said in an unconvincing tone of voice while running her hand over the fine glass beadwork on the white gown. She wondered if she'd be able to dance in it until she saw the long slits on each side that would allow her to move freely.

"I'm sure these are nicer. Put them on and come down to the reception room," Apollonia said. "Your audience awaits."

After Apollonia left the bedroom, Tentopet stood up and a young harem girl stepped out of the shadows to help dress Tentopet. She was the one who had brought her a drink when she arrived.

"I'm Harere," the girl said, helping Tentopet out of her clothes with quick and efficient movements. "If you ever need anything, I'm here to take care of you."

"Thank you, Harere," she said, remembering that she was supposed to be in disguise. In reality, she felt special, because these were services that the younger harem girls performed for the consorts of Pharaoh—services she had performed herself up until recently. "I can do the rest myself."

Harere shook her head. "My lady was very clear that I was to help dress you properly."

Tentopet plucked the dress from the bed and slipped it over her head. It settled over her body like a cloud, making her skin tingle with pleasure.

Harere pressed her hands together and looked like she was going to cry. "Please, Tyti. I don't wish to be beaten."

Alarmed, Tentopet sat on the bed and allowed Harere to attach a series of anklets made of tiny bells to her ankles. These were followed by jingling chains that went around her waist, attached at her hips so that the loops could dangle and glitter when she moved. Then came the wig, the perfumed wax cone for the top of her head, and the slow process of painting her face. The process was slower than usual because Tentopet wanted extra kohl applied around her eyes and a heavy coating of powdered green malachite for her eyelids to help disguise her face. Harere studied her face with care, painted her lips with henna, then attached a jeweled collar around her neck.

Harere stepped back and appraised her appearance, then leaned in to study her fingers and toes. "Your nails should be darker. When we have more time, I'll mix the henna paste and apply it for you."

"I'll tell Apollonia you were very helpful," Tentopet said.

Harere knelt and rested her forehead on Tentopet's knees. "Thank you. I want to keep my job. My parents depend on the grain that I earn here."

Tentopet stroked the hair of the strange girl. "It will be fine. I'll tell her."

"Please stay. You'll like it here."

"I'll stay if they want me," she said. "I have to go down and audition for them now."

Harere stood with a smile and guided her toward the door. "Oh, she's already decided. That's why she brought you here."

"Really?"

"And I know that Thales will like you. He tries all of the new girls, but you're special."

"Is Thales the lord of this house?"

"Oh, no." Harere tipped her head and gave her a half-smile. "He's a Greek merchant who visits here often. An old friend of Apollonia's. He's a customer."

Puzzled by Harere's description of the mysterious Thales, Tentopet made her way down the stairs, her bare feet whispering across the cool stone as the numerous tiny bells on her body jingled with every step. The fabric of her dress flowed across the smooth skin of her legs in the slight breeze. Confused about the harem girls she'd seen earlier, she wondered why a Greek merchant would be among them if he wasn't their lord.

Apollonia greeted her at the bottom step and guided her into the reception room where the feast was arrayed on the table, still smelling and looking as good as it had when she arrived hours earlier. At the far end of the table stood a man with a round face and body dressed in a green linen tunic and cloak. He wore many jeweled rings on his rough fingers, frequently brushing them through his curly brown hair and short beard. His eyes widened when Tentopet entered the room, immediately swooping in to take her hands, spread her arms wide, and look her up and down. "Charming," he said. He spoke Egyptian, but his accent was hard to understand. "Charming, charming."

Tentopet glanced at Apollonia, waiting for permission to speak. She nodded. "Tyti, this is Thales, master of the Great Green and trader in exotic goods from distant lands."

Tentopet gave Thales a nervous smile, wishing he'd let go of her hands. His palms felt cold and sweaty. "Welcome, Thales. May all the gods of this land give strength and health to you. What manner of goods do you trade?"

"Many things, my girl. Strange and wondrous things! I have things that delight the tongue, the skin, and the eye. Pretty things that delight the women, and even prettier things that delight the men," Thales said with a wink. "Much as you delight me."

Apollonia clapped her hands. Several of the harem women entered the room carrying bronze sistrums, golden harps with twelve strings, lutes with colored ribbons dangling from their necks, and wooden flutes with two pipes. Some of the women began to clap in rhythm as the others settled in to play their instruments.

Apollonia gestured to Tentopet. "Gladden our hearts with your songs, Tyti, and rejoice with your dance."

Thales smiled and moved away to sit beside the musicians, picking up figs as he passed the table. Tentopet stepped to the middle of the floor and began the slow, sinuous movements she had learned from her teachers in the palace. These would be punctuated with backbends and leaps as the pace increased, but the key to the performance was always to start slowly and build the excitement of the audience. She began to sing a hymn to the Great River. The clappers responded by altering their rhythm, and Tentopet's movements flowed like water.

"Songs to the harp are made for you,

One sings to you with clapping hands..."

Thales glanced at Apollonia, who signaled for Tentopet to continue dancing without singing. She didn't know why, but perhaps Thales had heard that song too many times, or he wished to hear the voice of a favorite girl. One of the harpists began to sing:

"While unhurried days come and go,

Let us turn to each other in quiet affection,

Walk in peace to the edge of old age.

And I shall be with you each unhurried day,

A woman given her one wish:

To see for a lifetime the face of her lord."

As the music swelled, Tentopet swirled and jumped, demonstrating her skill and balance so that Apollonia would offer her work in this pleasant harem of fine clothes and excellent food. She couldn't remember why she had worried at all about her future when her talents would certainly be enough for her to live well and prosper wherever she went. While the harpist began to sing again, Tentopet twirled faster and faster, dazzling her audience with the speed and grace of her hypnotic movements.

"With a beaming face, celebrate the joyful day and rest not therein,

For no one can take away his goods with him.

Yea, no one returns again, who has gone hence."

Raising her arms with the last beats of the music, Tentopet jumped into the air and landed in a graceful pose, bent forward and breathing hard, her eyes locked on the face of Thales, who dropped the fig he was eating and jumped to his feet to applaud.

"Excellent! Excellent!" He rushed forward to grasp both of her hands and kiss them.

Apollonia stepped forward. "Did I not tell you what a wonder she is? A beauty like this, with so many skills, brings only joy to her man and wins the favor of the gods."

"Yes! Yes!" His head waggled up and down as he licked his lips. "I'll pay whatever you wish."

"Whatever I wish?" Apollonia tipped her head with a smile. "Have you forgotten that you're a trader, my lord? I had expected you to haggle with me like a dog over a cattle bone. You must really like her."

"I'm a trader, not a fool. And she is a goddess. Your price will be reasonable, for we all know what she is worth."

Tentopet didn't understand the conversation. Were they discussing how much she would be paid for her employment? When Harere pressed a lotus cup, glazed with blue faience, into her hand, she barely noticed herself drinking from it as she watched Apollonia conclude the conversation by whispering into the Greek's ear. He nodded.

"My men are outside. They will pay you," he said. Then he looked at Tentopet with a bright gleam in his eye.

Apollonia smiled and kissed Tentopet on the cheek. "You're hired, my beautiful one." She winked and walked out the front door.

When Tentopet's eyelids grew heavy, she remembered the cup of lotus wine in her hand and set it down before she dropped it. She had only sipped a little of it, but the room was starting to spin as if she were dancing again. Thales saw her sway and stepped forward to put his arm around her. "I'll take you to your bed, Tyti."

She thought it was nice of Thales to help her, but his grip was unpleasantly tight as he helped her up the stairs. Harere led the way back to her room. Once they were inside, Harere quickly scattered red rose petals on the bed before leaving the room. Two more blue cups of lotus wine rested on a low table. When Thales sat her down and removed his cloak, Tentopet's head cleared a bit and she realized what was going on.

"No, my lord. I'm not ready."

He laughed and offered her one of the wine cups. "Here. This will help."

She glanced at the closed bedroom door. On the other side of the bed, a window looked out on a narrow alley. "I'm sorry, my lord. You are only a—merchant."

After she said it, she realized she'd made a mistake. Thales glared at her and quickly began to remove his tunic, pulling it over his head. "Don't play innocent with me. Not good enough for you, am I?"

While his face was covered, Tentopet rolled across the bed, ran to the window, and jumped out. The two-story drop was scary, but not as scary as Thales. She hit the ground hard, hurting her right ankle and rolling sideways, her flimsy gown swirling. When she stopped, her head still spun from the wine. She heard a roar overhead and his head poked out through the window.

"Get back here! I paid well for you!"

She staggered to her feet and ran down the long alley, hoping he wouldn't jump to follow her. If she could get far enough away before he left the building through the front door, she knew she'd have enough time to lose him in the crowded streets.

The alley kept curving, running between dwellings of mud brick and stone temple walls, narrowing until she could barely get through it, but there was little to obstruct her path. She stopped twice to catch her breath and allow her spinning head to settle, putting her palms flat on the walls to keep from falling. Finally, she emerged onto a major street under the light of braziers burning at a temple entrance.

"There! It's her!"

Her heart sank as she saw three men running toward her, one of whom was Thales. She started to run, but they were on top of her in an instant, and the world went black.

FIVE

1184 BCE—City of Thebes

Year 4 of His Majesty, King of Upper and Lower Egypt, Chosen by Re, Beloved of Amun, Pharaoh Setnakhte, Second Month of Akhet (Season of Inundation), Day 3

Wakhashem, Scribe of the Royal Granaries, a noble from a long line of scribes with great responsibilities to Pharaoh, a responsible man of great wealth and power, was nothing now but an empty shell bobbing in a pool of palm wine. The mortal body was merely the receptacle for the *ka*–the astral being that accompanied it throughout life. When the ka departed, the dead transformed from weak mortals to immortal spiritual beings, exchanging life on earth for the happiness of eternity.

Itennu worked the limbs of the corpse until he got a nod of approval from Ay. He was then allowed to climb out of the wine pool and let the body soak. As expected, he smelled like a drunk. He knew that some of the workers from the House of Beauty were free to go in and out of the temple grounds, but they rarely did so because the common people shunned the hooded caretakers of the dead. Now he knew why—they either smelled like drunks or like death.

Ay gestured broadly at the corpse pool. "Each new Osirid spends 15 days being cleaned and purified. Then we move them to the drying rooms for 40 days, and finish up with 15 days of wrapping and painting. The cheap jobs don't get as much attention, and if we get backed up we move things along a little faster, but we always keep the Osirid for 70 days. After they dry out and harden enough so they don't smell, we stack the cheap ones in the corner until we can do a quick wrap with 'yesterday's linen,' and then one of the apprentice painters practices on them."

While Wakhashem, Scribe of the Royal Granaries, humbly soaked in palm wine, Ay showed Itennu the next chamber. A short row of slanted stone tables, three of which were occupied, lined one wall. Bronze hooks, knives, tweezers, and needles were lined up in neat rows on each table. Canopic jars of blue faience and white alabaster stood by each table to receive the internal organs. Flaming braziers spaced evenly around the room smoked with incense, creating a permanent cloud that drifted heavily on the air. The flickering of oil lamps in the smoke created a ghostly effect close to the tables.

"The skull mush is removed first. Then we fill the head with resin and take out the internal organs to slow the process of decay," Ay said, noting how the head of one man hung facedown over the low end of his table. A bowl beneath the head collected the gray skull mush that dripped from his nose. A trough collected blood and other fluids from the table.

"I thought a priest removed the organs."

"Priests!" Ay spit on the ground. "The *wetyu* do all the work. The *Hery Sesheta* is supposed to manage the process—that's Setau, you met him earlier. He's the Overseer of the Mysteries. The only time he ever touches a corpse is when he makes the cut in the side of the body, and he can barely see to do that through those little eye holes in his Anubis mask. With that sharp obsidian blade of his, he has almost cut off his own hand *twice* since I've been here. *We* do all the wet work of removing the organs. Then the *Hetemu Netjerm,* the Sealer Bearer of Osiris, is supposed to help Setau, and he places the ritual objects in the mummy wrappings, but he's drunk most of the time anyway. Then the *Hery Heb* reads the spells and the prayers while everyone else is working on the body, but do you see *him* standing around here? Do you *hear* him reading the spells? The only time I've ever *seen* one is when they bring a royal stiff in here, and then some royal busybody scribe is here to keep an eye on things. *We* store the organs, *we* clean the body, *we* dry it out in the natron, *we* wrap it in the linen, *we* haul the heavy coffins around, and the sem-priests get all the credit and go home at night because they don't *stink* like we do!" Ay kicked the bowl of skull mush across the floor and spit on the ground again.

Itennu stepped back for a moment until Ay's breathing returned to normal. "Perhaps you should get outside more often, Ay. "

Ay let out an exasperated sigh and glared at Itennu. "I don't know who you think we are, boy, but I'm not allowed to go out when I want to! *Most* of us can't. We're all criminals, misfits, outcasts, and people who were stupid enough to irritate high officials—like you. We're prisoners here. The only good part about this whole deal is that we get free mummification when we're ready for it—if the priests aren't mad at us for some reason. In that case, our bodies just get pitched out onto the hillside for the jackals to eat. No happy afterlife in the Field of Reeds when that happens, which is why you don't want to mess around with the bosses. Just shut up and do what they say, no matter how disgusting it is."

Itennu felt trapped and alone; a forgotten prisoner placed here as punishment by the gods for reasons he didn't fully understand. The more he learned about his situation, the more he felt like his life was over. For the first time, he was glad that his mother wasn't alive to hear about his failure. Of course, if his father ever heard that he was a corpse washer in the House of Beauty, he would die of humiliation, then tell his mother in the afterlife about how their idiot son had disgraced the family. He was fortunate that he had no wife or family of his own to dishonor. He resolved in that moment to do his assigned work and become another anonymous handler of the dead, untouched by the living, never to leave this place, and hope that his good behavior would keep anyone, especially his father, from learning about his disgrace.

Ay picked up one of the canopic jars and opened the lid, holding it up toward Itennu's face. "Smell that."

Itennu got a whiff of what was in the jar and gagged.

"That, my boy, is your life now. Everything that we take out of a corpse goes into one of these jars, and then it gets buried with the stiff in his tomb."

Itennu took a few deep breaths through his mouth, but the smell didn't want to leave his nose. He supposed he'd have to get used to it. "Does the skull mush go in one of those also?"

"No, we throw it out. It's not important. We keep the organs, but not the fluids. And the heart stays in the chest," he said, tapping the closest body in the center of its chest. "The heart has to be weighed in the presence of Osiris because it holds all your memories and thoughts, so it stays attached to the corpse."

Itennu knew the story. It was part of every Book of the Dead buried with every sarcophagus and painted on tomb walls. The heart was the source of human wisdom, memory, personality, and emotions—the king of all the organs. On the Day of Judgment, Anubis leads the deceased into the Court of the Two Truths to declare his innocence before the great god Osiris and forty-two divine judges holding knives. There, the heart of the deceased is weighed on the scale against the feather of Truth where it reveals the person's true character. Ammut, Swallower of the Damned, stands ready to devour the false heart of a wicked person, causing the deceased to die a second time and suffer oblivion. A true heart allowed Anubis to lead the deceased to Osiris, seated on his throne of the underworld. If he got that far, the deceased would live forever.

Ay gestured for Itennu to take a close look at the cut in the side of a corpse. It started at the rib cage and extended in a jagged line to the hip. "Behold! A good *Hery Sesheta* will make an even cut along the side even with his vision restricted through the Anubis mask, but Setau couldn't keep this one straight. The Ethiopian blade is obsidian—certainly sharp enough to make a neat cut—so what was his problem? You know, if there are unnecessary cuts in the body, the spirit might not be able to recognize its owner, dooming it to wander the earth and possibly even haunt the priest responsible for its mutilation. I'd say Setau has something to worry about, because I've watched his shaky hands mutilate many a corpse."

"Is that so?" boomed the voice of a god. Anubis stepped from the shadows.

Ray had to admit to himself that he was lost. It seemed like everyone who lived in Thebes, or anywhere near the city, had converged on the central marketplace and its surrounding streets, making movement almost impossible. Important people carried in litters by their slaves vied with sleds carrying market goods trying to make progress through the streets. Unburdened by heavy cargo, Ray was able to squeeze between people, slide along walls, and slowly maneuver around the stalls of merchants to make some headway through the narrow streams of humanity, but after a while it seemed that all of the streets and buildings looked the same. There were no familiar landmarks. How could anyone live in such a place? All he wanted to do was find his way to his father's house, but he was starting to think he might have to sit huddled in a doorway until nightfall when he could move more freely. He didn't remember the city ever being this crowded when he was a child and his father brought him along to the market. He also didn't remember seeing so many strange faces and unusual styles of clothing.

Stopping to catch his breath in a narrow alley between a beer hall and a temple to some minor god, his senses were confused by the sweet smell of incense mixed with the stronger scents of beer and urine. He scanned the crowd, thinking that if he stood there long enough he might spot the friendly face of a relative or a family friend who could help him.

When he finally did spot someone he recognized, he ducked down lower to hide between the walls. A gang of four Medjay policemen—two Nubians and two Egyptians—was led by the swaggering Sermont, a neighboring boy who had been fond of tormenting Ray before he moved away to the palace. Since Sermont's Nubian father was the Chief of Police in Thebes, he had always been free to terrorize the other children without fear of reprisal. Now that he had donned the leopard skin and carried the spear of a policeman himself, Sermont seemed to have found the perfect occupation where he could beat people and take their belongings in the name of justice. If the Medjay had been alerted to watch for Ray, Sermont would certainly recognize him despite the noisy crowd that surrounded them. Ray breathed a sigh a relief as Sermont moved past, shoving people out of the way to clear his path.

Ray slowly rose to his full height again, watching Sermont continue around the corner into the main market square. A slight commotion to his left caused him to turn his head and see yet another face that he recognized and would never have expected to see that day in Thebes. At first, it looked as if the burly Greek sailor was carrying a dead animal over his shoulder, but it would have been unusual indeed for an animal to be wearing a fancy linen skirt. Ray's heart almost stopped when he saw that the woman's face was that of Tentopet, eyes closed, her hair and arms dangling down over the man's back. Beside the Greek walked an Egyptian sailor, and they both followed what appeared to be their master, a wealthy Greek merchant. Although this was an unusual sight that drew a few curious glances, no one seemed surprised.

Stunned for a moment, Ray tried to sort out what he was seeing, but could only conclude that these men must be working with the assassins who had attacked the palace—and had apparently kidnapped the princess. Before he realized it, he was shoving his way through the crowd to reach her.

As he drew near, he saw Tentopet's eyelids flutter. Either she'd been drugged or knocked out; he couldn't be sure. He was only dimly aware that there were three large sailors and only one of him, but he didn't stop to work out the numbers—he only saw that she was in trouble and needed him. His mind flicked to the memory of Sermont walking past just moments before, but he was unlikely to get any help from the Medjay even if he were able to get to them fast enough. No time for thought, only time for action.

Hopping over a small pile of fresh bricks someone had made to repair the crumbling wall of their house, Ray turned around and hefted two of them. Now, the people in his path seemed to sense that he was coming and moved aside to let him pass. Just as the sailors were about to wade into the sea of people in the crowded market square, Ray hit the Egyptian sailor over the back of the head with a brick. His companion, the Greek sailor carrying Tentopet, reacted slowly, hampered by the crowd and the weight of the victim on his shoulder, and this gave Ray time to slam the brick into the sailor's stomach. With a groan, the man doubled over and dropped to his knees, giving Ray a clear shot at his head so that Tentopet wouldn't be harmed. Breathing hard, startled by his quick success, Ray took her arm as the sailor slumped onto his face. Her eyelids fluttered and she mumbled something, but he couldn't make it out as he rolled her onto his back and straightened up, prepared to run back the way he had come.

The Greek merchant, however, had other ideas. Ray felt the hairs on the back of his neck stand up as the man roared like a lion and ran toward him. He knew that the roar was loud enough to have drawn the attention of Sermont's gang of policemen somewhere nearby.

"Stop, thief! That's my property!"

Out of bricks and out of time, Ray looked around for help. Seeing no one willing to get involved with his dire situation—probably with many of them wondering whether he was the good guy or the bad guy in this situation—he stumbled away from the Greek and turned to make his escape, immediately running into a wall. Stumbling sideways, he fell into the soft sand of an alleyway with Tentopet, who shook her head and blinked in confusion. She kicked Ray in the side and rolled away from him just as the Greek roared again, a dagger in his hand now as he shoved people out of his way to get into the alley. Ray jumped up, prepared to block the Greek's path, having no idea how he would stop a madman with a dagger without getting himself killed, wondering what Pasai would do in this situation, when he heard Tentopet squeal and run away behind him. With a quick look over his shoulder, he saw her staggering along with one hand on the wall for balance, but she was making good progress.

Ray reached down, grabbed a handful of sand, and tossed it into the Greek's face when he was almost on top of him with the dagger. While the man sputtered, wiping the sand from his eyes with one hand, Ray turned and ran after Tentopet, wondering whether the police would be waiting at the other end of the short alley. Thinking of that moment later on, he realized how sharp his senses had been, memorizing the feel of the soft sand under his pounding feet, the familiar smell of urine and incense, the reddish-brown color of the walls fading toward black as the sun raced into the underworld beyond the horizon, the roar of the Greek merchant running after him mixed with the pounding in his ears and the hissing of his own rapid breathing, the faces of wide-eyed children watching him from second-story windows, and the look of the sweat and the sand on Tentopet's bare back as she turned the corner without looking to see who had rescued her—if she were even aware that someone *had* rescued her.

It was his last glimpse of the beautiful young princess before she vanished into the shadows and crowds of the ancient city of Thebes.

The city of Thebes was starting to settle in for the night and Tentopet felt like she could breathe again. After escaping from the Greeks, the running and the pain in her foot had helped to clear her head of the drugged wine, and she was able to make her way down to the small harbor outside the Theban Temple of Amun-Re—the one area she knew well enough to feel a bit safer. For the first hour, she had hidden under a dock of rotting wood that had once been used by the royal boats arriving for the festivals. As the area got quieter and the bats and night birds began to cry out in the night, she became aware of dark shapes moving along the muddy bank and decided that it would be safer to spend the night out of easy reach of the river creatures that might eat her. After rinsing off the mud she had collected from crawling around under the dock, she dried off in the warm breeze at the end of a stone jetty, wishing she had been able to bring the rest of her clothes and cosmetics with her when she left Apollonia's house. The dancing skirt that Apollonia had given her was torn and she felt even less prepared to take care of herself now than she had when she first arrived in Thebes. She still had the anklets and bells, but she wanted to look her best when she auditioned for work.

Tomorrow, she would seek out the Street of the Performers and try, once again, to find respectable employment there, hoping that she didn't run into Thales or Apollonia along the way. With luck, she thought she could join a traveling troupe of performers who would leave town soon, avoiding any further unpleasant incidents. She shivered as she thought of what Thales and his men might have done with her, and she felt lucky to have escaped from slavery. The foreign women in the harem had often mentioned how lucky they were to be there, telling tales of how slavers captured and sold their captives in distant lands where they would bring a higher price for their exotic appearance and customs. At the time, Tentopet thought perhaps they were exaggerated stories intended to shock the Egyptian women, but now she realized they were telling the truth. She would have preferred it the other way around.

Keeping to the shadows, she walked up to the outer walls of the temple complex on the narrow strip of dry embankment that provided a barrier between the temple and the river during its annual flood. She spent a few minutes collecting reeds and grasses to provide some cushioning for a bed, then lay down on her back and looked up at the mass of twinkling lights in the sky. Her hips were sore where the sailor had carried her over his shoulder, her feet and ankles hurt, and her skin was scratched where she had fallen in the alley, but at least she was free and safe.

Fatigue would bring her rest very soon. Before she crossed the border to the land of dreams, her mind drifted and she thought about Ray. What was he doing now? Was he safe at the palace, or had Teya been unable to keep his visit to the harem with her a secret? He was a smart boy and a good friend, so with luck her brothers would be able to keep him safe from Pharaoh's wrath, knowing that he would never take advantage of her or the other women in the harem. Perhaps her own reputation would be saved, and she would learn that she could return home without fear of punishment. Her own mother, Queen Isis, would certainly defend her if necessary, but she had to be careful because of her important position as the Chief Royal Wife of Pharaoh—without proof of her daughter's innocence, her own reputation could be harmed, and Teya would take advantage of that weakness. If the situation improved and it was safe to return to the palace, Teya would find a way to let Tentopet know, for it had been her idea to contact the dancer in Thebes about finding work. In any case, the truth about Ray would be apparent if anyone heard about her taking him to the harem after they had worshipped Sekhmet at the home of the respectable high priest Bakenkhons. Ray's father was a respectable scribe and teacher, and the son was a reflection of the father, so they would have to believe he was innocent. At least, Tentopet needed to believe that. There had to be stability someplace in the world.

Ray had hunted for Tentopet for over an hour, but she had somehow managed to vanish in the crowds of the marketplace. In a way, Ray supposed that this was a good thing—it would be just as hard for anyone else to find her, and he knew they were looking. Attracted by the shouts of the Greek merchant, Sermont and his gang of Medjay policemen had caught up with the fat man, and Ray watched from a safe distance as he presumably gave them Ray's description and told them how he had attacked the sailors in the street and taken "his property." Ray was outraged that the Greek could possibly have called Tentopet his property, for it simply wasn't possible that a princess would be removed from the palace and sold to a slave merchant like some commoner. In fact, he had no idea how she could have gotten to Thebes in the first place, but it was too late to worry about that now.

Dodging the Medjay and the Greek merchant, Ray knew he was risking discovery by hanging around the market area for so long, but he had to be certain that Tentopet was safe. Satisfied that none of them had been able to find her, he finally gave up as the crowds began to thin. To reorient himself, he ventured back down to the public landing on the river and retraced the steps he'd taken with his father before he was sent off to the Karnak temple complex. At that point, with fewer people in the streets, he recognized the way he had known as a child and eventually found the wealthier neighborhood that his father called home. A servant gave him entry to Hapu's house.

Inside, where Hapu was settled in on the master's chair on its dais in the reception room, Ray learned that the physician from the House of Life, Khaemope, had already come and gone. After a thorough examination of Bull, Khaemope determined that nothing could be done to help Bull recover his memories that had been washed away by the waters of the Nile. They knew that Khaemope could not have communicated with Seini at the palace in such a short time if he had suspected Ray's true identity, so he couldn't possibly be covering for an inferior diagnosis by Pharaoh's palace physician. Hapu also seemed certain that Khaemope hadn't recognized Bull, although he had admired the expensive furnishings and decorations in Hapu's home, prompting Hapu to take the hint and give him two silver rings as an additional payment for providing his services in the evening. Khaemope had gone away happy, making his skills available to them at any time of day or night should he be needed.

As Bull snored away in one of the bedrooms, Ray related the story of Tentopet and the Greek as he hungrily bit into bread and fruit served to them on platters by the household servants and slaves. He hadn't realized until now how hungry he was, being distracted by the wild events of the day.

"And you're sure it was the princess?" Hapu asked again with a look of extreme concern.

"No question," Ray said between bites. "I would never mistake her for anyone else."

Hapu nodded. "I thought not. This is very distressing, my son. Not having heard any other news from the palace, I have to think that the assassins made their way into the harem. Tentopet was either captured by them, or she escaped and was captured by someone else. Strange that we've heard no news of this in the city, though. Perhaps word will reach us in another day or two. Pasai will certainly know more when he arrives."

"You mean *if* he arrives?"

Hapu scowled at him. "We must remain hopeful. You know Pasai. You know that it would take an army to slow him down, let alone stop him or kill him. Both pharaohs have complete trust in his skills, and so should you."

"But he hasn't found us yet, father."

"As I said, we must allow another day or two to pass before we start to doubt him. News only travels as fast as the river."

Ray let out a heavy sigh. "I want to go and look for Tentopet tomorrow."

"We need to remain here in case Pasai returns."

"She might need help. She could still be in danger."

"And the city is very large. You have little chance of finding her."

"I'll have even less of a chance if I don't look."

Hapu nodded his head toward the bedrooms. "You must remember the importance of what we do here. Bull must be protected. The future pharaoh is our first concern."

Attempting to stop his reply, Ray tore off a big chunk of the gritty brown bread and stuffed it into his mouth, but he couldn't help himself. "Bull can never be pharaoh. You've seen him. You heard what Khaemope said. The waters of the Nile have made him simple. He's my friend and I'll take care of him with all of my ability, but we shouldn't think he'll be pharaoh one day because he won't!"

"That is not for you to decide, Ray. Many things could happen between now and then. He could get better. This could be a passing illness. When the time comes, the gods may choose to heal him. For all that we understand, this may be the way that the gods are protecting him until they need him to rule the Two Lands."

"Pen could have been pharaoh."

Hapu looked down and nodded. "If Bull dies before Ramesses III descends beyond the western horizon—may he live a long and healthy life—Pentawere would have been the logical choice. I'm sure that his mother would have wanted that, in any case, but Teya is only the principal wife of pharaoh. Bull is Queen Isis's son, and therefore he's fit to rule."

"Why? Because the gods say so?"

Hapu closed his eyes. His jaw muscles tensed, then relaxed again. "I know this is hard to understand, my son, but there are rules that govern these things. The rules are set by the gods. As their representative, pharaoh—the living god—leads his people with their wisdom informing his actions. A mortal man would not be able to accept such a responsibility. Therefore, the royal descendants of pharaoh are the only people who have the ability and the training to govern the Two Lands, defend us from our enemies, and feed us. The royal blood gives them the divine right to do so. While it may appear that our young Ramesses IV is incapable of ruling the country at the moment, his blood will know what to do when the time comes. The gods will see to it. In the meantime, we must protect him."

Ray knew that it would be pointless to argue any further. He still didn't understand why any man or woman with the proper training, and the proper spirit, wouldn't be just as capable of becoming pharaoh. There might even be commoners that could match the grand accomplishments of a Ramesses the Great. He wouldn't be ridiculous enough to think that a slave could be pharaoh, but there had to be other possibilities. If an entire royal family was killed, as they must have been in the past despite numerous children, how else could a new pharaoh be established? Setnakhte, mighty of arm and heart, had almost been such a person, even though he was a distant relation of Ramesses the Great. What if he had not existed to reunite the country during the time of chaos?

Ray drank his thick beer. Such matters were beyond him. He was not a learned priest who could understand such things. Besides, his stomach was full, his body was sore, and he needed his bed—assuming that the next pharaoh's divine snoring would allow him to sleep.

The partial moon provided just enough silvery light for Khait to make her way through the garden in the harem courtyard to the large pond. Night birds hooted and clicked, and she heard the scuttling of little monkeys in the trees. The air smelled of jasmine and citrus. The harem was quiet now with everyone else asleep, but she liked the occasional swim in the cool water at night to relax her mind and body. When she returned to her bed, she would be able to achieve the rest and dreams that had eluded her so far this evening.

At the edge of the pond, Khait slipped out of her gown and let it fall, then silently stepped into the water so that she wouldn't draw any unwanted attention with her splashing. The water felt so lovely, the coolness inching up her skin as she walked toward the center of the pond where it was deeper. She was not surprised that sleep was harder to find this night. Queen Isis had opened up more of the world to her, and granted her an additional income, by making her a servant of Hathor. She had not yet told her father of her good fortune. She wanted to savor the idea and play with it in her mind before telling anyone else about it. Speaking of the queen's gift would only spark jealousy in the harem, although they would learn of it eventually. Her father was another matter; after his initial surprise, he would start thinking about how he could use her new position to further his own goals at the royal court. That was how he always thought about things, and he had tried to teach Khait to think the same way, looking for advantages or for weaknesses in others that made them amenable to persuasion, but such thoughts were not natural for Khait. She appreciated what Panhayboni had taught her, and it had clearly helped him reach his elite position as Overseer of Cattle, but she wanted to prove herself and achieve successes of her own without manipulating others. Well, to be fair, she sometimes manipulated others, and she did look for opportunities to better herself and protect her position in the golden house, but she did not feel the same predatory instincts that had served her father so well.

Swimming slowly, she gasped as she bumped into something soft in the water. That something then pushed her away.

"What do you think you're doing?" Queen Teya demanded. Her words were slurred as if she had been drinking too much wine.

"I'm sorry, Majesty! I didn't see you!" Khait tried swimming backwards, but the queen grabbed her wrist.

"Of course you didn't see me, you fool. That's why I'm out here in the dark. Come closer."

Khait didn't have a choice as the queen pulled her wrist and peered into her face. The smell of wine assaulted Khait's nostrils. "It's you, dressmaker."

The queen was much too close, pressing against her, but she sounded less angry now. Khait tried to move to one side, but the queen grabbed her other wrist. "Remain here. You will keep me company under the moon-god's special light."

"As you wish, Majesty."

The queen freed one of her wrists and ran the backs of her fingers along Khait's cheek, leaving a trail of water droplets. "You will entertain me now, dressmaker."

Khait felt a shudder and hoped the queen couldn't feel it.

"I'm told you have a beautiful voice. I want you to sing for me."

"Now, Majesty?" She realized she was breathing faster than normal. The queen shut her eyes for a moment and stroked Khait's thigh under the water.

"Yes, now," the queen said, slurring her words so much that she was hard to understand. "Sing anything I might like."

Khait cleared her throat and hummed a tune that her nurse would sing to her when she was a child in her father's house. The queen settled her head back against a patch of papyrus along the bank that she was using for a pillow. As Khait was about to start singing the words, she felt the queen's hands drift away, so she just kept humming. When the queen's mouth opened with a soft snore, Khait saw her chance to escape and began drifting away. She continued humming as she worked her way back the way she had come, careful not to make any splashing noises. If the queen remembered what had happened in the morning, Khait would hear about it and there might be some form of punishment waiting for her, but she would hope for the best.

Didu's stomach fluttered as he walked between the long rows of guttering torches that defined the broad path between the camp tents and piles of war equipment. At the end of the path stood the square command tent of Pharaoh Ramesses III, son of Re, Beloved of Amun, Lord of the Two Lands. They were still many days away from Pi-Ramesses, but well within the controlled area of Egypt's boundaries. Many hours of darkness had passed that night before he received the royal summons. Due to the strange hour, Didu could only think that he had done something so horrible, or made such a horrendous mistake, that he was roused from a deep sleep and summoned to the command tent so that he could be executed in Pharaoh's presence. Still, he walked with straight back and defiant eyes as was appropriate for a soldier of his stature, until he neared the white linen walls lit from the fires within. He met the gaze of the two muscular guards, one wearing a terracotta hawk head of Horus and the other wearing the dog head of Anubis. Their long spears, made for stabbing enemies at a safe distance, were tipped with shiny bronze. Having performed such guard duty himself, Didu knew that they looked intimidating but could see little through the eye slits of their masks, but that only meant they were more likely to spear an unwanted visitor if they didn't identify themselves fast enough.

"Behold! I am Didu, Standard-Bearer on Pharaoh's Right Hand!"

The guards stepped sideways out of his path. Horus lifted the tent opening.

Didu stopped just inside the tent, blinded by the light of the fires, and bowed with his arms extended.

Ramesses flicked his hand. "Enter, Didu."

As his eyes adjusted, Didu stepped forward and saw that Ramesses was seated behind a desk of ebony and gold. An array of shields, armor, and weapons were arrayed on stands or planted vertically in the sand. On the floor near his feet, Pasenhor the Truth Scribe scratched his reed pen across the papyrus on his writing plank. Oil lamps and braziers provided so much light that a blind man might see within this tent.

Pharaoh held up a hand to keep Didu silent as he completed a thought he was dictating to Pasenhor. "With mighty arm and bow, he did slay the enemies of the Two Lands like the god Montu, crushing their bodies beneath his chariot wheels, cutting them with his sword, smiting their skulls with his club, piercing them with his arrows, burning their tents with his torch, and teaching them the constant fear known by those who would defy Pharaoh in his lands."

It sounded like the usual report of Pharaoh's actions in battle. Didu waited patiently for him to finish, trying to breathe quietly, afraid to move a single muscle for fear of disturbing him.

Pharaoh turned his gaze on Didu. "What do you think, Didu? Does that sound like an accurate report?"

"Of course, my lord." He knew enough not to contradict Pharaoh.

"You would not like to expand upon the description in any way?"

"Only the Great One has the wisdom to properly interpret the events of battle," Didu said, fervently wishing to survive this conversation.

Pharaoh nodded, keeping his eyes locked on Didu's face. "There's something missing. Ah, I know. The object of the description. The name of the mighty warrior who risked his life to defend the Two Lands."

Didu let out his breath as Ramesses looked down at Pasenhor. "Note this. Behold! Thus did Didu, Standard-Bearer on Pharaoh's Right Hand, accompany the living god into battle, slaying Pharaoh's enemies with his own hand, driving the royal chariot over the bodies of the cowardly Tjehenu, the Libu, the Meshwesh, and all the tribes assembled to defy the Two Lands. Behold! Thus they did die at the hand of Didu."

Didu couldn't believe what he was hearing. To have his name recorded with Pharaoh's name in the histories was the highest honor he could receive. He swallowed.

"Sit," Pharaoh said, indicating one of the leather stools reserved for the generals.

Didu sat, happy to remove the weight from his trembling knees.

"Are you familiar with the story of Thuthuti at Joppa?"

"No, Highness." Of course he was familiar with the story. Both his father and mother had wanted him to seek a military career, so they told him stories such as this when he was a child. Still, it seemed safer to feign ignorance in case Pharaoh was testing him.

"Well, Thuthuti was a general in the army of Tuthmosis III. He followed the pharaoh on all his campaigns to the north and the south, and with him he crossed the great river Euphrates that runs upside-down. He fought in all of these places as the head of the soldiers and was rewarded for his service with the Gold of Valor. When Tuthmosis heard that the King of Joppa had revolted against the Egyptians, killing the soldiers and charioteers and murdering the Egyptian vizier, he called his nobles, and wise men, and generals, and scribes together to seek their advice. General Thuthuti jumped up and volunteered to lead a troop of foot soldiers and a chariot battalion to Joppa. He asked only that he be given the pharaoh's curved sword to overcome the enemy. Pharaoh gave Thuthuti his sword and told him what an excellent thing he had said."

It occurred to Didu that Ramesses might be preparing him to go on a suicide mission, or getting him to volunteer for one, which only made him more nervous.

"Well, what do you think Thuthuti did? When he arrived in the land of Djahy where Joppa was, he set up camp and caused five hundred pottery jars to be made that were large enough to hold a man. He then sent a message to the King of Joppa, identifying himself and saying that the King of Egypt was jealous of Thuthuti because of his many victories. He said that he had stolen the great sword of Tuthmosis and would give it to the King of Joppa, along with his infantry, his chariots, and many jars of treasure if the King of Joppa would let Thuthuti live in that wondrous land that was strong enough to defy Egypt."

Didu licked his lips, thinking that of course the King of Joppa, a complete idiot, believed this ridiculous story.

"The King of Joppa believed his story," Ramesses continued, his gaze never wavering from Didu's eyes. "He believed it because of his own greed. He wanted the sword of Tuthmosis more than anything else in the land, believing that it would make him an invincible warrior. Thuthuti said that he could have the sword and all of the other great things if the king would come out of the city with his soldiers and meet them on the hill beyond the gates. The king did so. In the meantime, Thuthuti hid the sword of Tuthmosis in a sack of grain. When the king arrived, he opened two of the large pottery jars and showed the king the gold and other treasures that filled them, saying that there were 500 of these jars he had brought as gifts for the king."

Didu tried not to blink or move. He could only wonder how a king could be a king and still be dumb enough not to check all 500 of the man-sized jars before allowing them into the fortress city of Joppa.

"The jars were carried through the city gate by a thousand Egyptian soldiers. Once they were inside the walls, the soldiers inside the jars jumped out with their weapons and took the city with those who had carried the jars. Hearing the screams of his dying people in the city, the king of Joppa asked Thuthuti what was happening. Thuthuti explained that his men were taking the city of Joppa, and then he removed the sword of Tuthmosis from the sack of grain, saying: 'And here is the great sword of the king that you were so anxious to see.' He then cut the King of Joppa in half with the sword. When he was done, he sent the head of the King of Joppa to Tuthmosis, saying: 'Rejoice, for I have taken the land of Joppa. Send men to take these people to Egypt as captives, that you shall fill the house of Amun-Re, King of the Gods, with servants and slaves, and that the treasures of Joppa shall go to adorn his temples and your palaces.' Thus did Thuthuti take the fortress city of Joppa by using his own thoughts as strategy."

Didu wondered where Pharaoh was going to send him. So much for his plan of leaving the army as soon as they returned to Pi-Ramesses.

"Stand and approach me, Didu." Pharaoh reached into a leather bag by his chair and withdrew a gold chain adorned with three gold flies, which he then placed over Didu's head. "Behold! You are my Thuthuti. I present you with the Gold of Valor in the name of Amun-Re, and Montu, and Horus, in full view of the gods and the witness, Pasenhor. Behold! Your deeds will be enshrined with mine on the walls of the Temple of Amun-Re in Pi-Ramesses and on stelae throughout the country."

Didu bowed deeply, extending his arms. The gold flies on the necklace dangled in front of his face. "Thank you, Great One. I am humbly grateful for this honor. At the feet of my lord, the sun, seven times seven times I fall down, the dust of thy feet."

"Of course. Sit with me another moment, Didu."

Didu sat down again, his head spinning.

"When we return to Pi-Ramesses, you will have a choice to make. You can remain with my army, in which case your military career will advance as it pleases me. You also have the option of leaving the army, in which case I have high hopes that you can find a suitable place in the royal administration. You would leave with the rewards you have earned, and additional land I'm giving you now for your long and faithful service. However, all of this depends on what we find when we return to the city. If the situation is stable, all will be as I have said. If the city has been attacked, you will remain in my service until I give you leave to go."

"I understand, my lord. I am, as always, at your command."

"Of course you are. Know that I have watched you here in my service, and that you have the skills of a leader, perhaps a general. The soldiers listen to you and follow you. This is a rare ability, for men do not wish to be led by others they know to be inferior. When their lives depend on correct decisions by their leader, they must trust them completely. As Pharaoh, I also must trust the men who surround me, for they are my eyes and hands on the battlefield, and my eyes and ears in the royal city. Know that if you stay in my service, you will achieve great responsibility in time, for I am a judge of men, as the gods are judges of men, and I see into your heart, which has the spark of greatness."

At that moment, if Pharaoh had asked Didu to attack Joppa all by himself, he would have done so. He had the Gold of Valor, slaves, land, riches, and the promise of a fine career whether he stayed in the army or not. He started to bow and thank Pharaoh again, but the living god raised his hand to stop him.

"Go and rest, Didu. Prepare for our triumphant return."

Khenti, son of Kemosiri the stonecutter, rested his head on his thick fore-arm and relaxed his grip on the copper chisel. On his stomach in the narrow passage, he tried to take a deep breath but coughed in the dust his digging had raised. The oil lamp sputtered and he hoped it would last a little longer, for he hated crawling across the rubble in the dark tomb shaft as he had already done twice that night. He was tired and wanted sleep, having already spent his usual work day farther up the valley in the old, unused tomb of Queen Twosret, part of the gang replacing her name and images with that of Pharaoh Setnakhte, who was likely to need his resting place in the very near future. Setnakhte had become Pharaoh at an age when he was too old to have a new royal tomb cut from the rock; one had been started, then abandoned when the tunnel ran into an older tomb, so the only practical choice was to use the tomb planned for Twosret. Because of this work on Twosret's tomb, Khenti had met the mayor of Thebes, Paweraa, and the potential for a better future had opened up before him. The powerful

Paweraa had known Kemosiri, his father, and had taken a liking to Khenti on an inspection tour of Twosret's tomb. Invited to visit Paweraa at his home, long discussions over much beer and wine had led to an offer that would raise Khenti out of his life of drudgery in the stonecutting business; an occupation inherited from his father, who had inherited the position from his grandfather, and so on. Khenti wasn't sure when the first of his ancestors had become a stonecutter on the privileged work gangs in the Great Place—the final home of the earthly remains for the Pharaohs and their families since the beginning of time—but it seemed as if his family had always been here. It was a physical job, better than working in the hot sun like a farmer, or going blind by writing all day like a scribe, but stonecutters were not known for their long lives, being prone to dying from the dust in their lungs, being crushed under rocks, or falling from high places. He would never be hungry, but he would also never be wealthy, and he would have to work until the day he died, for he had no family to support him if he survived to an old age. In his late twenties now, he had not found a woman in the worker's village who wanted him as a husband, and he wasn't sure that he wanted to be tied to a home in the Great Place for the rest of his life anyway.

Then Paweraa had offered him a way out.

For almost a full season, Khenti had spent his nights digging through a hidden construction shaft built for noble parents of a forgotten wife of Pharaoh Amenhotep III. Assisted only by a boy named Ruta who dragged the reed baskets of limestone chunks out of the tunnel—rocks placed there by priests of the royal necropolis to block potential tomb robbers who might find the hidden shaft—they had almost reached the burial chamber of the tomb of Yuya and his wife, Tuyu. Ruta dumped the rocks where they would not be noticed—in a recent rubble pile from another tomb. Mayor Paweraa had come into ownership of a tomb map made by two necropolis officials who had broken into this tomb shortly after the burials of Yuya and Tuyu, stealing the perishable but valuable oils, perfumes, and cosmetics that were easily carried away. The robbery had been discovered, and the two necropolis officials confessed to the robbery under torture by the Medjay police who guarded the valley of the sleeping pharaohs. Before they were executed by impalement, the prisoners had given the police their map of the tomb and a description of its contents. The map was hidden for almost 150 years before Mayor Paweraa discovered it in the Theban archives. The original tomb robber entrance had been resealed and trapped by necropolis priests of the Osiris cult, but Paweraa had also learned of the construction tunnel that Khenti was clearing now—a secondary route that the tomb robbers had not needed.

The deal was simple—Paweraa and Khenti would split the value of the gold and other valuables that Khenti recovered from the tomb. Khenti would arrange for the sale of the stolen objects to the Greek or Syrian merchants who were known to trade in such items, despite the obvious dangers involved in that kind of smuggling. From the proceeds, Ruta would receive a token payment for his work before returning to the household of Paweraa. Some of the gold would be melted down so that it could be used again without being traced back to the tomb of Yuya and Tuyu. Even a small amount of gold would be enough for Khenti to create a new life for himself—and he would have to create it elsewhere so that he wouldn't have to explain his newly acquired wealth to his neighbors or to suspicious authorities. Since the death of his father, he had also been the sole supporter of his mother and two sisters, so some of the gold would be for them and he'd have to come up with a reasonable explanation for it.

Khenti drank from the jar of water he had brought with him, then gripped his mallet and chisel to attack the flat wall at the end of the tunnel with renewed enthusiasm. He would soon reach the burial chamber. There was a small fear in his heart that some avenger of the underworld would take his life when he finally broke through, but Mayor Paweraa had reassured him that the gold in the old tombs had already served its purpose. Yuya and Tuyu didn't need such great wealth in the afterlife; it was merely there as a convenience they might use in starting their new adventures. Paweraa also believed that the wealth of the tombs should be recirculated among the living to maintain the public welfare instead of hoarding it underground where it would serve no social benefit. Paweraa was an educated man, and it all made sense to Khenti, but he hoped that the gods also understood the mayor's reasoning.

Chipping around the edges of a final limestone block, Khenti finally loosened it enough to push it through into the dark chamber beyond. Cool air wafted past his face, carrying with it the smells of incense and ancient dust. Sound seemed to vanish into the black hole. A scorpion scuttled past. He lifted the sputtering oil lamp with a shaky hand and held it in the dark opening. On the other side, he saw the shiny glint of gold.

Khenti jumped when he heard the small voice behind him. "We will not die?"

"Not if I can help it," Khenti said, reaching back to pat the boy on the head. He thought there was an excellent chance that the gods would kill them for violating the tomb, but there was no need to worry the boy.

"Can I see?"

Khenti pushed to one side of the narrow tunnel to let Ruta crawl up beside him. The boy's eyes widened when he looked through the hole. "Shiny."

"Very shiny," Khenti said. Worried that Ruta would lean too far into the hole, he pulled back on the boy's dirty robes. "It's not safe. You wait here while I hand things out to you."

"Shiny for me?"

"Shiny for you, shiny for me, shiny for everyone," Khenti said, wondering if the boy's accent was Meshwesh or Sherden.

Ruta backed out of the way and allowed Khenti to crawl forward into the hole. Then Ruta tapped him on the foot.

"What is it?"

"A man was outside. I forgot to say."

Khenti stopped breathing. If there was a man outside—

"Man is the painter," Ruta said, stroking the air with an imaginary paintbrush. "Back tomorrow for talk."

Khenti relaxed. The painter was his partner in crime who had been called out-of-town for the last month, leaving him to do most of the digging. But that was okay. Now that he was back, his partner would be able to help him sell the tomb objects since he had a much better idea of what they were worth. Khenti would still be the one to deliver payment to the mayor because Khenti was the only one who knew his identity as the mysterious tomb map provider.

While Khenti pulled himself forward into the new opening and prepared to drop to the floor beyond, he held up his lamp for another look. He had the feeling that evil things were waiting for him in the burial chamber, and he wanted to be sure he could reach the floor without breaking his leg or a valuable piece of tomb furniture. The glint of gold was everywhere, but he gasped when he saw that the protectors of the tomb were everywhere as well.

Wherever he turned, the eyes of the watchers were upon him.

Paniwi's dance troupe was practicing in the shade of a giant palm tree when Tentopet found them in the Street of the Performers. Despite her common manner of dress, or lack of it, and paint on her face she had been unable to fix without her cosmetics, she was pleased to see that she caught the attention of the performers as she approached. She now hoped that she would be allowed to audition, and could perform well, despite the little sleep she had managed to get on her makeshift reed bed near the river. With any luck, she would have a bed indoors that evening.

Tentopet studied her "competition." The eight female *khebeyet* dancers were professionals from various regions with muscular thighs visible beneath their diaphanous short skirts. They wore decorative white headbands and jingling bells around their waists and ankles. The acrobatic *hebi* dancers wore only beaded leather belts with bells so that clothing wouldn't interfere with their tumbling and leaping. There were five singers in pleated white gowns who weren't singing at the moment, and six male musicians in loincloths who were seated on the ground playing their flutes, drums, and oboes for the dancers.

As Tentopet neared the tall woman with smooth, caramel-colored skin who directed the activities of the dancers—the *Weret-khener*, or "Great One of the Musical Troupe"—she smiled and asked for work. Paniwi, who appeared to be in her early thirties, looked her up and down, then asked Tentopet to list her talents, which she did. The small group of musicians playing for the dancers looked at each other with skeptical expressions when she mentioned all of the different instruments she could play, but she was particularly surprised to see the exaggerated rolling eyes and looks of disdain that the dancers and singers gave her in between bouts of giggling. She knew this reception did not bode well for her future.

Paniwi sighed. "Did someone send you? Is this one of Khuy's little jokes? Did he tell you to come here and tell Paniwi that you had every imaginable performing talent and that I'd be a fool not to hire you? Did you lay with him?"

Tentopet was taken aback. "No, mistress! I was sent—" She caught herself before she said that Queen Teya had sent her, remembering that her identity needed to be kept a secret.

"Yes? Who sent you?"

"The goddess Hathor. She visited me in a dream."

"Did she? How convenient. Did she mention me by name, or just tell you to go and seek your fortune here in Thebes?"

This conversation wasn't going at all the way Tentopet had planned. She figured she would have auditioned and had the job by now. She was also annoyed at the way Paniwi was treating her, but she didn't want to say anything that might prevent her from getting a job. This might be the only chance she had left for sleeping in a real bed in Thebes that night.

"May I sing for you, mistress?"

"We're very busy right now." Paniwi said. Seeming uncertain now, she looked at her waiting performers.

One of the singers, a light-skinned girl with delicate features who also had the muscular legs of a *khebeyet*, stepped forward. When she spoke, her sweet voice captured the ear like honey. "We should give her a try, Paniwi. You know that Hekenu is ill, and who knows how long she will be away?"

Paniwi bit her lip. "Yes, Kiya. And we have the festival coming up in two weeks." She thought about it for a moment longer, then turned to Tentopet again. "I don't just need a temple singer. I need someone who can sing all of the forms. And dance when necessary. Can you do that? Sing something short."

Tentopet smiled at Kiya, then cleared her throat and sang:

"The King comes to dance, he comes to sing.

Sovereign lady, see how he dances.

Wife of Horus, see how he leaps!"

Tentopet saw that the singers were avoiding her eyes. Kiya looked down at her feet. Paniwi shook her head. "I don't know who told you that you could sing, girl. I'm guessing that it wasn't Hathor."

Speechless, Tentopet could only stand there with her mouth open. Everyone had always told her what a wonderful voice she had—lyrical and beautiful enough to please the gods!

"Go and don't waste any more of our time," Paniwi said, shooing her away while prompting her performers.

"But I can dance," Tentopet said, finding her voice as the musicians began to play and the dancers started into their routines once more.

Paniwi ignored her. However, having come so far, and desperate to avoid going back to Apollonia's house again, Tentopet started dancing, listening to the music with her eyes closed. She tumbled, leaped, and flowed like the river, swaying in time with the double oboe, then twirling with the notes of the flute, bending over backwards to touch the top of her head to the ground, then sinuously shimmying to the steady beat of the small drum. When she opened her eyes again, breathing hard, the music had stopped and the dancers were all watching her.

"Interesting," Paniwi said. "Where did you learn to dance?"

"From my mother," Tentopet said. "She was trained in a harem. And my grandmother knew many dances that she had learned on her travels."

"I see. What's your name?"

"Tyti, mistress."

"You understand that my troupe travels throughout the land? If you join us, you may not see your family or friends for long periods. We move like the wind from place to place, sleeping where we can, but we are paid very well for our services. If you are with child, you will not be allowed to dance. If you promise not to sing when we perform, you can join us as a dancer. Even then, you must remember that I am the main attraction, so don't try to draw attention away from me with your acrobatics when I'm performing."

"I can remember that," Tentopet said, barely containing her excitement—and relief.

Paniwi offered her hand. "Then welcome, Tyti. You have a job."

It had taken Khenti and Ruta almost three hours to drag the sled loaded with gold tomb objects around the far side of the hill to the river, barely avoiding the Medjay desert patrols in the darkness. Usually, nobody was stupid enough to drag such a heavy load this far around the mountain to reach the tombs in the Valley of the Kings, so they had only seen two patrols. Waiting by the river would actually be riskier. While they crouched among the reeds near their sled, which was covered with rocks to disguise it in the black desert night without any moon, they slapped at the insects seeking their blood and listened for larger creatures from the river that might think of them as an easy meal. Khenti's own father, a tomb foreman, had been killed by a hippo a few months ago, leaving him as the head of their family in the village of the tomb workers. This meant that they'd had to start living on Khenti's income, with grain payments that were much smaller than what his experienced father had received for his services. His mother kept asking why he didn't try to do more with his life and advance in the family business that had supported his ancestors for the last two hundred years, but her real concern was how she and Khenti's sisters were going to survive on his pitiful income. Her own grain ration from the government was not enough to support a family, and his sisters were too lazy and unpleasant to have found husbands to support them or find useful work that would feed them. Khenti didn't have good answers to his mother's questions, but he felt the pressure of his family responsibilities, which was why he had taken the great risk of robbing a tomb for Mayor Paweraa.

Ruta gasped and Khenti's heart leaped into his throat when they heard footsteps snapping reeds nearby.

"Khenti?" whispered a man's voice.

Khenti lifted his head just enough to peer over the reeds along the riverbank. "Neferabu?"

"Of course," whispered the painter. "Did you think the Medjay would call your name when they came creeping through the mud and the reeds?"

"I don't know. The Medjay are very clever."

"Well, not *too* clever, I hope. Otherwise, we're dead."

A few more reeds snapped and Neferabu sat down beside them, brushing mud off his knees.

"Where's the boat?" Khenti asked.

Neferabu indicated the broad expanse of water beside them. "On the river, I assume."

"Are we in the right place?"

Neferabu looked around. "He said we should wait just above the Osiris landing where the two stones form a little pyramid."

Ruta nodded his head and pointed at the nearby stones jutting out of the river mud. "There."

"So we just have to wait, then," Khenti said.

"Keep your eyes open," Neferabu said, settling down where he could put his feet up on a rock. "I'm going to take a nap."

About an hour later, they all sat up when they heard wood scraping along the reeds a short distance away. A Syrian river boat with one mast hove into view, visible only as a darker object outlined against the river. Neferabu stood and grabbed a line hanging from the boat's prow, which he then threw to Khenti to tie off on the pyramid rocks. As the boat settled into place, Neferabu took the hand of a silent man who reached out for him and jumped up into the boat. Motioning for Ruta to remain where he was, Khenti waited for the side of the boat to come around his way and hauled himself aboard.

Neferabu stood between three bearded Syrians wearing linen gowns ornamented with diagonal stripes of black beads. All three sailors wore curved daggers at their waists, but their captain also wore a long sword hanging from a leather belt.

When Khenti first arrived, the captain had been smiling. Neferabu's whispering gradually got louder and his gestures more animated, but Khenti couldn't make out all of his words. He didn't seem to be happy about the arrangement. The captain's smile gradually faded into a scowl.

Finally, Neferabu turned his back on them and walked over to whisper at Khenti. "Pretend that we're talking."

"We are talking," Khenti whispered.

"They think we're stupid," Neferabu said. "The captain says only the son of a goat would pay the kind of price I'm asking for. I explained that these are probably the highest quality tomb objects that they've ever seen and he just said everyone says that."

"Have you shown him anything yet?"

"Just this," Neferabu said, opening his hand to reveal a protective charm in the shape of a hippo with detailed features. Lotus and flower symbols were engraved in the hippo's sides. This heavy gold symbol of the goddess Taweret would bring good luck and protection from storms.

"They didn't like it?"

"I should have brought a gold dagger or a spear. The Syrians like that sort of thing. We can also say they have magic powers—they aren't going to know the difference."

"I can have Ruta bring a dagger from the sled."

"Wait a minute, and then we'll both go. We'll pretend that we're leaving. I don't know if I trust them, anyway."

Khenti shrugged. "What did you expect? They're Syrians. They'd probably trade their mothers and sisters for what we've got on our sled."

"Unfortunately, I have no use for their mothers and sisters. I want gold, and a lot of it at that."

Neferabu glanced over his shoulder and waved, then he and Khenti jumped down into the mud. As they crawled up onto the reeds where Ruta was kneeling, one of the Syrian sailors untied their mooring line and the boat began moving away.

"They're leaving," Khenti said, a little too loud.

"I can see that. Have patience. And send the boy for some more gold trinkets," Neferabu said, lying back on the reeds so that he could put up his feet again.

As Ruta left, the boat continued moving away. Neferabu seemed unconcerned. Khenti tapped him on the foot. "They're definitely leaving. Should I say something to them?"

"Why bother? They can barely understand us anyway. They speak gibberish."

Faced with the prospect of hauling the heavy sled all night to get back to the tomb before dawn, Khenti started pacing, wondering what to do. "Why aren't you worried? How are we going to sell these things?"

Ruta returned and handed a large gold dagger to Khenti along with some smaller items. "Shiny."

Neferabu nodded at Ruta. "As the boy said, we've got many shiny things. And Greeks like shiny things."

"What are you talking about? What Greeks?"

They heard the gurgling and scraping of wood on reeds once again. Thinking that the Syrian boat had turned around, Khenti was surprised to see a larger Greek vessel moving into view. It had two masts and a variety of colorful faces painted along its hull. Two weighted ropes landed among the reeds and the boat came to a smooth stop by the rock pyramid.

While Khenti wondered how Neferabu had managed that performance, and how many smugglers actually knew about this "secret" spot on the river, the painter took the gold dagger and the other shiny objects from his hands and climbed into the boat. If he hadn't known Neferabu and his family of artists for a long time, he might have worried that he would never see him again, but despite his superior manner—which was not all that unusual for the families of tomb painters and sculptors who lived there in the tomb worker's village—he knew that Neferabu was an honorable fellow. Neferabu's father was a famous sculptor who didn't like his son's nontraditional work, but Khenti had suffered some of the same problems with his own father. In Neferabu's case, he had been banned from sculpture in the tombs and forced to paint. In Khenti's case, he had not shown the leadership qualities that his father expected of him, so he had remained a simple quarryman, able to identify the good stone and cut it from the living rock or cut a deep and strong hole into the mountain by studying the way the limestone fractured, but not good enough to design a tomb or manage a work gang. He could follow a plan, but he wasn't a planner himself. However, he knew that he was good at getting the best tomb jobs for himself and his family, and the tomb architects always said that he had a golden tongue, which was partially why his father had such a high income. Now that his father was gone, and his brother had been killed in a tunnel collapse a year earlier, his golden tongue wasn't good enough to get the highest-paying work that required management. Never having been trained as a scribe, which his father considered one of the weaker occupations—despite the fact that they all worked under scribes—Khenti had few other options. Now, here he was, robbing tombs at night and risking his life to sit in the mud waiting for smugglers to buy his stolen goods.

Neferabu looked over the boat railing and down at Khenti with a smile. "Who is the king of negotiation?"

Khenti frowned. "I don't know."

Neferabu hopped over the side and thumped into the mud. "Me, of course. The Greeks will pay my price once they see the sled. And they loved the dagger."

Two sailors drew the boat in closer to the pyramid rocks so that their captain could hop down without sinking into the mud. As the big merchant stepped across from the rocks to the reeds, Neferabu smiled and introduced him to Khenti.

"This is Thales, master of the Great Green Sea."

SIX

1184 BCE—City of Thebes

Year 4 of His Majesty, King of Upper and Lower Egypt, Chosen by Re, Beloved of Amun, Pharaoh Setnakhte, Second Month of Akhet (Season of Inundation), Day 14

Over two weeks had passed since Ray last saw Tentopet in the Theban market, but he worried about her every day and occasionally sneaked away from his father's house to hunt for her in the city streets. Without any idea as to where he should look for Tentopet, he walked around hoping to run into her if she went outside, no matter where she might be staying. Still not having heard anything from Pasai, and mindful that Sermont or the other Medjay policemen might see him wandering around the city, Ray limited his trips and kept to the shadows whenever possible. However, he felt that today would be different. Today, everyone in Thebes would be out in the streets. Today, the Beautiful Feast of Opet would begin.

More than ever, the streets of Thebes, particularly near the Temple of Amun-Re at Karnak, would be thronged with people of all classes of society—over 50,000 of them according to the last count by the royal tax collector. With the Nile flood at its peak, work was suspended in the fields, allowing the farmers and their families to travel to the city and join in the 24-day celebration with the rest of the population. All would be heading for their favorite places along the two-mile route to watch the festivities, starting with the dramatic procession of Amun-Re and his priests through the Karnak temple complex—stopping so that Amun-Re could commune with the other gods at their shrines—then out onto the river on his floating temple barge, *Userhetamon*, "Mighty of Brow is Amun." The procession would end at the Theban Temple, where the god would commune with another holy image of himself—Amun-Min, who inseminated the earth and brought about plentiful harvests. In the Theban sanctuary, Pharaoh would also have his divine strength renewed by Amun-Re.

During the Opet Festival, Amun-Re bequeathed his might and power to his living son, Pharaoh, and this annual rite during the second month of Akhet reaffirmed that transfer of power. The priests of Amun-Re would distribute free loaves of bread that could be dipped in olive oil; festival beer flavored with figs, mint, pomegranates, honey, or grape juice; ox and gazelle meat basted in honey; spit-roasted Nile duck; lumps of fat spiced with cumin and radish oil; and bowls of brown beans or chick peas spiced with cilantro, dill, wild sedge, parsley, and coriander. Arrayed along the processional routes were large stalls shaded by papyrus garlands of white and blue lotus, chrysanthemum, red poppy, white acacia, red safflower, and blue cornflowers. Within these stalls were tables loaded with sycamore figs, pomegranates, heads of roasted garlic, celery, leeks, lettuce, honey cakes, and large wine jars where young priests mixed white and red wines into serving jars. Wine was a special treat, not appreciated by everyone, but it made the common people feel like royalty. Within the restricted confines of the temple, the more refined priests and important guests would be offered special vintages, such as the locally produced *Gift of Amun-Re* or the ever-popular *Hathor is Pleased*. This was all food that Pharaoh had donated from the royal warehouses for the festival, demonstrating how he loved and cared for his people as the source of bounty and well-being for all of Egypt.

Hapu and Ray had discussed a strategy for this day, hoping that they could speak with Pharaoh while he was in Thebes, or at least talk to someone who knew of the situation in Pi-Ramesses. If Pasai had been held up by his duties to Pharaoh Setnakhte, he might also have sought this opportunity to accompany the pharaoh to Thebes to communicate with Hapu. Since it would be hard for Pasai or Pharaoh's messengers to traverse the crowded streets during the festival, Hapu believed that their best chance for contact would be to find a vantage point as close as possible to the Theban Temple and watch for an opportunity there.

Hapu had taught at Amun-Re's school for scribes in Thebes for many years. This experience, and his later success as tutor to Pharaoh's children in Pi-Ramesses, gave him the authority to join the other senior teachers to watch the show. They occupied the rooftop of the four-story school overlooking the massive stone entrance to the Theban Temple with its tall lotus columns and colorful wall paintings. The temple roof adjoined that of the school with a slight gap between the two, but its ornamentation and skylights would make watching the festivities from there a dangerous business. It was possible that Hapu might run into old friends at the school, but he knew they were likely to keep his visit a secret if he requested it. In the event that Hapu and Ray were able to contact Pharaoh, it was also possible that they would no longer have a need for secrecy and could return to their normal lives in Pi-Ramesses. In case they had to leave quickly with Pharaoh, Bull would be there with them.

The ancient scribe Khamenwati, who was now overseer and head teacher of the scribe school in Thebes, sat in the shade of an awning on the balcony. His chair was made of ebony with carved lion's feet. Student scribes created a breeze for him with their large fans made of white feathers. Supporting his upper body on an ivory cane shaped like an ibis, Khamenwati's chin rested on his right hand, which gripped the bird's head as he looked out over the throng below. Beyond the crowd lay the sparkling waters of the Nile, now colored brown by the fertile silt that the river was depositing in their fields. Long white pennants and colored streamers drifted on the breeze from their flagpoles atop the gleaming bronze caps of obelisks and pylons. Boats of all kinds lined the banks, dominated by the large rowing and sailing boats of the royal family. The royal boat of Pharaoh was moored at a private dock on a manmade river channel that ended at the temple's Sun Court. Pharaoh wanted the people to see and worship him when he appeared, but he didn't want them close enough to touch him.

For some reason, possibly due to his advanced age, Khamenwati didn't seem surprised to see Hapu standing next to him on the roof. They exchanged pleasantries as if they'd seen each other only yesterday. Ray and Bull stood a few paces away from Hapu and pretended not to notice. In Bull's case, he probably *hadn't* noticed since he was busy slapping at flies.

"Have you heard the rumor?" Khamenwati asked as he studied the crowd. A student poured some red wine for him in a flower-shaped goblet of blue glass, the likes of which Ray had only seen in Pharaoh's palace.

"There are always so many rumors, which one did you mean?" Hapu asked, leaning closer to the old teacher despite himself. There were a couple of other teachers on the roof that Hapu didn't recognize, but apparently they had already heard the rumor because they didn't seem interested.

"They say that Pharaoh Setnakhte—may he live a long, prosperous, and healthy life—is visited by evil spirits these days and does not feel well."

Hapu glanced at Ray. "What does his physician say?"

Khamenwati snorted. "Seini has not spoken to me since I called him a fraud in front of Pharaoh twenty years ago. Any physician who still depends on magic for most of his cures is behind the times. Unfortunately, the living god Setnakhte is bound to tradition, and he likes Seini despite my advice. That divine stubbornness may well lead to his departure from this earth one day soon."

"What are his symptoms, teacher?" Ray asked.

Khamenwati raised an eyebrow without looking at Ray. "Who is this pup, Hapu?"

"My son, Ray. He was much smaller when you last saw him."

"So small that I couldn't see him, apparently. I don't remember meeting the boy."

"As I said, it was some time ago," Hapu said with a smile.

"Are you teaching him the ways of the scribe?"

"Of course."

"Did you leave out the part where he would have learned manners? He spoke to me as if I were his doting grandfather."

Hapu sighed. "I shall beat him when we get home."

"I humbly apologize, teacher," Ray said with a slight bow. He really had no idea of what he'd done wrong by asking a question. As teachers went, Khamenwati seemed even stricter than Hapu.

"And who is the other one? He looks familiar."

Hapu motioned for Bull to stay back with one hand while gesturing toward him with the other for Khamenwati's benefit. "My son's friend. A farmer's son come to Thebes to seek his fortune."

Khamenwati nodded and continued looking down on the crowd. "As to what I was saying before the pup interrupted me, it will be a bad omen if the living god does not make his appearance today. The people expect to see him come out of the temple looking like he could fight the whole lot of them without getting winded. If they have to bring him out in a chair, the crops will fail, the harvest will be poor, and the people will starve. So, we must hope that Seini, that young fool, can draw a little more life out of Pharaoh to make this one public appearance. Otherwise, that worshipful crowd down there is going to turn into a raging mob. And that won't be a pretty sight."

"You must have heard a very detailed rumor," Hapu said.

Khamenwati shrugged. "All I heard was that Pharaoh was ill and the co-regent isn't here. Let's hope the rest is speculation."

Hapu focused on the temple entrance, waiting for a sign of someone he recognized from the royal party that would have accompanied Pharaoh Setnakhte. "Were you here when Pharaoh's royal boat arrived?"

"I was. It's always good to get here early. You never know what you're going to see."

"Did you see who accompanied Pharaoh into the temple?"

"Four big Nubians carried Pharaoh's chair into the temple, which was unusual since he normally walks. Then there were the usual priests, Queen Teya, some harem women, and Seini, of course. The usual hangers-on. The rest of the court is stuck on the other boats until they allow them into the Sun Court outside the Chamber of the Divine King. Mayor Paweraa met Pharaoh at the landing along with the High Priest of Amun-Re, what's-his-name—Bakenkhons—and his sycophant, Merubaste."

Ray leaned over to whisper to his father. "Pasai?"

Hapu whispered over his shoulder. "Doesn't sound like it, but he could be elsewhere. There are other boats."

"Queen Teya may have news of Pen," Ray whispered.

Hapu nodded.

"Another odd thing," Khamenwati continued, "was that Pharaoh never came back out. He usually starts the procession at Karnak where the triad joins the parade."

"The triad?" Ray asked. He felt like an idiot for not knowing these things.

Hapu turned to Ray. "The priests at Karnak dress the *ka* image of Amun-Re in colorful clothes and jewelry, then place him in his golden shrine on top of the ceremonial boat. They carry the boat on their shoulders to the Khonsu Temple, where offerings are made and Khonsu's *ka* image joins the parade. Then they proceed down the Avenue of the Sphinxes to the Temple of Mut to pick up her *ka* image. That's the Theban triad. They all travel together on the Nile, on the golden *Userhetamon* barge, to the western gate of *this* temple, where Pharaoh's power is reborn. Mut and Khonsu aren't allowed in the Chamber of the Divine King, of course—they have their own chapels outside the Chamber."

Khamenwati snorted. "How old is the pup? He knows nothing of this?"

"He has been away," Hapu explained.

"Across the Great Green Sea, apparently, if he doesn't know about the Beautiful Feast of Opet."

Ray started to say something, but Hapu stopped him with a hand on his shoulder.

"That is odd that Pharaoh hasn't joined the parade already," Hapu said, trying to change the subject.

"We're doomed, if you ask me," Khamenwati said. "This doesn't look good at all. Might as well start loading my tomb with the things I'll need for the journey so that I can beat the rush."

Hapu looked away and coughed to stifle his laugh, sitting down on the edge of the roof.

As Ray scanned the crowd, he noticed some people he didn't want to see. Sermont and the Greek merchant had climbed onto the base of a statue to watch while four Medjay circulated through the crowd, mainly focused on the people accepting free bread and beer from the young priests on the temple steps. Could they still be looking for Ray and Tentopet two weeks after she escaped? It made him feel better, in a way, since it might mean that Tentopet was still free.

The babble of voices and singing among the crowd on the river bank got louder as the massive cedar wood barge of Amun-Re came into view, glittering in the sunlight. Towed by gangs of bald, white-clad priests on the embankment, the barge was covered in gold from the waterline all the way up to the sculpted heads of rams that decorated the high prow and the stern. The tall shrine of Amun-Re—gold studded with dozens of precious gems—rested on its own ceremonial golden boat placed on a raised platform toward the front of the barge. The god himself was hidden by yellow curtains that rippled in the breeze. The high priest and lector priest stood on the deck with their arms raised up to Amun-Re; blue incense smoke swirling around them as they chanted prayers. The boat shrines of Mut, the consort of Amun-Re, and Khonsu, their moon-god son, sat on lower platforms behind that of the King of All Gods. The three of them were known as the Theban Triad, the protectors of Thebes. The priests towing the barges were escorted by units of the Egyptian army in chariots and full battle gear, marching behind standards adorned with colorful streamers and brilliant plumes. The crowd cheered and chanted and rattled sistra while trumpets and drums played. Female dancers performed in the procession on the banks, their naked bodies shining with sweat as they leaped and twirled, keeping pace with the military escort ahead of them.

As the procession neared the Theban Temple, the high officials, nobles, and members of Pharaoh's court joined the line to enter the eastern Sun Court gate with bouquets of flowers. They were followed by cattle, decorated with feather plumes and dangling gold ornaments, ready to be sacrificed as offerings by Pharaoh.

When the golden barge made the turn into the manmade channel leading up to the ritual western gate of the temple, Ray noted something unique about the way that one of the dancers moved in the procession. When her head turned and he saw her smiling face, he realized why her movements looked familiar. It was Tentopet.

"She's here," Ray said, tapping Hapu on the arm and pointing before he ran for the stairway.

"Wait!" Startled, Hapu blinked and looked where Ray had been pointing, then jumped up to follow him. He motioned to Bull to stay where he was. "I'll be back. Stay here. Do you understand?"

Bull nodded.

Thinking about the dense crowd in the street and how hard it would be to force his way through them, Ray turned from the stairway and jumped off the edge of the roof. His arms flailing to help his balance, he sailed across the gap and landed on the flat roof of the temple. He fell and rolled, barely avoiding falling through one of the many spaces between the high columns that supported the Sun Court's ceiling. Unable to follow, Hapu ran toward the stairs.

It was harder to cross the temple roof than he had thought. He also had the problem of how he was going to get down. Climbing up on a limestone slab that supported a flag pole, he looked down at the long drop to the crowd in front of the temple, wondering whether he should go back to the school's roof and take the stairs down. On the temple steps, Sermont was huddled in conversation with the Greek merchant while pointing at the western end of the temple where Tentopet was approaching in the procession, now almost out of Ray's view from his high vantage point. She would be entering through the western ritual gate at the far end of the temple, while Sermont would only have access through the eastern gate of the Sun Court, assuming the priests would allow him inside on official business—which they might not on this special day. Apparently, Sermont came to the same conclusion. He signaled to two of the closer policemen and started to shove his way through the crowd with the Greek merchant in tow. Ray knew he had to act now.

The smoothest path to the western end of the temple was along the front ledge of the roof—it was narrow, but at least it didn't have any holes in it. He couldn't remember ever having been this high off the ground before, so the potentially fatal drop made him nervous, but he kept his mind fixed on his goal of warning Tentopet. Perhaps if they were able to escape, they would finally have a chance to talk and he could find out why she was wandering around in Thebes by herself. Ignoring the flutter in his stomach, he slowed his breathing, then released the flag pole and started his walk along the narrow ledge of hot stone. Although he tried not to look down and think about his impending death, he saw that the Medjay were making progress through the throng by shoving people out of the way. The occasional shout of dismay was lost in the ongoing roar of the crowd, which sounded like the Great River where it flowed over the rocks of the cataracts. Incense drifted up in clouds from the extra braziers added to the temple for the day, and the smoke made him dizzy. Why had he not taken the stairs and circled around through the edges of the crowd? The Medjay were getting through, so perhaps he could have as well. But it was too late now. If he turned back, Tentopet would be caught by the police, and probably returned to the Greek merchant as his property, and he couldn't allow that to happen.

At the western edge of the roof, a long wall ran parallel to the manmade boat channel and angled down toward the royal boat landing. The angle was steep and appeared to have been added after the stone temple was built, for it was made of mud brick, some of which had crumbled over the years. It was the only way down that Ray could see, and much steeper than he would have liked, but at least he wouldn't have to turn around and go back. The soldiers had turned away from the procession, leaving only the priests and the performers to accompany the ceremonial golden shrines of the gods through the ritual gate. Amun-Re's processional boat shrine had already been lifted onto the soldiers of the senior priests and the other two gods were about to be lifted from the barge. Tentopet and the others performed a dance of greeting, tossing flower necklaces at the gods from the stack by the gate as the ritual Second Song began:

Hail, Amun, primeval one of the Two Lands, foremost one of Karnak,
in your glorious appearance amidst your fleet,
on your Beautiful Festival of Opet—
May you be pleased with it!

Although it was quieter on this side of the temple, the singing and music kept Tentopet from hearing Ray's yells from the roof. That left no other option than to walk down the wall.

Although there were spots where bits of crumbling mud brick gave way beneath his feet, the stone caps on the wall continued to hold. He had covered about half the distance to the royal landing when people started to notice that he was up there. Faces looked up from the crowd. Unfortunately, some of those faces belonged to the Medjay, and bits of crumbling brick landed on their faces when they looked up. Sermont gestured for his policemen to move faster, but they were approaching a wall of veteran Egyptian soldiers assigned to keep the crowd back from the royal dock and the ritual gate. Even the Medjay would have trouble getting through them, for these soldiers were dressed for the parade in full battle gear, including chariots, spears, and swords.

Ray thought he might actually make it to the royal landing unharmed when another chunk of the wall crumbled beneath his feet. He dropped to a crouch to try and recover his balance, but he only managed to bump his shoulder and the back of his head as he fell, tumbling in the air until he hit the water of the boat channel below.

Disoriented from his fall and the bump on his head, Ray spluttered to the surface in time to see Sermont, the Greek merchant, and his policemen come around the end of the royal landing escorted by two soldiers. By the time he swam around Amun's barge and climbed out of the water, he saw the frightened look on Tentopet's face as she and the other performers turned in the entrance to the temple to see what was going on. She said something to the older woman in charge of her group and immediately disappeared inside the temple. Knowing that Sermont would quickly catch up to her, Ray dove back into the water and swam across the gap to intercept the policemen on the other side of the channel.

He arrived just in time to receive a beating by the two Medjay. Sermont simply kicked Ray and ran past him with the Greek merchant. The soldiers looked confused, then decided that Ray was capably being beaten by the policemen, so they ran after Sermont. While Ray wondered if the Medjay would ever stop pounding on him, he heard a commotion at the ritual gate where Tentopet had disappeared, and caught brief glimpses of the older performer in the doorway shouting at Sermont and the Greek. When the two soldiers caught up to them, they drew their swords and threatened Sermont when he tried to get past her into the temple. With his lungs seemingly on fire, and barely able to breathe now, Ray was pleased that something had worked out right. Then he passed out.

Didu and Nebamun were once again sharing a chariot at the head of the long army column that stretched away to the dunes on the horizon. Bringing up the rear, currently out of Didu's view, were the captives from their most recent battles, eating dust and probably getting excited as they spotted the Great River nearby. The army was back in the fertile Black Lands along the Nile Delta, and they could now see the royal city of Pi-Ramesses rising ahead of them like a mirage in the hot desert. Didu also knew they were approaching the river due to the character of the flies that now buzzed around their heads, which were smaller and lighter than the three gold flies that hung around his neck. Ten days had passed since he'd received Pharaoh's gift, but he was still undecided as to the best course for his future. Nebamun had not helped him decide, as he tended to focus on the things that would make him happier sooner rather than later, and he didn't understand why everyone else didn't think the same way.

"You'd think those three gold flies would have given you more wisdom," Nebamun said, shifting his grip on the division standard that flew above their heads.

"They're not gods. Gold doesn't bring wisdom all by itself."

"Doesn't hurt. You can buy wisdom with gold, right? You could ask a temple oracle what to do. The priests would probably let you spend all day in Amun-Re's Hearing Ear shrine for the price of one of those flies."

"I'm not giving them away. Pharaoh gave them to me."

Nebamun shrugged. "That's true. It might not make the best impression on him if you gave them away as soon as you got back to the city. Best to wait a while."

Didu sighed and looked at Pharaoh's chariot. He was busy dictating the truth to Pasenhor, who was having a difficult time trying to take legible notes in his hieratic script while the chariot bounced around. Didu had seen some of his notes and wondered how Pasenhor could read them at all.

"Did General Hori have any advice for you?" Nebamun asked.

"The general has more important things to worry about."

"So he hasn't spoken to you?"

"No."

"Maybe that's why he's moving up beside us."

Didu glanced over his shoulder, surprised that Hori's chariot had managed to get so close without him seeing it. Too much daydreaming could get a man killed in the army.

When Hori pulled up alongside their chariot, he stared at Didu for a moment as if he'd already asked him something.

"Yes, general?" Didu asked.

"Pharaoh wants your decision. And so do I. Don't think that things will get any easier for you either way. Just because the living god has taken a liking to you doesn't mean that I can't have you executed if you get out of line. I think you've got a long way to go before you could be promoted to command, although I'm willing to teach you if Pharaoh orders it. That's if you stay in the army, of course. If not, you're on your own, and you're not going to like it."

Since Hori was staring at him with an expectant expression, Didu felt like he had to say something. "Yes, general."

"Made up your mind yet? Or are you as undecided as an old woman choosing fruit at the market? Not a good quality for a commander, if you ask me."

"I need to think about it some more," Nebamun said.

Hori rolled his eyes and pulled his chariot ahead to talk with Pharaoh, spraying them with dust at the same time.

"I think he just gave you advice," Nebamun said.

"Was he trying to encourage me to stay, or does he want me to go?"

Nebamun shrugged. "I'm not the one wearing the Gold of Valor. I'm just a simple soldier. You tell me. I never understand a word he says."

Didu wished he had a better understanding of the ways of generals. They knew so many things that it could be hard to understand them at times. Maybe that's what Hori meant when he said Didu still had a lot of things to learn.

Nebamun nudged him in this side. "What's this?"

A light chariot was hurtling toward them from the city. When it got closer, Didu saw that one of the princes was driving it—Pentawere.

Pharaoh looked up and said something to General Hori, who raised his arm to halt the long column. The signal rippled back through the long procession, which would take a while to stop because it was only a little easier than trying to halt the flow of the Nile.

Pentawere slowed his horses and stopped between Didu, General Hori, and Pharaoh. "To the great king of the Two Lands of Kemet, my lord Pharaoh, Beloved of Amun, favored one of Re, father of us all, king of battle, may you live a long life of great prosperity and health forever and ever. Behold! The city weeps and its tears fill the Nile after so long a time without your great wisdom and divine guidance. Help us, my father, and rescue this land from the hands of those who bring evil. Let the city and the royal house of Pharaoh not perish. May all be well with thee and your mighty arm that will deliver us to safety. The evil ones will be like birds in a net as soon as you return bringing divine justice. This is for the information of the king, my lord!"

Pharaoh waited a moment, then twirled his hand. "Go on, young Pentawere. What is your urgent news that prompts you to interrupt us out here after our long journey?"

"There are many ears in the city, great Pharaoh. I bring you news that you may decide how to respond before those who would make you blind by day are able to speak. Three weeks ago, the palace was attacked by assassins in the night."

"I know of this," Pharaoh said.

"Of course, my lord, your eyes and ears are everywhere. So, you must know that your son, Amanakhopshaf, is on his way to join the great god Osiris beyond the western horizon? You know also that your son, Ramesses IV, who shares the great name of the conqueror with you, has been captured by these same assassins?"

Didu had never seen that look of horror on Pharaoh's face before. If the gods had told him of the death of Amana and the capture of Bull, this could just be a clever performance for those who were watching, but it certainly seemed as if this were news to the living god.

"Meryey's men," Hori growled. "As Mesher foretold."

"Did you see these assassins?" Pharaoh asked Pentawere, his voice flat.

"I saw only men dressed as priests of Osiris who brought death in the night. Cowards who would not dare to face the mighty arm of Pharaoh in open battle. I, myself, did what I could to stop them, receiving many injuries in the attempt, but some of our own people—may their names be erased from the tongues of the living and from all monuments that they may die the true death—they helped the assassins with their evil and cowardly tasks."

"If you speak the truth, say the names of these men that they may die the true death without delay," Pharaoh said.

"My efforts to save Bull were thwarted by the formerly trusted Pasai, who waits for you in the palace to spread his lies. And he was helped by the formerly trusted teacher, Hapu, and his son, my former friend, the formerly trusted Ray, whose name I can now barely speak without spitting on the ground."

As each name was spoken, Pharaoh's eyes got wider. First Pasai, whom he had entrusted with the combat training of his children, then Hapu, who was like his own brother and was acknowledged as one of the wisest men in his administration. But when Pen spoke the name of Ray, royal friend and trusted companion of his children, the breath seemed to leave him and he sagged against the side of the chariot, the horse reins falling from his hand, alarming Pasenhor, who didn't know whether to risk catching Pharaoh to support him. No one touched Pharaoh without permission, and Pasenhor made the wise decision not to set a precedent.

After a moment, Pharaoh looked up at the sky and raised his arms. "Why? Why have you forsaken me, Amun-Re? Behold! Have I not built for you many temples and statues? Have I not brought you offerings of food, incense, and riches of all kinds? Have I not accepted the office that you, in your divine wisdom, and my father have given me as the great chief mouth of the lands of Egypt and commander of the whole land united in one? Have I not brought you captives and enriched your temples and your lands? Have I not stopped the enemies of Egypt and brought Maat back to the world, though the task was like gathering the wind between my two hands? All this, great god, and yet you allow an abomination in my household while I fight your wars? Why have you forsaken me?"

Didu realized he was watching something that he shouldn't be seeing. He wished he could back the chariot away from the scene before him, but to do so would draw attention, so his only hope was to disappear by not moving. He knew Nebamun was staring at him, and he fervently hoped that the gods would keep Nebamun's mindless tongue silent a while longer until they were a safe distance away from Pharaoh's ears. As for General Hori and Pasenhor, they stood transfixed, afraid that the gods might strike them down at any moment, or that Pharaoh might turn his anger on them. The only person who didn't seem to think he was about to join the great Osiris was Pentawere, who was nodding in agreement at everything Pharaoh said.

Pharaoh looked down and slowly turned smoldering eyes on Pentawere. "Where is my father, the breath of Horus, the living god Setnakhte?"

Pentawere seemed uncertain for a moment, glancing at the rest of them, then returned his eyes to Pharaoh. "It is the Beautiful Feast of Opet, my lord. Pharaoh Setnakhte—may he live a long life of prosperity and health—is in Thebes to celebrate the festival."

Pharaoh nodded, calmer now, his eyes haunted by death. "So much time has passed. I had forgotten. You have done well to bring this news,

Pentawere. You will return to the city with me in my chariot and I will honor you for attempting to save your brothers. And then we must get to the palace immediately, for our borders have been invaded from within, and I cannot allow that to continue."

Pasenhor quickly stepped out of Pharaoh's chariot and scuttled to safety so that Pentawere could take his place. One of Hori's generals took the reins of Pentawere's chariot.

With a look back at Didu, who stopped breathing when he saw Pharaoh's eyes, the living god beckoned for him to follow in his chariot. "Your decision is made. I have a task for you."

Inside Pi-Ramesses, seated on a leather stool in the audience chamber of Queen Isis, Pasai felt uncomfortable. Having never been alone in the presence of Pharaoh's Chief Royal Wife, he found the scent of her perfumed oils disturbing. As usual, she was immaculately dressed in a pleated white gown with gilded sandals, her delicate lips and eyebrows painted for maximum effect, her long black wig layered and shaped to perfection. She wore less jewelry than the rest of the harem women, possibly because her own beauty was enough, limiting herself to a pair of gold anklets and two gold bracelets set with blue lapis lazuli. Her posture was perfect and her expression calm as she rested on an ebony chair set with ivory and colored stones. More so than the other wives of Pharaoh, she actually looked like a queen.

"This delay worries me," Isis said. "Sesi—my husband—should have been here by now."

Pasai nodded. They would wait in this audience chamber until they were summoned by the living god Ramesses III. Pasai could do nothing about it, so he simply sat and waited as a military man always waited. Of course, there were better rooms in the palace to do this waiting. The audience chamber had light-colored walls painted with relaxing floral motifs and river scenes of water birds and fish. The strange tiles on the floor were made of blue glass, giving the odd sensation that they were sitting on water that didn't move. A woman's place. In Pharaoh's audience chamber, designed to intimidate foreign kings and commoners summoned into the royal presence, the wall decorations were not relaxing, and bound enemies were depicted on the floor so that Pharaoh could walk on them.

"Do you say nothing, Pasai? I don't see how my husband could be so attached to you when you don't even talk. I know nothing about you. Were you born, or were you hatched from an egg like an eagle?"

"I was born into a poor farming family, my queen. My father's father was a member of the royal bodyguard for Ramesses the Great when he built Pi-Ramesses, but my own father lost his land after Ramesses died and became a great god. The Tjehenu tribes crossed the border and raided the area of our farm many times, killing my mother and father, and taking me as a captive. I was young and they worked me hard until I managed to escape into the desert."

"Ah, so you're a hardy creature of the desert, is that it? I can see how my husband would like that. Is there more to the story?"

Pasai shrugged. "I lived in a cave for many years, hunting game and watching the horizon for anyone who might come after me, but they never came. They probably thought I'd die out there too quickly to bother about. There was a spring in the cave, so I had water to drink, food to eat, and plenty of time to think."

A slight smile lit up her face. "Some would say living in a cave and hunting every day would be the ideal life for a man."

"Yes, mistress. And some would not," Pasai said. "When I was sure the Tjehenu wouldn't come after me, I watched for trade caravans passing through the area. I found one heading toward Thebes, and one of the traders found work for me when we arrived. I was big, so they made me a stonecutter in the granite quarries of Wadi Hammamat."

Isis's eyebrows rose to form two neat arches over her dark brown eyes. "Apparently you survived the quarries."

"I was still young. I know that many of the slaves and the foreigners died there, but many said it was better than working in the mines. The quarry foreman fed me and watched out for me as if I were his son, so he eventually advised me to leave. I was old enough by then, so I joined Pharaoh's army when I reached Thebes."

"I'm surprised that you didn't go with my husband to fight the Tjehenu this time. Don't you hate them for killing your parents?"

Pasai studied her a moment, thinking about his answer. "I've killed many Tjehenu. I would kill more if Pharaoh wishes it. But this time, he asked if I would stay and teach his children the ways of war. He sees no lasting peace in our future. Our lands are rich and we have enemies on all sides. The children must learn to defend themselves and lead armies into battle."

Isis's voice lost its warmth as she looked at the ceiling with its pattern of blue lotus blossoms. "As Amana was learning? It did him no good when his time came. How can our children protect themselves from cowards who attack in the night? And what of Bull? He may also have gone to join Osiris." She looked away and brushed at the tears on her face. "Tentopet is missing. Perhaps she ran away with Ray with Hapu's help. Perhaps she was taken by the assassins. Who can say? So many children lost in such a short time. The news will destroy Sesi. As it has destroyed me."

Isis sagged in her chair, the tears flowing freely on her face. Pasai had not told her the truth of what he knew. When he returned to the palace after safely leaving prince Ramesses IV with Ray and Hapu in his own home, he felt that there was no one he could trust with the information until Pharaoh returned. He also felt a duty to protect Queen Isis, now weakened by the loss of her children. He had managed to watch her from a distance each day, keeping her safe while keeping his own secrets. Although he wanted to do so, he couldn't tell her the truth because she might tell others who would use the information against her and the rest of the royal family. There were too many ears and too many tongues in the palace to keep such secrets, especially among the harem. However, seeing her now, seeing how she grieved for her children, and aware that he could break his silence in a private audience with the living god Ramesses when he returned, his own resolve weakened. He had to say something.

"I've had reports, my queen. I know that young Ramesses IV escaped from the assassins that night."

Her head snapped around to face him, her eyes flaring. "You've had reports! Why would you keep this from me, Pasai?"

Pasai felt uncomfortable again. Women were so unpredictable. "For your own safety, my queen."

"My safety! Do you understand the world that I live in? You know nothing of life in the palace, or the constant, quiet wars of the harem! My life is at risk every day! If you have information about my children, your duty is to give it to me, their mother, immediately!"

Pasai bowed his head. "I'm sorry, mistress. I am but dust on your feet; a humble defender of your family who has no right to keep information from you. But I must do what I feel is right for the safety of you and your family. When Pharaoh arrives, I will say everything I know."

The heavy door to the chamber burst open and Pharaoh Ramesses III strode into the room. "Then you would do well to speak the truth, Pasai! And quickly!"

Pasai dropped to his knees, bowed, and held out his arms with his palms up. The gold fly on the chain around his neck dangled against his chin. "My lord Pharaoh—may you live a long life of prosperity and good health! Great is the pleasure in my heart at your return—"

Pharaoh bent down and pushed Pasai's head so that he sat back on his heels. The eyes that stared into Pasai's face looked like those of a god prepared to engulf his victim in fire. "Enough! Give me your news, Pasai!"

Surprised by Pharaoh's reaction, Pasai started to speak, then saw prince Pentawere appear in the doorway with armed soldiers standing behind him. "Young master!"

"You seem surprised to see my son," Pharaoh said, gripping Pasai's face with his right hand. "Did you think he was dead?"

Queen Isis answered first. "Pasai may not have known he was in the palace." She gave Pasai a significant look. "You see, I have secrets of my own."

"I don't understand," Pasai said, thoroughly confused now.

Pharaoh released his grip and took a step back, looming over him. "You don't have to understand, Pasai. What you must do is speak the truth. Now."

Pasai glanced at Pentawere, suspicious of his presence. If he had returned to the palace freely and without deception, Pasai would have known about it. Something must have happened to prince Ramesses, Ray, and Hapu, but why would Pentawere keep that a secret? And why would Queen Isis keep Pentawere's presence a secret?

Pentawere stepped into the room, the soldiers moving up behind him in the doorway. "See how he takes too long to respond? He's going to lie. He can't be trusted now. We should take him outside to interview him properly. "

"Why would I lie?" Pasai asked, looking up at Pharaoh, whose hand was now resting on the haft of his curved khepesh sword. "I will speak the truth, my lord, but I can only do so in your presence. Alone. My information is too important for other ears."

Queen Isis hissed through her teeth. "Then you just lied to *me*, Pasai. Who do you think you are?"

"My queen—" Pasai began, only to find the tip of Pharaoh's sword in front of his face.

"I trusted you, Pasai. I let you teach my children. And guard them. Your people have been loyal to us for generations. You fought bravely for me in many battles. Why have you done this? Why should I not kill you immediately?"

Before Pasai could answer, Pentawere took another step forward and beckoned to the soldiers, who swarmed into the room to surround Pasai while keeping well back of the angry Pharaoh. "We must question him first. We will encourage his tongue to give us the truth."

Pharaoh stood up straight, his face a mask of stone. Then he yanked the gold chain around Pasai's neck, taking back the Gold of Valor. "Take him."

Sermont smiled as he punched Ray in the stomach again. "Just like the old days, eh? Remember how I used to greet you in the street?"

Ray groaned, knowing quite well how Sermont would beat him in the street whenever he showed any sign of weakness, or illness, or simply not paying enough attention to him. Now, he felt as if he'd gone back in time to when he was young and living in Thebes. He leaned against the crumbling mud brick wall of the dark cell to steady himself.

"Not feeling talkative? Don't you want to tell me why you keep interfering with Thales?"

"Who is Thales?" Ray croaked. A torch in the hallway provided sufficient light for him to look down and see the blood and the bruises on his body.

Sermont punched him again. "Come now, Ray. You must know Thales. He's the Greek merchant you stole from."

"I didn't steal anything."

"You stole the woman. Tyti. His property. He has the legal papers recording the sale."

"No. I don't understand. She's—" Ray cut himself off before he blurted out her identity.

Sermont leaned in close to his face. "She's what? Did you think she was your own personal toy? Many men have had her, you know. She worked for the House of Kifi."

Ray shook his head. "I don't know the place you're talking about. You're lying."

"Oh? Bold words for a thief." Sermont tipped Ray's head forward and studied the bloody bruise where he had hit his head on the wall during his fall into the boat channel. "That's a nasty looking bump you've got there." Then he slammed Ray's head back against the wall. The pain that had been lurking in the back of his head suddenly overshadowed every other pain that he was feeling. He bent over and dumped his morning meal on the floor of the cell.

Sermont nudged him in the side with his foot. "Stealing a woman is not a minor offense, Ray. The magistrate will not be pleased. If you tell me why you stole her, perhaps I can say that you feel sorry for the damage you've done to Thales and his reputation. Maybe I can get Thales to accept an appropriate payment from you for his loss."

Ray opened his eyes. "For his loss?"

"Yes. The loss of his legal property. I'm sure he'd want to make a profit on his purchase, of course, but he seems like a reasonable man. There will be other costs, too, to pay for my time, the use of my best men, court fees, and so on. But I'm sure you can afford all that."

"Did she escape?"

Sermont laughed. "Ah, I see! Now that we get down to it, you're hoping to give her up in exchange! What a weak little man you are, Ray. You steal the woman, but you won't fight to keep her. Typical of you scribes—you all think you're so superior until you need people to fight your wars or grow your grain. So, tell me where she's hiding and I'll see what I can do."

Ray looked at Sermont's foot. He was too tired and sore to be clever, but he felt better knowing that Tentopet was still free. "I don't know where she is."

Sermont sighed. "You must think I'm a fool, is that it? Are you trying to trick me?"

"No," Ray said, sitting down on the floor, his head spinning with the drumbeat in his skull. "I don't know where she is."

"I'm sorry to hear that." Sermont reached behind his back and pulled a short leather whip with multiple tails out of his loincloth's waistband. "You know, people misunderstand me. I don't actually *like* inflicting pain—most of the time. I represent the law. Justice. I'm the only thing that stands between the average person in this city and people like you who don't think you have to follow the rules. You can't go around stealing things just because you feel privileged. We all belong to Pharaoh—even me—and I have to enforce his laws to maintain order. If someone gets out of line, I pull them back into line. The law is the law."

"I can't help you," Ray said, bracing himself for the blow of the whip.

"Stand up," Sermont said.

Ray slowly stood and turned to face the crumbling mud-brick wall of the cell. He closed his eyes so that he'd have a chance of keeping his eyes if he survived.

Ray heard footsteps in the hard sand of the corridor.

"Sermont. Wait," said a deep voice that Ray didn't recognize. Someone else gasped.

"Mayor Paweraa," Sermont said. "How nice to see you. Did you come to watch?"

Ray turned and saw a fat man dressed in a pleated white gown of fine linen. He wore a heavy collar of office around his neck that appeared to be made from electrum, shiny with golden highlights, colored stones, and a red scarab in its center. It looked heavy enough that he had to be wearing a counterweight behind his back, but Ray couldn't see it from where he was standing. He also couldn't see the man standing in the shadows behind him.

"Certainly not," Paweraa said. He spoke with a slight accent that sounded like he might have been schooled in Memphis, but he pronounced each letter of each word with sharp clarity. "You will release this man. He is free to go."

Sermont dropped his whip. "What?"

"You will hold him no longer. He can go."

"Why? Do you realize what he's done?"

Paweraa stared at Sermont as if he were an idiot. "Of course I know what you *think* he's done, but there is no proof. I've already spoken to the magistrate."

"No proof? I was there when he took the girl from the Greek!"

"No, you were in the area, but the Greek came to you with his complaint. You saw nothing."

Sermont spread his hands. "That's not true! Ray ran from me with the girl! He interfered with the Greek when he tried to catch her! They both got away the first time, and if it weren't for my watchful eyes that see everything in this city, he would have gotten away with his crime. Then he interfered with me again at the temple this morning!"

Paweraa waved his hand to dismiss the argument. "As I said, you have no real proof. You have a frightened young woman and a man who tried to save her, or so he thought."

"Thales has legal documents! He owns the woman!"

"Documents can also lie. There isn't enough proof to hold him. And you've beaten him sufficiently if there was, in fact, any wrongdoing. Now, release him!"

Sermont took a step back when Paweraa raised his voice. "Someone has paid you, Mayor."

"The government of Pharaoh has spoken," Paweraa said.

"Then I should be paid as well. Who *is* that behind you in the shadows?"

Hapu stepped forward into the light, glaring at Sermont.

"I see," Sermont said. "Scribe, you have placed your trust in the wrong person. You don't think our good mayor will remember you after you leave this place, do you?"

Paweraa put his hand on Hapu's shoulder and stared at Sermont. "You will get nothing. You will do your job. Let the boy go."

Grumbling, Sermont grabbed Ray by his most injured shoulder and shoved him out of the cell. Hapu caught him before he fell.

As they turned to leave, Sermont laughed softly. "You've made a mistake, scribe. Both of you have. You don't want me as your enemy."

"You are your own enemy," Hapu said over his shoulder, guiding Ray down the corridor with the mayor's help.

Just after dawn, Didu received the summons he had been expecting. The anticipation of this meeting had interfered with his sleep, which was difficult enough on the mats in the Pi-Ramesses barracks. Noise wasn't a problem, as most of the soldiers had crossed the river to seek entertainment that night and had not returned afterward. He could only imagine what it had been like when thousands of the men had descended on the town like ravening locusts. No, his problem with sleeping had more to do with his recent fear of being enclosed, as if any building he slept in represented the tomb he would someday occupy. Unlike many of his compatriots, he did not look forward to the eternal sleep of death or the rewards he might receive from Osiris in the afterlife. He was not a rich man who could afford an elaborate tomb or beautification by the sem-priests. He preferred to sleep out in the open, under the night sky, with rocks or sand under his back and weapons for a pillow.

Wearing the clean kilt that a servant had provided, Didu acknowledged the guards at the entrance to the public throne room of Pharaoh's golden house and was allowed to enter. He'd been in this room twice before for ceremonial occasions, but never for a private audience with Pharaoh. Limestone columns carved and painted to look like giant lotus flowers held up the high ceiling. The light from the small windows near the ceiling was not strong enough to make out a lot of the details on the columns. He liked the walls, which were decorated with scenes of bound captives and lions eating prisoners. The floors continued that style of decoration. Yes, the Two Lands had many enemies, and it took a strong Pharaoh to maintain control over such a vast country. Food was laid out on a low table with a variety of meats, bread, fruit, and milk, but Didu knew it wasn't meant for him.

The incense burning in the braziers made Didu sneeze. As his eyes adjusted to the dim light of the few lamps that were burning, he detected the odd sight of a dwarf eating Pharaoh's food. When he got closer, the dwarf gave him a menacing look.

"Are you supposed—" Didu began.

The dwarf cut him off. "I'm Pepi, Steward of the Pantry and Protector of Pharaoh. You're Didu, I assume?"

"I am."

"Don't speak again until someone speaks to you."

Didu raised one eyebrow. He didn't feel like conversing with the dwarf, but it annoyed him to be told to remain silent. He started to respond when the living god Ramesses III quickly walked into the room and sat on his golden throne on its raised dais. His elbow bumped a small bowl of dates that had been placed on the armrest.

"Get out, little man," Pharaoh said, waving him away from the food.

"My lord, I'm not finished tasting yet."

"Go eat somewhere else. I have no need of you."

"My lord, it's my duty to—"

Pharaoh picked up the bowl of dates and threw it at Pepi, who ducked just in time to avoid having a dent made in his head. "Get out, or I'll have your head!"

Pepi scuttled away and Pharaoh turned his gaze on Didu, who immediately dropped to his knees, placed his forehead on the stone floor decorated with enemies, and held out his arms. "My lord, the good god of the Two Lands, great in—"

"Get *up*! We don't have time for these formalities!"

Didu had never seen Pharaoh in such an anxious state. Even in battle, he rarely raised his voice. He stood up and fixed his eyes on the wall beyond Pharaoh's head, not daring to look him in the eyes.

"You recall I said I had a task for you yesterday?"

"Yes, my lord."

"The task has become urgent. You will leave here today with a sealed order that will give you access to whatever you need." He paused for a moment. "Didu, what *are* you looking at?"

"Sorry, my lord." He shifted his gaze to Pharaoh's face.

"Am I boring you? Do you have better things to do? A woman to see? Beer to drink?"

"No, my lord."

"Then pay attention because I'm only going to say this once. I'm giving you a task. It could take hours to complete, or it could take months. If you succeed in this task, you will have no worries for the rest of your life. You will have a house, a comfortable job for your old age, and a tomb. However, if you *fail* in this task, as the gods are my witness, your life will be too short for you to worry at all. Do you understand me?"

"I do, my lord Pharaoh."

"Take this. It will give you power." Pharaoh tossed a sealed papyrus roll on the floor in front of Didu, who picked it up while keeping his eyes on Pharaoh's face.

"You are to choose one man to go with you. This must be a man you can trust, who will obey without question and act without details. The particulars of this task will be known only to you. If you're killed along the way, the other man must destroy that document and report back to me without delay. If you're gone for more than two weeks, you must send me reports on your progress. Use the Medjay as messengers. Do you understand?"

Didu nodded. "I do, my lord."

"As to the task itself, you must never give anyone else these details. General Hori is the only other person who will know what you're doing. Pentawere may ask, but you should not speak with him. You are to seek out three people who left this palace on the night that Meryey's assassins attacked. Witnesses have told me that they may have been involved with the assassins, whether because they were bribed or for some other reason, I don't know. I'll have to question them myself. When you find them, they may not wish to return with you freely. Tell them that I've summoned them myself. If they don't comply, you can do whatever is necessary to bring them back. Use force if you must, but do *not* kill them under any circumstances. One of them is my son, Prince Ramesses IV, whose thoughts were invaded by evil spirits when he nearly drowned in the Nile. He, most of all, must be kept safe. Second is Ray, son of Hapu, whom you've seen in the presence of my children. Do you remember what he looks like?"

Didu remembered seeing Ray practice with weapons alongside Pharaoh's children. "Yes, my lord."

"The third person is Hapu, tutor to my children. I am most suspicious of his role in this matter. I know of no reason that would have caused him to harm Amanakhopshaf or my other children, but the palace breeds strange relationships and people's minds can be twisted. The palace is a nest of vipers, especially when I'm away for any length of time."

As Didu suspected, this all had to do with the report Pentawere had made to Pharaoh outside the city walls. He nodded, glad that he'd be out in the open air again, at least for a while.

"General Hori will give you the supplies you need. He'll also tell you where to start looking. We have a captive who provided us with the necessary information, but we can't say for certain what may have happened to them after they crossed the river."

Didu wondered if Prince Pentawere had caught one of the assassins, which would explain why he was able to supply Pharaoh with this information. Then he remembered that the prince had mentioned Pasai being a traitor, which he found hard to believe. He didn't know Pasai that well, but he had seen his accomplishments on the battlefield, and he had never seen a better, or more loyal, soldier in Pharaoh's army.

"I see what you're thinking, Didu. Yes, Pasai is our captive. The vipers of the palace can reach anyone. Pasai will remain alive until you return. If Pentawere interpreted the events correctly, Pasai will be executed when you return. Do you have any questions?"

"No, my lord. My heart is filled with gladness at this opportunity to demonstrate, once again, my complete loyalty to you. May you live a long, prosperous, and healthy life with many children—"

Pharaoh waved him away. "Yes, yes. The children. Get to your task! You have no time to waste, for your life truly does hang in the balance before Osiris."

Didu bowed and backed away.

Once he was across the river, Didu started at the beer hall that he knew to be Nebamun's favorite. Smashed furniture, broken beer cups, and unconscious soldiers lay strewn about the room. When Didu entered, a frightened old man jumped up from a chair with a battle axe in his trembling hands. After Didu explained that he only wanted to find Nebamun, the man gestured at the broken furniture and told him where Nebamun probably went after he was thrown out the previous night. From one beer hall to the next, the story was the same. Along the way, Didu looked in on the House of Kifi, where a young woman named Harere said Nebamun had left only two hours earlier. She had no idea where he went, but he had seemed at peace when he left.

Annoyed, frustrated, and anxious, Didu slowly walked down the nearly deserted early morning streets of the city. The air was filled with the odors of urine and fish. He sighed—at least Pasai's house wouldn't be far from here. Almost ready to give up hunting for Nebamun and start his quest without him, he stopped suddenly when he heard a familiar voice drifting through the open doors of the Temple of Montu, the god of war. Knowing he might be hallucinating, he ascended the stone steps and penetrated the thick cloud of incense to view the dimly lit interior of the audience room. One large man was kneeling in front of the shrine to Montu. The image of the god—"the raging one who prevails over the serpent-demon"—had a man's body with the head of a falcon. He was crowned with the solar disk, adorned with two vertical feather plumes and two snakes. In his hands, he held two spears. A god favored by soldiers, he was also known as the protector of the happy home.

"Tell me, great Montu. Answer my prayer," Nebamun said, spreading his arms.

Didu saw fresh offerings of meat and fruit on the altar in front of the shrine.

"Hear me, Montu. Take of my offerings and give me your guidance."

Finally, Nebamun sighed and dropped his arms to his sides. He bowed, rose to his feet, and turned to see Didu standing there waiting for him.

"Didu! How did you find me? Did the god send you?"

"Actually, Pharaoh sent me."

Nebamun looked back at the image of Montu. "Thank you, Montu. You've given me the answer. You are wise."

"I have a task," Didu began.

"Of course you do," Nebamun said, quite cheerful as he took Didu by the arm and led him out into the street. "And I'm going with you."

THE END

For more information, and to sign up for the newsletter, please visit https://brucebalfour.com

Here's your chance to read the first chapter of the next book in The Harem Conspiracy series, *The House of Death*:

ONE

1184 BCE—Thebes

Year 4 of His Majesty, King of Upper and Lower Egypt, Chosen by Re, Beloved of Amun, Pharaoh Setnakhte, Second Month of Akhet (Season of Inundation), Day 18

Khenti and Ruta followed the same route from the Valley of the Kings to the river that they had used successfully on their first trip. The sled was heavier this time since Khenti had widened the tunnel opening enough to get larger gold and silver objects out of the tomb. Only one Medjay patrol passed them in the darkness, and then they were past the high point of their trail and it was easier dragging the sled down the long slope to the tall reeds of the river bank. With his usual timing, Neferabu met them at just the right moment to avoid having to drag the heavy sled any farther. He had, however, arranged for the Greek trading boat to meet them at the pyramid rocks once more.

"It will be our old friend, Thales, again," Neferabu said, making a little bed out of the reeds so that he could rest. "He has three boats with him on this trip, with just enough room left to take tonight's cargo. The rest of what we dig up will have to be sold to someone else. Or we can wait a few months until Thales returns from the Great Green."

While Neferabu settled himself down and closed his eyes, Khenti looked up into the partial face of the moon-god, Khonsu. "Perhaps we should stop."

Neferabu sat up, his eyes alert. "Stop? Why?"

"Because this is a dangerous occupation," Khenti said. "Because it's hard work digging at night after I spend the day digging somewhere else. Because I'm tired!"

"Quiet," Neferabu whispered. "Keep your voice down."

"Will you listen to me if I do?"

"Of course, my old friend. I always listen to you. And I understand how tired you must be. What if I help you dig?"

"Not to offend, Nef, but you're an artist, not a quarryman. Your arms are small and weak. You would only be in my way in the small spaces of the tomb."

"Ruta helps you," Neferabu said, pointing at the silent boy watching them with wide eyes.

"Yes. He drags rocks out of the tunnel. He scampers like a ferret among the rubble and carries small things to the sled. He brings me water. So, you see, I don't need your help in the tomb."

"Ah, but can he help you lift the heavy things? Can he entertain you with his amusing stories? These are things only I can do."

Ruta stuck his tongue out at Neferabu, but then he smiled. His teeth glowed in the moonlight.

Khenti sighed. "I don't know. It seems to me that the longer we spend digging in the tomb, the more likely it is that the Medjay will find us. Or the necropolis priests. I'm a simple man—I don't wish to be impaled on a stick or have my nose and ears removed. I like them right where they are."

"Just think of the wealth we'd be leaving behind, Khenti. Think of all we could do with it. We could live like pharaohs ourselves with nice houses, our own harems, many children, plenty of food, and our own harems."

"You said harems twice."

Neferabu smiled. "Maybe I did. A man can always use more than one harem. And what about your family? I know you're thinking of your widowed mother and what she'll need now that her husband is gone. And your sisters can't support themselves. They all depend on you. What would it hurt to give them a little more than you had planned?"

Khenti slapped at a big mosquito on his arm. "I must think on this."

"That's all I ask. I'm sure that my old friend will arrive at the best decision for himself, for me, and for his family. Not to forget little Ruta here." Neferabu said, patting the boy's head.

The sound of wood scraping along the reeds warned them that the boat was coming. A silhouette appeared against the moon. The boat was about the same size as the last one with two masts and the same gaudy decorations painted on the outside. Neferabu stood so that he could help tie the mooring line to the pyramid rocks.

While a sailor helped Neferabu into the boat, Khenti and Ruta started removing things from the sled to speed the unloading. They had been fortunate so far to avoid the Medjay patrols, but he didn't want to push their luck. A few minutes later, Neferabu and the sailors brought nets to help them load the cargo onto the boat. Thales watched the entire process from the bow with a big smile on his face.

Ruta was just going back for two gold *ushabti* figures—servants intended to help the tomb owners in the afterlife—when he heard the sound of a chariot moving slowly toward them on the the path beside the river. Leaving the gold figures behind on the sled, he turned and ran back to the boat to tell Khenti and Neferabu what he had heard.

Thales reacted quickly. A sword appeared in his hand, which alarmed Khenti and Neferabu, but he used it to cut the mooring line that secured the boat to the pyramid rocks. Motioning for his passengers to remain quiet, he disappeared beyond the cargo stacked on the deck. The boat turned in graceful silence and moved off toward the middle of the river.

When they were a safe distance away from the bank, Thales returned with what appeared to be two big jugs of beer cradled in his arms. "Your payment, my friends. It has been a profitable evening for all of us."

Khenti wondered why they were being paid in beer, but he started to catch on when he noticed the loud thump each jug made when Thales set them down on a crate in front of them. Neferabu smiled and reached inside one of them, withdrawing a handful of silver ingots and gold rings. As each one dropped back into the jug, it made a metallic *tink*! sound.

"Music to my ears," Neferabu said.

Khenti looked into the other jug and saw shiny things in the moonlight. He plucked out one of the rings and put it on Ruta's thumb, which made him smile. "Shiny!"

"I don't think the patrol saw us, so I'll drop you off at a safe distance downriver," Thales said. The jugs are heavy, but it shouldn't be too far for you to hike back to your village."

Remembering his appointment, Khenti looked up. "Perhaps you could let me off at the main landing in Thebes? I'd like to spend some of my earnings tonight."

"Of course, of course," Thales said with a broad smile. "A man needs his little celebrations of life, eh?"

Neferabu didn't look convinced. "Are you sure that's wise, Khenti? Someone will see you if you wait until morning to go back to the village from Thebes. We don't want to draw any suspicion."

"I understand. I'll be back before the *Manzet-boat* of the dawn rises above the horizon."

"Then maybe I should go with you. Thebes can be a rough place at night."

Khenti smiled and shook his head. "Thank you for your offer, Nef. I'd actually prefer some privacy where I'm going."

Thales laughed, nudged Neferabu in the side, and winked at Khenti. "Try not to spend it all in one place, my friend."

After all the years he'd spent carrying stone out of the tombs, like his ancestors before him, Khenti looked powerful enough that few people would bother him in the streets of Thebes at night. Despite that, the big clay jar that he carried would have been certain to draw the attention of risk-takers who would try to take it away from him if anyone could have seen the silver and gold that it contained.

The buildings still burned with the heat that they had absorbed during the day, but he felt a pleasant current of cooler air blowing past his bare legs while he strolled toward the administrative core of the city. Enough torches, temple braziers, and oil lamps continued to burn to light his way along the stinking streets. He knew he was drawing close to the residence he sought when he passed the House of Kifi, where two young women smiled at him from the front doorway and beckoned him inside. Continuing on, he passed the home of the vizier and arrived at the door belonging to the three-story house of Mayor Paweraa.

Diligent knocking eventually roused one of the slaves, who opened the door just enough to peer outside. Khenti saw only one eye and part of a man's face.

"Who dares to disturb the residence of his lordship, Mayor Paweraa?" asked a grumpy male voice.

"Tell him Khenti is here."

The slaved looked doubtful.

"Khenti, Quarryman of Pharaoh on the Right Side in the Great Place of the western horizon. I have a delivery that he requested."

"A delivery? Then leave it by the door and I'll bring it in after you're gone."

"I must place this delivery in his hands myself," Khenti said, holding up the heavy jar. "And your punishment will be great if you don't tell your lord that I'm here waiting for him."

The slave took a step back, studied him for a moment, then shrugged. "All right. I'll get him. But don't say I didn't warn you."

Before he scuttled away, the slave allowed him through the door into a pleasant courtyard with two trees overshadowing a small pond. The face of the moon-god was reflected in the still water. On the other side of the pond, Paweraa's stately home loomed over his head. A few minutes later, the mayor himself shuffled out into the yard, yawning and blinking. Whenever he saw the mayor, Khenti thought how large his head looked compared to his body, even though he had the round shape of a well-fed city administrator who rarely, if ever, had to labor outside.

"Khenti, my good friend, it's always a pleasure to see you, but my heart would be filled with much more joy if you had delighted me with your presence in the morning."

Khenti nodded his head and held out the clay jar. "Unfortunately, my movements are restricted during the day. I have a delivery for you, my lord."

Paweraa's eyes widened and he beckoned Khenti into the house. They entered his spacious audience room, cooled by high windows just below the ceiling, and Khenti studied the fancy chair of ebony wood centered on the raised dais. The chair was inset with colored stones to form a scene of a man hunting from his boat with a long spear among the river weeds. Paweraa dismissed the slave that Khenti had met at the front door, then settled into the big chair with a grunt. However, he jumped up again when Khenti emptied the contents of the jar on the dais. Gold and silver clattered onto the wood platform.

"May you live a long life of good health and prosperity, Khenti! Is this my share of the proceeds from our little enterprise?"

"Half of it is yours, my lord."

"You have done well! Very well, indeed!" Paweraa's eyes glittered and danced as he stared at the pile with a big smile. "The great Amun-Re, king of the gods, has smiled upon us this day. And how fortunate you must think you were to have met me, eh? Without my map and my knowledge of the best tombs, you'd be forced to spend your life breaking rocks deep beneath the earth!"

Khenti nodded. "I humbly appreciate your wisdom and trust in me, my lord. I know that the great Amun-Re must love me, for he has allowed us to meet and become wealthier for having met."

Paweraa's fingers twitched until he finally kneeled beside their pile of earnings and ran his hand through the shiny rings and bars. Khenti felt fortunate that Thales had been able to pay with valuable metals since it would have been time-consuming and awkward to lead cattle or goats or carry bags of grain or other goods of equal value. He couldn't *eat* the metals, of course, but grain was easy to come by when one could afford it.

"Yes, we are favored by the gods," Paweraa said, looking up at Khenti with a serious expression. "And it would be unfortunate to lose the great wealth that we've acquired, would it not?"

"Of course, my lord," Khenti said with a frown. "Why do you say this?"

The metals clinked together as Paweraa stirred his fingers through them. "Although I don't know why, Vizier To has become suspicious that tomb robberies are increasing in the Great Place. You know as well as I that the treasures of the long-dead nobles are no longer of use to them. Wealth is wasted if it's buried permanently under the ground. With each piece that we bring to the light, the more prosperity is returned to the people of Thebes. However, not everyone is so enlightened and progressive in their views. Men are still impaled upon the wood when the magistrates find them guilty of tomb robbing."

Khenti didn't like this kind of talk. "Then I should stop and seal up the tomb again."

Paweraa waved his hands. "No, no, no! Let's not be hasty. There will be time enough for that later. In the meantime, we must redouble our efforts to ensure that our futures will be secure, prosperous, healthy, and safe. Our wives, our children, our parents—they all depend on us to give them good lives. And we deserve to live well ourselves! While the gods continue to smile on us, we must work even harder to bring more treasures to light."

"But, my lord, you say that Vizier To is aware of us!"

"I said no such thing, young Khenti. I said he is merely suspicious of the activity in the Great Place. I thought you might hear of this from other sources and I didn't want you to panic. Tomb objects have been appearing for sale in the local markets, and they could only have come from one place."

Khenti gasped. "I was told that they'd only be sold in Greece!"

Paweraa shrugged. "Such is the way of traders and merchants, Khenti. They cannot be trusted. They seek profits as quickly as they possess a thing. But we must not let this deter us from our efforts, for I have a solution that will focus Vizier To's eyes on other likely offenders."

"How is that possible? Are there others working for you? Or are there others digging among the ancient tombs? I've seen no sign of such activity."

"Leave these things to me, Khenti," he said, resting a fatherly hand on Khenti's shoulder. "There is an answer for every problem."

Mayor Paweraa always enjoyed making the Medjay police kneel when they entered the audience hall of his elegant home. Sermont, in particular, needed to be reminded of his lower status, otherwise he would become uncontrollable. The stonecutter, Khenti, had made his delivery an hour before Sermont's arrival, giving Paweraa time to summon the police captain and develop a plan to intercept some of the problems that were developing in his life. His ability to plan for potential unfortunate events had always been the key to success in his career, and he had no desire to have his nose and ears cut off, or to die upon the stake, for his small part in redistributing the wealth from a forgotten tomb. However, the purchasers of the stolen goods had shown poor judgment by selling their wares in Thebes, bringing the tomb robbery to the awareness of Paweraa's superior, Vizier To. The vizier, an ambitious man who took his job seriously, always sought swift justice for those who would defile the tombs of the Great Place. The Medjay were already under orders to increase their patrols of the west bank tombs and to conduct investigations into any rumors of unusual activity among the tomb workers. Therefore, a tomb defiler had to be found. Khenti was too valuable a worker to sacrifice, and he might reveal Paweraa's part in the robbery if he were tortured during his interrogation.

"May the light of Re shine upon you, my lord mayor," Sermont said, kneeling in front of Paweraa's chair on its raised dais. "How can I be of assistance at this dark and very late hour of the night?"

"You have many talents, Sermont. You never sleep, you have no hesitation when it comes to violence, your mind is clean and uncluttered by complex thoughts, and you have flexible morals."

Uncomfortable kneeling on the hard floor tiles, Sermont nodded and started to rise, but Paweraa motioned for him to stay down.

"These are all excellent qualities, Sermont. A man in your line of work could have a very successful career by applying his talents for me when special situations arise."

Sermont smiled. "I am ever at your service, my lord mayor."

"Of course you are. You're like one of Pharaoh's faithful greyhounds, ever ready to kill something and bring it back to Pharaoh for his next meal. And you should be rewarded for such faithful devotion to your craft. You may stand up."

Sermont nodded and stood up.

Paweraa gestured at a dark wood chest inlaid with ivory at the edge of the dais. "Open the chest and remove what you find inside."

When Sermont lifted the lid, his eyes widened. He removed three objects fashioned in the old style: a female ushabti figure made of ebony wood and electrum, a pair of formal sandals inlaid with gold and precious stones, and a hawk pectoral on a gold chain with blue and green stones set in its spread wings. When he was able to tear his eyes away from the objects, which were probably the most valuable items he'd ever touched, the look of hope in his eyes was almost enough to tug at Paweraa's heart.

"For me?" Sermont whispered.

"Don't be a fool, Sermont. I could buy the services of a Medjay army with those. There are other rewards waiting for you once you've completed a task for me."

"What's that?"

"You must arrest Hapu the scribe."

Sermont frowned and tipped his head to the side, once again reminding Paweraa of a dog. "Happily. But why?"

Paweraa sighed and shook his head. "Some unfortunate news has come to my attention. Hapu is a greedy man. He lives in a big house with many servants and a family to support, and he somehow manages to do that on a scribe's earnings. You may wonder how this is possible?"

Sermont shrugged. "Scribes are paid well."

"Obviously, you've never been to Hapu's house. He lives well beyond his means. And now I know why." He pointed at the expensive tomb objects. "He robs the honored dead. He steals from the tombs of the nobles on the west bank."

Sermont gasped and took a step back. "Hapu? The scribe? He never does anything wrong."

"So you would think, but he's a very clever man, this Hapu. You saw how he humiliated you by making you release his son after you arrested him. How do you think he managed to do that?"

Sermont frowned. "You were the one who told me to release Ray."

"At Hapu's insistence," Paweraa said. "He has powerful friends, which is why you'll have to arrest him quietly. No one must know. His neighbors must not see you take him, and he must not have any visitors."

"Ah," said Sermont, pretending to understand.

Paweraa sighed. This was almost too easy.

"And what about Ray? Arrest him, too?"

"Ray is another matter. Do you recall hearing that the great General Hori, the most favored of Pharaoh's generals, sent a message to all the cities upriver from Pi-Ramesses?"

Paweraa watched in silence as Sermont shook his head. He obviously couldn't read, and he wasn't smart enough to pay attention to what was going on around him. Hori's message had been relayed along the command chain to the city administrators and the police units all along the Nile.

However, since Sermont hadn't heard the news, he saw no need to go into details. Sermont could remain in the dark.

"Hori's message can be ignored for now. Hapu is your first priority. Leave the son free. Once you have Hapu in your custody, Ray will come to us, most likely with a hefty bribe to have his father released. We will confiscate the bribe as evidence against Hapu, then report to Vizier To that you've captured a tomb robber and a fugitive who flees from the wrath of the living god. I can assure you that the vizier, and General Hori, will be pleased."

Please buy *The House of Death* (Book 2 of The Harem Conspiracy series) by Bruce Balfour.

About the Author

Bruce Balfour, PhD, is the national bestselling author of *The Forge of Mars* (Ace Books) and its sequel, *The Digital Dead*. You can find the full list of his novels, computer games, and comic books on his website as noted below. He would greatly appreciate it you would buy every book with his name on it. As certain characters in this novel would say,"Thank you. A thousand times thank you."

Bruce lives north of Phoenix, Arizona with his wife and a fierce Chihuahua named Bug.

For more information, and to sign up for the newsletter, please visit https://brucebalfour.com

Printed in Great Britain
by Amazon